SEA CHANGE

HIGH SEAS #1

DARLENE MARSHALL

SEA CHANGE

High Seas #1

DARLENE MARSHALL

SEA CHANGE

…Charley buttoned her coat and brushed her short hair off her forehead.

"Take care of yourself, Mrs. Denham, Captain Denham. Thank you for all you have done for me."

"We will name him Charles!" Charley heard Mrs. Denham call out as the pirate took her by the upper arm to haul her from the cabin.

The cabin doors were smashed in, but Charley saw no injured crew, and when she was pushed up the ladder ahead of the pirate captain, she blinked in the bright sunlight. The *Lady Jane* was alone in the vast and empty sea, save for the vessel nearby, the one distinguished by the black flag flying over it.

The pirate took her arm again, Charley tried to shake him off, but she might as well have tried to shake the mainmast.

"I said I will come with you, you do not need to manhandle me."

He did not reply, and did not let go as he looked at a sailor standing at the rail.

"Did you find it?"

"Aye, Cap'n. We cleaned out the sick bay to the bulkheads."

"My belongings!"

"Are all aboard my ship now, Doctor, which is where you are going."

He pulled her forward and Charley stumbled along with him to the rail. She did not know what her fate would be aboard the pirate's vessel, but she knew one other thing after listening to the men talk. Her captors were Americans…

"I love that you've staked out early 19th century... sea captains, privateers and pirates. David and Charley are...matched perfectly with strength meeting strength.-- Recommended Read"--Dear Author

"I got sucked into Charley's story right from the get go and about halfway through, I knew I was reading a book I'd be listing as a top read for 2011. And I was right. Sea Change is going to be in my top 5 reads for this year."---Book Binge

AUTHOR NOTES

Some of the sites mentioned in this novel are real, others, like Santa Rosa, are fictional.

Lest you think I made this all up out of whole sailcloth, gentle reader, there have always been women who went to sea, sometimes going disguised as men. According to Suzanne J. Stark, author of *Female Tars*, there were more than 20 *known* cases of women disguised as men in the Royal Navy and Royal Marines from the late 17th to mid-19th centuries. Those are the cases of known women, so the true numbers are no doubt even higher. Some of the women continued to serve aboard ship with zeal and honor after their identities were uncovered, and some died for King and country. There were iron women on those wooden ships.

The medicine practiced in this novel was the medicine of the time. Just as we wince at the idea of bleeding patients, no doubt there will be readers 100 years from now who will read accounts of our medical treatments and wince at the idea of treating disease with radical surgery, poisonous chemicals and radiation.

DEDICATION & ACKNOWLEDGEMENTS

For Howard, who tells the whole world that Darlene Marshall is his favorite author.

Thanks go to:

My incredible beta readers: Janice Gelb, Connie and Bob Stern, and Cindy Vallar. As always, any mistakes are mine and not theirs.

Captain Vic and First Mate Ellen of the good ship Liberty for ending my status as an armchair sailor.

Eleni Polopolus for help in how to pronounce "Caeneus."

John Barreiro of the Compuserve Languages Forum.

Cornelia Olifiers Stern and Robert Stern for the "Careful, or you'll end up in my novel" shirt.

Dr. Mark Sherwood and Dr. Amarilis Iscold for help in maiming characters.

The Compuserve Books and Writers Forum for helping me blow things up and find great metaphors.

The Alachua County Library District. I couldn't do it without reference librarians and Inter-Library Loan. You guys are the best!

CHAPTER 1

1814

No one was bleeding or vomiting or oozing, so Charley Alcott decided to take a stroll. There wasn't much room to walk around the deck of a brig in the middle of the Atlantic Ocean but sick call was over, the captain's lady was below taking a rest, and the fresh air was welcome. Charley wandered over to the larboard side of the *Lady Jane* where some of the crew gathered, watching the gunnery practice of their escort frigate, the fifth-rate *Caeneus*.

"Afternoon, Doctor," the cook said.

"Are you still using that ointment on your hand, Johnson?"

"Yes, sir. Cleared that problem right up."

"Keep up the treatment then, and see me if you have need."

"Aye, Doctor."

Charley didn't know anything about guns, but the sailors and Mr. Silas Stuart, the mate, seemed impressed with the speed of the "Cannies" at their stations. Naturally, they placed bets on whether the next shot would hit the barrel floating off the starboard bow.

"They're fast, but accuracy counts," Stuart said. "Now, if you want to see real accuracy, watch the Americans. 'Cousin Jonathan' is so skinflint about outfitting ships I suspect the cost of each ball that doesn't hit its mark is deducted from the sailors' pay!"

"Those Yankees cannot stand against our big Navy guns," the cook said with a grin. "When you're going broadside to broadside it ain't accuracy, it's blowin' up as much as you can in as sho—"

His words were cut off by the noise of an explosion aboard the *Caeneus*. Smoke erupted from a gunport, and the yells of the crew could be heard across the water.

"Gun exploded," was the guess of the blacksmith.

"Mr. Stuart, they may need help with the injured. Can you take me over in the boat?" Charley said, watching the frantic activity aboard the frigate.

"Let me hail them, Doctor," the mate said.

He got his speaking trumpet and yelled across the water.

"Ahoy, *Caeneus*! Do you need assistance from our surgeon? Or our carpenter?"

The disaster aboard the frigate had the look of organized effort to Charley's eyes. Men rushed to help and everyone seemed to know what to do. Pumps were manned to put out the fire, and the ship's carpenter gestured at the blackened hole where the neat gunport had been moments earlier. The other naval escorts on this journey to the West Indies were not as near as the *Lady Jane*, and a young officer picked up a trumpet and called back to them.

"Yes, send your doctor over." He consulted with the officer next to him. "Thank you for the offer of the carpenter, but we have that in hand."

Charley ran below to throw together extra bandages and

gear. The wounded would have burns and splinters for certain, but direction for other wounds would come from the *Caeneus's* surgeon.

The boat was ready when Charley came back up on deck, passing the satchel to one of the sailors and clambering awkwardly down into the craft. The sailors pulled hard to get over to the frigate as quickly as possible.

"This is Dr. Alcott," one of the *Lady Jane's* men told the officer there to meet them, a midshipman younger than Charley.

"Follow me, Doctor," he said.

The smell of charred wood and hot metal lingered in the air as they made their way to the frigate's cockpit, and a handful of less seriously injured men were arrayed outside the door, waiting their turn. The young officer knocked once, then entered.

"Dr. Murray, I've brought the surgeon from the *Lady Jane,*" the midshipman said.

The surgeon was a broad man with powerful shoulders beneath his bloodstained leather apron, his unkempt hair patterned with gray and russet. A spare tourniquet dangled from his coat pocket. He didn't look up from the seaman strapped to the table, his left leg hanging in shreds, the shattered bone clearly visible. The man held a piece of leather clamped between his teeth, tears streaming through the soot and blood on his face.

The middy left to return to his duties, and Murray paused for a moment and looked at Charley.

"I have to tell you, Dr. Murray, that I am not a certified surgeon," Charley said quickly. "I was apprenticed to my physician father, but have not begun my formal studies. The crew on the *Lady Jane* call me doctor because I tend them on this voyage."

"Did you ever assist at an amputation?"

"Yes, a farming accident caused a man to lose his leg. My father performed the surgery and I assisted him."

Murray grunted in approval. "My assistant is down with a flux, so you're the best I've got right now, Mr. Alcott. Do not disappoint me."

"No, sir," Charley said, swallowing. All of a sudden the room felt like it was devoid of air, but Charley stepped closer. The injured man needed help, collapse could come later.

"Spencer, I am ready to begin," Murray said briskly, looking into the face of the weeping seaman. "It will be over quickly."

The instruments were covered with a cloth to keep them from the eyes of the injured, and Murray threw back the cover now and turned to Charley. His lined hazel eyes were intent and Charley felt pinned by their gaze, like a specimen beneath a magnifying glass.

"This is not a theater, Mr. Alcott, nor are you my apprentice. The operation will be done quickly to spare Spencer as much agony as possible, so save any questions until after."

"Yes, Doctor."

"Apply the tourniquet."

Charley took a knife and cut the seaman's trouser leg open, then put the tourniquet on his thigh, positioning the screw and its pad over the large artery and tightening it as quickly as possible while Spencer jerked against the straps binding him to the table. He held the leather in his teeth and his screams were muffled.

"Here we go," Dr. Murray said under his breath in his lowland Scots accent, and then he began. His hands moved almost too quickly for Charley to watch as fresh blood leaked out from beneath the tied-off thigh. He directed Charley to draw the skin back for the flap that would cover the stump.

With saw in hand he hunched over the man, his shoulders bunching as he bore down and cut through the bone, the entire procedure taking less than ten minutes. Fortunately, Spencer passed out and no longer fought against the surgeon's saw, so Murray kept up a quick commentary as he worked, showing Charley where to close and suture the vessels.

The discarded limb thumped to the floor, the sand scattered on the deck absorbing blood to keep the surgeon from slipping in the mess. The heavy copper smell of fresh blood, the stench of urine, and the sweat of the men added to the reek of the small space. Charley noticed none of that, intent on making the most of this opportunity. It was a tragedy for Spencer, but an invaluable experience for a young apprentice from a small village.

Murray told Charley to pinch off a splinter of the bone with the nippers, then showed how to take the cotton bandage, a piece of cloth about two feet long torn halfway up the center, and bind it around the flap of skin and the stump, sealing the end of the damaged leg before the tourniquet was removed.

"Notice that the cut was made well above the wound. While a surgeon should never remove a limb without cause, once you make the decision you do the patient no favor by being too conservative and not allowing the stump to heal properly."

Spencer was carried to a hanging cot in the sick bay and covered well, the braziers in the room warming him so he would not go into shock. His were the worst of the injuries, and the rest of the session in the cockpit was spent removing splinters, treating burns, setting a fractured arm and examining the boatswain's mate, who complained of a ringing in his ears from the exploding gun.

At the end of the day Charley stretched cramped muscles

as Dr. Murray put his instruments away and removed his bloody apron. Charley, too, was covered with gore, reddened sand clinging to bloodied clothing.

"I will arrange for a boat to take you back to your vessel, Alcott, but perhaps you would care to join me in a glass of wine first? I have a fine Madeira in my cabin, and if you have any questions about the procedures today I would be glad to discuss them with you."

"Thank you," Charley said, looking forward to a restorative glass of wine, then a good washing aboard *Lady Jane*. Charley followed the *Caeneus's* surgeon to his tiny quarters, a space barely large enough for his cot and a chair.

Murray motioned to the chair and Charley fell into it ungracefully while the doctor poured wine for them both.

"Now then, Alcott," Dr. Murray said after they'd each enjoyed a restorative sip, "would you please explain to me how a woman came to be masquerading as a surgeon?"

CHAPTER 2

"**D**o not look so surprised. I am a surgeon, and one of the first things we're taught in anatomy class is how to distinguish one sex from the other. I have become quite adept at it over the years."

Charley gripped her glass with fingers that shook and took a fortifying swallow of her wine.

"Are you going to reveal my secret?"

Dr. Murray was difficult for her to read, neither old nor young, he could be any age from thirty to sixty. Her fate rested in his hands, and he studied her with interest, his craggy face reflecting curiosity rather than condemnation.

"I would have to say that depends on what you tell me, Miss—it is *miss*, is it not?—Alcott."

"Yes, I am Miss Charlotte Alcott, though on the *Lady Jane* I am known as Charley Alcott. My father was Horatio Alcott of Little Abbot, and I did assist him for many years. I did not lie about that."

"Oh, I have no doubt that you had medical training. I watched you this afternoon and you have some skill. Of course, the idea of a woman being a surgeon is patently ridiculous, so I would like to know what your game is."

Charley bristled at the idea of her skills being "patently ridiculous," but she needed to stay on this man's good side. She had no idea how Captain Denham would react to her ruse being uncovered, and there was no place to run to in the middle of the Atlantic Ocean. Denham might accuse her of defrauding him and demand payment for her passage and additional compensation, or he might try to have her arrested.

"My father is dead and I needed to leave England. I am going to Jamaica to live with my godfather, Dr. Curtis Wilson. Disguising myself as a man and working my passage across the Atlantic was the most expeditious means of making the voyage."

"I know of Dr. Wilson. Is he part of this scheme?"

"No!" she said quickly. "It is all my idea."

Murray made a noncommittal noise and sipped his wine. He appeared to be thinking, and working around to his next statement.

"I will not reveal your secret, Miss Alcott. *Primo no nocere* means—"

"'First, do no harm,'" Charley said with some asperity.

"Amazing. She knows Latin, also. You likely have not killed anyone—yet—with your amateur efforts, and you were an able assistant today. Taking you off the *Lady Jane* could harm the crew that has come to depend upon your skills, lacking as they are. I cannot imagine Dr. Wilson would allow a gentleman's daughter to work at such a task, but if you feel you must push yourself forward in caring for people, consider midwifery as an outlet."

Now she really had to keep hold of her temper, telling herself nothing would be gained by antagonizing this arrogant medico. She simply said, "Thank you for keeping my confidence," and rose to take her leave.

"Sit down, Miss Alcott."

Charley sat.

The surgeon reached for a piece of paper and a pencil that he put on the table next to her.

"I watched you removing splinters today and while a probe can be best, sometimes there's no substitute for an index finger feeling the foreign object, especially with thinner fingers such as yours. Miss Alcott, if I am speaking, you should be taking notes." He gestured at the paper. "Now, for example…"

And to Charley's amazement the gruff Scotsman discussed wound treatment for what she might encounter at sea, including removing bullets and the treatment of burns. The hours passed so quickly that she was startled when a knock at the door announced the boatswain's mate with the news that the boat was ready to take her back to the *Lady Jane*.

Dr. Murray rose and reached up to the railed bookshelf attached to the bulkhead over his desk, his hand resting on a thick volume.

"Take this with you, Miss Alcott. Study it. You will find it useful."

It was a worn copy of John Woodall's *The Surgeon's Mate*, and Charley took it, clasping it tight to her bound bosom.

"I have heard of this book but my father did not have a copy! Thank you so much, Dr. Murray!"

He looked at her steadily.

"I am not gifting you with this volume to make you happy, Miss Alcott. I am hopeful that the solid medical advice and common sense in that volume for treating men at sea will keep the numbers you kill to a minimum."

On that humbling note, he reached around Charley to

open the cabin door, hesitated, then said, "I am being posted to the Jamaica station. If you encounter difficulties with Dr. Wilson, come see me. I may be able to be of assistance."

"Thank you, Doctor, that is a most generous offer."

He simply made that noncommittal noise again and ushered her out of his cabin and up to the deck.

The seamen from the *Caeneus* were ready to take her back to the *Lady Jane*, and she received the thanks of the officer on the watch for her assistance. The crew pulled the oars in the moonlight, hauling her away from the frigate. Charley looked over her shoulder from where she sat in the stern and saw Dr. Murray watching from the rail. She almost raised her hand to wave at him, but instead turned forward again, toward the ship looming in front of her.

When Charley and Captain Denham struck their bargain in Plymouth, Charley acting as ship's surgeon in exchange for passage, it could have been a disaster but it was too good an opportunity for her to pass up. Long accustomed to dressing as a boy while assisting her father, she felt more comfortable as "Charley Alcott" than as "Charlotte Alcott" anyway. She knew her square face, blunt features and long frame might not get her dance partners, but they could fool people who expected to see a young man.

Except, it seemed, for an astute ship's surgeon.

But back aboard the merchant vessel, all was as it should be, and the days at sea passed with the convoy wending its way to the West Indies. Charley fell into the rhythm of the *Lady Jane* with a minimum of laughter from the crew at her landlubber ways. She was sure she would never learn the foreign language spoken by the crew, a language of "futtocks" and "shrouds," but at least by the end of her first day at sea she knew larboard from starboard (even if she had to remind herself "left for larboard" under her breath), and bow from stern.

Sick call was held in the morning and her cramped cabin that also served as sick bay was a popular destination. She learned how to distinguish the malingerers from those needing treatment, and her store of emetics helped convince the ones who weren't truly ill that it was in their best interest to return to duty. The ones she bled and plastered were soon bragging of her skills to their mates, each one outdoing himself in describing the pain, oozing or itching of his particular condition.

The sailors took Charley's youth in stride, and she realized after only a short time that being competent counted for far more aboard ship than one's age or appearance. But appearance did make a difference, as Charley knew all too well from every day of her life masquerading as a man. Aboard the *Lady Jane* she dressed in loosely tailored brown or dark blue coats, her bound breasts invisible beneath heavy linen shirts and unadorned waistcoats. The total effect was one of sobriety and competence. She learned from watching her physician father and was serious in her demeanor, which contributed to an air of masculine assurance.

She checked every day on Mrs. Denham, the captain's young and pregnant wife, and was pleased to see the lady progressing well. There was an initial bout of seasickness that sent Captain Denham into a panic, but some ginger tea and dry ship's biscuit helped both doctor and patient get their sea-legs.

Charley and Mrs. Denham fell into the habit of a daily walk around the ship. There was not far to go on the brig, but Charley was sure taking the sea air as opposed to the miasmic atmosphere belowdecks would do them both good.

"'Mornin' Doctor! 'Mornin' Mrs. Denham!" a sailor

called from aloft. Charley shielded her eyes and waved up at Ryan. He'd been to sick bay earlier in the week for the rheumatism that plagued so many of the sailors, working as they did in a wet and cold environment. One of her tasks while waiting for the *Lady Jane* to sail was to mix up plenty of the liniment she'd used with such efficacious results in Little Abbot. Some of the sailors swore by a cayenne pepper rub for their aches and pains, but Ryan said her preparation had given him relief and Charley heard the crew arguing at length over the best medical treatments they'd ever used.

She wasn't an experienced traveler, but to her eye the crew appeared content, not sullen or subdued, and she over-heard one say he liked being on a "hen-ship," because having the captain's wife aboard meant that in general there was better food and treatment for them than in an all-male company. And if Mrs. Denham—and Charley—had their vocabularies vastly expanded by contact with the sailors, they were polite enough not to remark upon it.

The brig was like a little village of its own, she mused to herself as she paced the deck. There was the steward and the carpenter, the cook and the boatswain, the sailors and the family who were the officers and owners of the ship. Everyone had a task and everyone knew his place in this village.

And Dr. Murray was a man of his word, for no communi-cations came from the *Caeneus* to the *Lady Jane* exposing their fraudulent doctor.

The weeks passed on the Atlantic crossing and Mrs. Denham grew large, her ungainly shape causing her to laugh at herself as she waddled through the daily walk around the ship.

"This may be the last walk we take, Mrs. Denham," Charley said. "Your baby has dropped and I believe your child will make his arrival aboard ship rather than wait for Jamaica."

She said this cheerfully, knowing from past experience that one of the most important tasks in dealing with a *primagravida* was calming her fear of the unknown.

"Cook told me that if I was aboard the warships escorting us and the babe was born there, then he would be a 'son of the guns.'" Mrs. Denham chuckled and gestured at the mound preceding her on their walk. "I would rather be here, away from guns and fighting. Do not tell my husband though, Doctor, that the babe might come earlier than expected. He has enough on his mind, and he'll realize soon enough that his plans for the child to be born on land may not come to fruition."

Today Mrs. Denham was wearing an emerald green wool dress that strained at the seams in front, but she dutifully wrapped herself in a heavy plaid shawl after her husband gently scolded her for risking herself in the sea breezes. Charley watched the way the aging Captain Denham treated his young wife, as if someone had handed him a rare treasure to guard. This was why he'd been so open to allowing Charley to barter passage on his ship in exchange for doctoring the crew and Elizabeth Denham. He cosseted her and pampered her as best he could in the middle of the ocean, and Mrs. Denham seemed genuinely fond of him.

"Y'see, Doctor," she'd confided to Charley on one of their walks, "my sisters always told me I wasn't pretty enough to get a husband of my own. When Ronald came courting they were sure he wanted one of them, but he said he'd have no one but me, if you can fathom that!"

She was not at all surprised, for despite eyes that were small and set close together, and a chin that had an unfortunate slope inward, Mrs. Denham had a way about her that made people feel warm in her presence.

"I would say that the captain was looking for a handsome lady of a sweet disposition who would make him a comfortable home after his years at sea. He is a fortunate man to have found you."

"Why, Dr. Alcott, are you flirting with me?"

"A doctor never flirts, Mrs. Denham. That was my professional observation."

Mrs. Denham smiled at this, and kept walking with a rolling gait that incorporated the ship's movement as much as her own bulk.

She peeked up from beneath her bonnet and saw Charley watching her progress. "Do not fear that I will overbalance myself, Dr. Alcott. I am comfortable with the motions of the *Lady Jane*. This is now my home. If I am to be a good wife to the captain, then I must make him feel I fit into his world. What of you, do you fancy a life at sea now that you have had a taste of it?"

"Absolutely not," Charley said with conviction, offering Mrs. Denham her hand to help her step around some lines. "This has been a wonderful adventure and opportunity, but I will be satisfied and relieved to stand again on a floor that does not shift beneath my feet!"

Mrs. Denham laughed at this, but pronounced herself well satisfied with life at sea, as long as she had Captain Denham beside her. Later that evening when Charley came above to take the air, she came upon the captain and his lady, but they did not see her. Captain Denham had his arms around his wife, his hefty bulk acting as a windbreak to shield her from the fog rolling across the water. She watched from the shadows, and swallowed down the lump in her throat. They seemed so content together, just standing at the rail and holding each other. Charley hugged herself to get a bit of extra warmth, then turned back to her solitary bunk.

She was awakened from a sound sleep that night by a

frantic Captain Denham pounding on her cabin door. She wasn't surprised, but got dressed in a few moments since she slept in shirt and trousers to maintain her disguise.

In the captain's cabin a lantern was lit, and Mrs. Denham was sitting on a chair in her nightdress, clutching her belly. A patch of wetness on the deck told the tale as much as her next words.

"I arose to use the chamber pot, and when I stood there was a rush of water from between my legs!"

"Is she well? Is something wrong?"

Charley turned to Captain Denham, who was wringing his hands and nervously shifting from foot to foot.

"Mrs. Denham's waters have broken and your son is going to make an earlier arrival than anticipated, Captain. Do not be concerned. Mrs. Denham and I have it all well in hand. You should go above now, and we will call you when it is time."

"But Elizabeth—"

"Listen to Dr. Alcott, please, Ronald," his wife said as she clutched her belly.

Charley took the captain by the arm and turned him toward the door.

"Your part is done, Captain," she said with a wink to convey masculine solidarity. "You don't want to be here now. It will not happen quickly and your presence is a distraction."

"Aye," the captain said in a daze as he allowed her to evict him from his own cabin. "This fog—I need to talk with the helmsman…"

He was still mumbling to himself as Charley closed the door behind him.

"Well!" she said, pushing up her sleeves. "Let us see what we can do to help the newest Denham into this world."

The fog closed 'round the ship like a heavy blanket during the night, cutting them off from contact with the convoy.

Sounds were muffled in the damp gloom and the lookout strained to keep the running lights of the other ships in sight.

Charley spent the pre-dawn hours helping Mrs. Denham pace the confines of the cabin, holding her when the contractions hit, bathing her forehead and soothing her fears.

"No, this is not unusual. A first child is a new experience for your body, so it is no wonder that it takes time to adjust."

"I have been laboring forever!" Elizabeth Denham moaned.

"Your contractions will start to come closer together, as we discussed they would. Now, you lie back and try to rest. Conserve your strength for you have a hard task ahead. I will return shortly."

Charley stepped out of the cabin and stretched with her hands at the base of her spine, easing the kinks in her back. She knew the babe wasn't going to emerge in the next fifteen minutes, so this was an opportune time for her to use the head and maybe get a cup of tea from the galley.

When she came above, the only sign that dawn had broken was a shift in the light filtering through the fog, but the gray shroud still covered the *Lady Jane*. Captain Denham was pacing the deck anxiously, and rushed over when he saw Charley.

"Elizabeth! What— How—?"

"Your wife is well, Captain, and all is progressing as it should."

"That's good," Denham said in relief, then looked out over water that appeared as bleak and washed out as the mist engulfing them. Droplets of moisture clung to his salt-and-pepper beard and beaded on his shoulders. He lowered his voice. "This damned fog has cut us off from contact with the other vessels. Do not tell Elizabeth."

"Of course not. She has enough on her mind."

"I can take a moment to visit with her," Denham said heartily. "That will cheer her."

Before Charley could stop him he was headed down to his cabin, and she followed behind.

"I am not sure this is a good idea. Ladies in Elizabeth's state are not always themselves—"

But it was too late. Captain Denham threw open the door of the cabin and started to say, "My darling Eliz—"

"You!"

His darling Elizabeth was sitting up in the bunk, clutching her belly, glaring at her husband. Lank strands of sweat-dampened hair fell across her face and she looked like a serpent-haired Fury come to deliver retribution.

And she knew just who to deliver it to.

"You!" She snarled again, pointing a shaking finger at her husband. "You did this to me, you—"

And then Captain Denham's demure and shy wife demonstrated exactly how well her vocabulary had been broadened by contact with the *Lady Jane's* sailors. She ended with a description of what she was going to do to her husband's private parts so that he would never be able to put her in this position again.

Charley escorted a white-faced Captain Denham from the cabin.

"Pay it no mind, Captain. Women in the midst of labor will say all sorts of things they do not mean."

"You don't think she really means it?"

"Wellll, she does mean it now, but once she's holding her babe she will forget she ever said these things to you."

Mr. Stuart was calling for the captain, so Charley clapped him on the back, said, "Buck up, sir, this will soon be over," and returned to her patient.

The contractions were gaining in intensity and she monitored Mrs. Denham, even as she heard the noise and commotion increase abovedecks.

One of the ship's boys threw the door open to reveal the news.

"Pirates! There are pirates, Doctor! The captain says to stay below while he talks to them!"

"What else am I going to do?" Charley said in asperity. "We are busy here, Lawton. Your job is to keep pirates—and anyone else—out of this cabin."

Mrs. Denham moaned, but she gave her a brief smile.

"Do not fear, Mrs. Denham. I know your husband will not do anything to put your life at risk."

The contractions were close now. Mrs. Denham was propped up against the bulkhead, and Charley was between her legs letting nature take its course. There was no more gunfire, but she could hear yelling and feet thundering through the lower decks.

"Won't be long now," she said cheerfully.

"That's what you said earlier, you pox-ridden bastard!" Mrs. Denham gritted from between her teeth, arching her back as the next contraction came.

"No, do not push! Not until I tell you to!"

The cabin door burst open.

"Are you the surgeon?"

Charley glanced over her shoulder and caught a glimpse of a tall, masked stranger.

"Get out," she said, turning back to her patient.

Mrs. Denham screamed, and the man raised his voice to be heard.

"If you are the surgeon, you're coming with me."

"Not before this baby's born."

She heard him walk across the cabin, and felt something cold placed against her neck. She angled her head to look at the cutlass resting just below her ear. Charley knew she should be terrified, but all she felt was aggravation that this pirate was upsetting her patient.

"I need a surgeon aboard my ship. You are coming with me."

Mrs. Denham panted in short gasps, her eyes darting between the man over Charley's shoulder and the doctor. Charley turned around and looked up at him. The pirate's mask covered his upper face, but she caught a glint of amber through the eyeholes, and saw a firm mouth set in a grim line.

"A dead surgeon is no good to you either, pirate. You are upsetting my patient. Get out. And take your sword with you."

"That's 'Captain Pirate' to you, leech," but the sword was taken away.

Elizabeth Denham took that moment to lean over and vomit, missing the bowl next to the bunk. A rush of blood-tinged fluid came out from between her legs.

Charley glanced back again and saw the pirate's jaw pale before he turned and fumbled for the latch.

"I'll be back, Doctor!"

She ignored him and turned to Elizabeth.

"Good work, Mrs. Denham. The baby's crowning!"

After that, things happened quickly. The baby's head emerged into Charley's hands and the body rotated for the shoulders to slip through on the next contraction, and in moments she had hold of a slippery, squirming son for Captain and Mrs. Denham.

The baby's lusty cries brought a sound of joy from his crying mother.

"My baby!" she cried, and laughed through cracked lips, and cried some more. "Give me my baby!"

"In a moment, Mama. We are not quite finished here yet."

She cut the cord and cradled the child, holding him up in

the lamplight to give him a quick examination. All the necessary parts seemed to be there, so she offered up a silent prayer of relief and thanks, wiped him with a soft cloth and wrapped him in an even softer blanket, then laid him on his mother's belly to stay warm.

"Now for the afterbirth, and then you can rest."

Charley was washing her hands and smiling at Mrs. Denham as she held her new son to her breast, cooing down at him, when the cabin door slammed open and Captain Denham was shoved into the cabin, followed by the pirate.

"Elizabeth!"

"We have a son, Ronald," his sweet wife beamed at him, "Oh look, is he not beautiful?"

Like most newborns he was red and wrinkled and squished looking, but to Charley's eyes he also appeared beautiful, for she had helped bring him safely into the world.

"This is all very touching," the pirate said, "but I have waited long enough. Captain, your strongbox, quickly now, before harm comes to these innocents."

He motioned a pair of his crewmen into the cabin. They took Captain Denham's money and papers while the captain and Charley stood guard in front of the bunk, keeping Mrs. Denham and the baby safe. It was a gallant gesture, even though they each knew they could not stand against armed pirates.

"And now for our final business. Come with me, Doctor!"

She took a step back from the pirate, who was standing holding a pistol loosely at his side, but he stood between her and the door.

"You cannot take Dr. Alcott prisoner, I will not stand for it!" Captain Denham said.

"Really?" the pirate drawled, and cocking his head to the side, looked down at the baby Mrs. Denham clutched to her chest.

"You would not harm a baby!" Charley said in outrage.

"You are correct, I would not harm a baby." The pirate looked at her, his eyes intent behind his mask. He was tall and loomed over her as he smiled coldly and said, "That child can, however, grow up without a father. You choose, Doctor. Now. Either you come with me, or I will shoot the good captain here."

"Ronald!" Elizabeth Denham cried out.

Denham did not plead for his life, but Charley knew she had no choice, not really.

"That baby needs its father more than you need a doctor, Captain Denham. Mrs. Denham, remember what I said— plenty of beef broth, have the cook kill one of those chickens and make a rich soup for you, stay in your bunk and rest. Your milk will be in in a day or two. In the meantime, let the baby nurse as he will and it will help you recover."

She turned back to her captor, who was standing silent during this speech, radiating tension.

"Very well, pirate, I will come with you."

"How accommodating you are."

Charley said nothing to this but buttoned her coat and brushed her short hair off her forehead.

"Take care of yourself, Mrs. Denham, Captain Denham. Thank you for all you have done for me."

"We will name him Charles!" Charley heard Mrs. Denham call out as the pirate took her by the upper arm to haul her from the cabin.

The cabin doors were smashed in, but she saw no injured crew, and when she was pushed up the ladder ahead of the pirate captain, she blinked in the bright sunlight. The *Lady Jane* was alone in the vast and empty sea, save for the vessel nearby, the one distinguished by the black flag flying over it.

The pirate took her arm again, Charley tried to shake him off, but she might as well have tried to shake the mainmast.

"I said I will come with you, you do not need to manhandle me."

He did not reply, and did not let go as he looked at a sailor standing at the rail.

"Did you find it?"

"Aye, Cap'n. We cleaned out the sick bay to the bulkheads."

"My belongings!"

"Are all aboard my ship now, which is where you are going."

He pulled her forward and Charley stumbled along with him to the rail. She did not know what her fate would be aboard the pirate's vessel, but she knew one other thing after listening to the men talk. Her captors were Americans.

CHAPTER 3

The mask obscured his vision, but Captain David Fletcher of the privateer *Fancy* knew better than to rip it off. He was already in danger of losing his bond to the United States if word of this escapade leaked out. Posing as pirates instead of legitimate privateers, taking a civilian prisoner—it was not how he wanted to deal with this situation, but he needed medicine and a doctor. He had anticipated the former would be on a merchant ship, but the latter was a stroke of pure luck and an opportunity he could not pass up.

He was having second thoughts about this surgeon, however.

Dr. Alcott was a weedy stripling who did not look old enough to run a razor over his face. He seemed competent with that screaming harpy—and that was a scene David would be reliving in his nightmares!—but was he competent to deal with life aboard the *Fancy*?

More importantly, and more urgently, could he heal Henry?

He looked over at his prisoner, who was making his way in a lubberly fashion down to the waiting boat. Likely this was the man's first sea voyage, and he felt his doubts blossom anew. An experienced sea surgeon was one thing, but some youngster more used to delivering babies and aiding old ladies in stimulating their digestion—

It was too late now, he thought as they rowed over in silence and boarded his vessel. He was stuck with what he had, and he had to believe that whatever assistance Dr. Alcott could offer would be better for Henry than David's own lack of skills.

"It was a good haul, Captain. Plucking this one like a fat goose right out of the convoy, slipping by those frigates as neat as you please…"

He turned to Mr. Bryant, who was acting as mate while Henry was laid up.

"We need to get under weigh before the convoy discovers one of its geese has wandered away. This doctor will tend to Henry, and I want everyone aboard to give him whatever assistance he requires."

Bryant's weather-beaten face told him that everyone on the *Fancy* knew healing Henry was a long shot, but David refused to give in to his fears. As long as he believed his brother could be cured—the alternative was not to be contemplated.

In the meantime, the doctor was watching the *Lady Jane* as it raised sail.

"Goodbye, Ryan! Don't forget the liniment!" Alcott yelled through cupped hands. The *Fancy's* crew was watching their unexpected prisoner, waiting to take direction from the captain on how to deal with the man.

David sighed, scratched his hot forehead through the mask, and went over to get the doctor. There was nothing to be served by putting this off.

"I brought you here for a purpose, Doctor…"

"Well, of course you did!" Alcott snapped at him. "I

cannot imagine you randomly kidnap surgeons off of ships. What is it you need? And who are you, anyway?"

He ignored the last and said, "Come with me."

Alcott followed docilely enough, stepping carefully around the pilfered goods waiting to be placed in the hold by the crew. When they got to the lower deck, and out of sight of the retreating *Lady Jane*, David removed his mask. In the lantern light Dr. Alcott glanced at him, then stopped and took a longer look, his gray eyes widening.

"If you are thinking you will memorize my features to testify against me, think again," David said harshly.

Alcott started, as if in a daze, and said, "No…that was not what I was thinking at all. Who are you?"

"I am Captain David Fletcher. Follow me."

"I demand to know what your intentions are, Captain Fletcher! Where are my instruments and the medicine chest? Why have you taken me off my ship? Where are my belongings?"

David's temper was already on its last nerve, and this arrogant, high-voiced sawbones had just stomped on that nerve. He grabbed him by his neckcloth and slammed him up against a bulkhead, gripping him so tightly the doctor's feet weren't touching the deck.

"You listen to me, you little runt!" he said through his teeth. "I give the orders and make the demands! You're going into that cabin and you're going to fix Henry! Because if you don't, I will dangle you over the side and feed you to the sharks from the feet up. Understand?"

The man's face was turning an alarming shade of purple, but he jerked his head in a nod, and David lowered him until he stood on the deck again.

"All you need to know for now is that your life depends on your medical skills."

He knocked at Henry's door, and it was opened a moment

later by Lewis, David's steward, who'd been tending to Henry since his injury.

"Is he awake?" David asked softly.

"Come in, brother," said a weak voice from the cabin. "I am awake."

He crowded into the narrow cabin, Alcott behind him. Henry Fletcher lay in bed with his injured left arm propped up on a cushion beside him. The hand was loosely wrapped with bloody bandages, and Alcott pushed past David into the small space.

"Get me more light in here, a basin of hot water, and my satchel," Alcott snapped out, leaning over Henry and looking at the bloody limb.

Lewis looked at David, who nodded and said, "Whatever Dr. Alcott needs, you give him."

Alcott looked back over his narrow shoulder.

"What Dr. Alcott needs is more light, more room, and less rocking of the ship!"

"I can give you more light, this is all the room in this cabin, and a ship at sea rocks," David said, his temper rising again at being ordered about by this green Englishman, but he reined himself in. The man was a doctor, or so he said, and knew what he needed. Lewis returned at that moment with his satchel and another sailor brought in a pair of lanterns. Alcott directed the placement of the light, and, straightening, turned to David.

"Go now. I need to examine my patient."

He was reluctant to leave Henry, and started to argue.

"Captain, you brought me here for a purpose," Alcott interrupted him. "Leave me to do my task."

His demeanor softened slightly as he looked over his shoulder at Henry, then turned back to him.

"He is your brother? I can see the resemblance. I will do whatever I can for him, and I will give you news when I know more. But I will not know more until you are gone and I can examine him."

David stared the man down, but Alcott didn't flinch. For all his youth and lack of bulk, he wasn't easily intimidated, and he could not help but appreciate that in any man.

"I will be back, Doctor. Be very careful."

Alcott said nothing to this, and David turned to Henry and forced a smile.

"See? I told you I would find a doctor, even if I had to raid every ship in the Caribbean."

"So you did," Henry said with a strained smile of his own. "Thank you."

"Now leave, Captain Fletcher," Dr. Alcott said, and with a last glance at Henry, David turned on his heel and exited the cabin.

He wanted to stay below, but there was too much happening aboard the *Fancy*, and with Henry out of commission David could not be spared. He went above into the sunshine, and took a deep breath, eyeing the black shadow of a frigatebird soaring overhead, envying the bird its freedom to just fly away.

The schooner was dancing over the warm Caribbean waters, and it was the kind of day that David would normally be celebrating—a good haul, a fair wind—but Henry's condition cast a pall over the ship, the men subdued as they all awaited word.

It seemed like hours later, though he knew not that much time had passed, that Lewis came above and told him the doctor was ready to talk to him.

When he re-entered the cabin, Alcott was sitting alongside Henry on the bunk, the injured hand loosely bandaged. Henry's face was white as bleached bone, tears trickling from the corners of his eyes, and the smell of blood filled the small space. The doctor's face was grim, and older looking than it had been an hour earlier.

"What is it? What have you done to him?"

Alcott sighed, and rose from the bunk.

"I must be brutally honest with you, Captain, as I was with your brother. Mr. Fletcher's hand is damaged beyond repair."

"What are you saying?" he asked, hoping for a reprieve. But he had spent years at sea, seen men undergo horrific injuries, and he knew the doctor would say what he'd feared all along.

Alcott looked at him.

"The bones are crushed, and soon the flesh will become corrupted. Mr. Fletcher's hand must be amputated. If the hand is removed now, I can save most of his arm. If it is left to fester, the corruption will spread and he will either have to have all of his arm removed, or he will die."

"Have you ever done this before? An amputation?"

He hesitated, then looked David in the eye.

"As I explained to Mr. Fletcher, I have not done an amputation, but I have assisted other surgeons in their operations."

David wanted to punch the doctor in the face. What good was this untried youngster, no more qualified than some ship's carpenter or the surgeon's loblolly boy, to be taking off a man's hand?

"Is there no port nearby where you can put in and take him to a proper surgeon?"

"If there was, I would not have needed to haul your skinny arse off that scow, would I?" he snarled. "That is the sawbones' solution to everything, isn't it? To cut and hack away at a man until there is nothing left!"

Alcott flinched, but held his ground.

"It is not a decision I, or any other surgeon, would make lightly, but there is no choice. Without amputation this hand will poison the rest of Mr. Fletcher's body. I cannot slow the spread of the corruption, nor can I heal a hand where the bones are ground to powder."

"David—"

He turned to his brother, who was staring down at the hand the doctor had decently covered. He did not need to see it again. He'd been there in the hold when the barrel slammed into Henry, pinning his hand beneath it. He would always hear his brother's screams in his nightmares and wonder if he'd only been a little faster, if he'd only been able to push Henry out of the way...

"Let the doctor do what he needs to do."

"But—"

"It is my hand, and my decision, David. You are not responsible."

Yes, I am, he wanted to shout. *I have been responsible since you were in clouts and I held your hand to teach you to walk! I have been responsible since father died! I was responsible for taking you privateering instead of leaving you behind as Mother begged me!*

He only looked at Henry and said hoarsely, "Are you certain?"

He nodded, his face pale and sweat streaked, but resolute.

"Dr. Alcott and I talked. He will see that I'm fixed up. And then," Henry swallowed, "when I am recovered I will talk to Purcell about carving me a wooden hand so I do not frighten the ladies."

David blinked his eyes and looked away, examining the lantern hanging aft of the bunk.

"Well." He cleared his throat and tried again. "I will leave you then, to get some rest until...until the doctor is ready for you."

He turned back to the silent doctor, who was swaying slightly, and not entirely from the motion of the vessel.

"Doctor!"

Alcott's head snapped up, and his eyes focused on David.

"You need to rest. Henry will not get any worse over the next few hours, will he?"

Alcott straightened up and looked at Henry.

"As long as he doesn't move about he should be able to wait that long. You may have small amounts of water, Mr. Fletcher, but no food until after—after we are finished."

"You will stay in my cabin since I don't have quarters ready for you, Doctor," David said.

Alcott looked prepared to argue, but nodded.

"If I can nap, I will be better able to deal with Mr. Fletcher."

He scrubbed his hand over his face, and David suspected the lad had been up all night with that laboring woman on the *Lady Jane*. He wanted to yell and rail at him, but knew in his heart that Henry's hand was beyond repair. Terrorizing the man who was needed to remove it would not do any of them any good.

"I will send Lewis to stay with Henry and see to his needs."

Alcott nodded again and, picking up his gear, followed behind him.

David glanced around his cabin, checking for any stray weapons or other items that might tempt a man held against his will, but everything was properly stowed away. Between Lewis and his own lifetime habits, there was not much to remark on in the sparsely furnished cabin.

Alcott set his bag down on the deck.

"Captain—do you have a sick bay or a cockpit aboard this vessel?"

"No. What do you need?"

"I need my own space," the doctor said waspishly. "A room suitable for operating on a wounded man."

David put a hold on his temper and crossed his arms over his chest.

"Tell me what you need, Doctor, and I will instruct the crew."

Alcott scrubbed at his face again. "A table long enough for a man to lie upon, with restraints. A brazier. A second table or shelf for my instruments. Plenty of hot water. Sand on the deck. Good light. As much stability as this ship can offer." He looked up at him. "Aboard the *Caeneus* the surgeon's cockpit was in the orlop and it seemed fairly steady."

"That was aboard a frigate. We do not have facilities like that here, but you will get what you need."

He nodded. "I will need an assistant also. Someone strong, who won't be too frightened to help."

"I will assist you."

"No, you will not. Do not argue with me, Captain. I am the surgeon and I say you are not suitable for this procedure. Find someone else."

David Fletcher was not used to being gainsaid, certainly not on his own ship, and not when his brother's life was at stake, but after a moment's hesitation he acknowledged it would be foolish to argue with the man who would be wielding the knives.

"Brown is the best man for the job. I will assign him to you."

David didn't want to ask, but he had to. All the doctors and surgeons he'd known had been mature men, steady and reliable for the most part, though some weren't worth the powder necessary to blow them away. This nondescript lad in his rumpled brown coat and stained shirt looked like he was more prepared to open his schoolbooks and wield a pen than use a knife on a man.

"Are you really a surgeon?"

"Will you throw me overboard if the answer is no?" Alcott said with the ghost of a smile.

"I cannot afford to do that."

The young man sighed. "No, you cannot. I assisted my father, a physician, for many years and I was heading to Jamaica in the hopes that I could apprentice myself to another doctor I know there. I assisted with an amputation some weeks back on a frigate—the *Caeneus*. Aboard the *Lady Jane* I doctored the crew and the captain's lady in exchange for passage."

"Kill many of them?"

"No, and some did better for my treatment. Face facts, Captain. Right now, I am your best hope for your brother's recovery."

"If Henry dies," David said softly, "I will have no further use for you."

"Henry will die if I do not operate, Captain Fletcher."

David stared at him, but the boy just looked back at him calmly.

"Very well. Stay in here, and I will call for you. There is water in that carafe. Do you need any food?"

"No, no food."

"Do not meddle with anything."

Alcott walked over to the bunk and sat, staring at the deck.

"Alcott."

He looked up, the shadows beneath his eyes stark against the pale skin.

"As you value your life, you will save my brother."

"Go away," he said tiredly.

When David returned some hours later followed by a sailor carrying a tray of food, Dr. Alcott was standing at the stern window, looking out at the schooner's wake.

"Did you sleep?"

"Some. Enough."

He turned from the window and walked farther into the room, the late afternoon light highlighting his plain face, his slender shoulders and arms that looked too fragile to wield a surgeon's saw.

"I am not hungry," he said.

"Eat anyway. I speak from experience," David said when Alcott frowned at him. "You will do better with some nourishment, and the coffee will combat your fatigue."

"A valid point," he acknowledged, seating himself at the small table. David sat on his rumpled bunk and watched the doctor drink some of the harsh but effective coffee brewed in the galley, and then spoon up the chowder.

"This is good," Alcott said in surprise.

"One of the advantages of cruising the islands, Doctor. More access to fresh food, and there are plenty of fish in these waters."

He stopped eating after just a few spoonfuls, but drank the rest of his coffee, a frown digging two lines between his brows.

"You will never grow to your full size by not eating," David said, injecting some heartiness into his voice. "I vow, at your age I could chase down a cow and consume it whole, then be hungry again a few hours later."

A smile twitched the corner of the doctor's mouth. "All young men are empty kettles that never seem full."

"How old are you?"

Alcott looked at him over the rim of his coffee cup. His face taken as whole wasn't going to win him the hearts of young ladies, but David suspected those thick-lashed eyes that tilted up at the corners got him his share of feminine smiles.

"I am twenty years old, Captain."

"You look younger."

"So they tell me."

"Twenty. That is how old Henry is."

"I could tell he was your younger brother."

"Yes, and a pestilent little puppy when he was growing up, always tagging behind me, imitating me, following every-where…even to sea."

David looked down at his hands, clenched into fists on his knees.

"Captain Fletcher."

He looked up. The doctor was watching him.

"Your brother lives, and while there is life, there is hope."

Alcott rose from the table and washed his hands at the basin near the bunk, then picked up his satchel.

"Is my room ready? Take me there so I can prepare, and then I will take care of Mr. Fletcher."

David escorted him to the room near his own cabin. Abovedecks he could hear the crew, one watch eating their meal while the others went about their work. They all knew their tasks, and the sounds and rhythms of the busy ship normally would have soothed his frayed nerves, but not this evening.

The doctor's room would never pass muster on a Royal Navy ship, but the crew had, to David's eye, done an adequate job. There was a table with ropes attached that made him wince to see them. Alcott saw the gesture and only said, "It is necessary, Captain. I have no doubt your brother is a brave soul, but it is too much to expect of any man, not to try and run from the knife."

David watched Alcott go to his instruments and prepare them, tourniquets and knives, saws and sutures. There was no hesitation in the man, and his assured manner gave the captain hope that Henry would be in good hands.

And as the doctor himself said, what choice did they have?

When he was satisfied that all was in order, Alcott took a clean cloth and covered his instruments so Henry would not see them when he was brought in.

"It is time, Captain."

David took one last look at the doctor, who pulled a stained leather apron out of one of his cases and tied it on. He felt the bile rise in his throat at the sight, but he knew what he had to do, and gathered two sailors who were waiting outside the room with a board to carry Henry on. He spent a moment with his brother in the cabin, because Henry insisted on giving him messages for their mother.

"You will come through this to see her again, brother."

"It is in the hand of God, and that surgeon you found for me," Henry said, pain etching lines in his face as he was lifted onto the board to be carried out. He wanted to walk, but David was afraid he might lose his balance and fall against his injured arm, and would not risk it.

Henry was placed on the table, and the sailors prepared to strap him down, but the doctor stopped them and turned to David.

"Leave now, Captain. I will send word when we are finished."

David Fletcher was a strong man and a seasoned warrior. He'd sent his share of foes to their graves, and captured ships of enemy nations, but at the moment he felt again like that little boy charged with taking care that his brother came to no harm.

"I will see you in a few hours," he said to Henry. He did not go to his cabin, but stood watch outside the door to the jury-rigged cockpit. The men stayed away, out of respect to the captain and the suffering mate. None of them saw the silent tears pouring down the captain's face as he listened to his little brother's muffled cries.

CHAPTER 4

Charley sat next to Henry Fletcher's bunk as he slept the pain-free sleep of opium, and she stared at her hands. During the operation they'd been steady. Now they shook like she was standing in a blizzard, and for a moment she watched herself in a detached manner, before tucking her hands in her armpits to still them.

"You cannot doubt yourself while you're working on a patient," Dr. Murray had admonished her, the same wisdom she had heard from her father so many times. But afterward there was plenty of time for reflection, dark thoughts on what she might have done differently, might have done better.

He would have died if not for me, she told herself again. And again. She knew it with a certainty that went deep into her bones, yet she needed to repeat it. Henry Fletcher might yet die. There were no guarantees in life, except that the same end awaited us all, for some sooner than for others.

But what I have done here today may yet allow Mr. Fletcher to live out his natural span, Charley thought, and brought her no longer shaking hands out from beneath her arms. Her back and shoulders ached, and she rolled her shoulders to loosen them. It was no easy thing to saw through human bone.

The door to Henry Fletcher's tiny cabin creaked open. Charley straightened up in the chair as Captain Fletcher stepped in quietly, lines of concern aging his face.

And what a face it was, she mused, allowing herself the small luxury of a brief distraction. In all her days she had never seen a more handsome man than this American pirate. To say he had the face of angel would be wrong, for the pictures of angels she'd seen showed beings of gentleness and light.

There was nothing gentle, or light about Captain Fletcher. One could see him as the angelic being who went after evildoers with a sword, not one of the ones who played the harp.

His eyes were like a tumbler of smoky whisky catching glints of firelight, his teeth were white and even, and his black hair was thick and lustrous, making her itch to run her fingers through it. What she saw of his skin, from the chiseled cheekbones down to the firm jaw and the broad column of his neck, was tanned and smooth. Even his voice was smooth, like cream laced with honey.

Really, it was not fair that all of this bounty had been bestowed on some sea-thief. No doubt when he went ashore the women flocked to him like bees to a blossoming rosebush, and he had his pick of the beauties in various ports-of-call. Miss Charlotte Alcott would never have been one of those buzzing around him, though. Ducks fly with ducks, and swans fly with swans, she reminded herself ruefully. Ah well, it didn't hurt to look.

"How is he?"

The question was asked in a low voice, but Captain Fletcher's eyes were all on his brother, not on her. Charley saw how his glance was drawn to the bandaged stump that looked so empty compared to the hand resting at Mr. Fletcher's side. She knew he was trying not to stare, but he couldn't look away.

"He is resting. Come, we will talk outside his cabin."

She preceded the captain into the narrow corridor and stepped back to give him room when he exited. Captain Fletcher's shoulders filled the space, but she no longer felt threatened by him, at least, not at this moment. He was just another family member standing by helplessly as someone he loved suffered. She had seen that before, and been there before, and felt a little of her anger at him recede.

"I have done what I can. Your brother will need observation and care until the stump heals."

He flinched at her words, but he might as well face the reality of the situation. Nothing was to be gained by pretending all would be as it was.

"Yes, Captain, his stump. Mr. Fletcher is a strong young man, and I am optimistic he will make a full recovery, but it is no small thing for a man to lose a hand. He will have a difficult enough time dealing with it, and you will not help him by pretending there has been no change in his circumstances.

"However, you also will not help him by over-coddling him. Does he favor his right hand, or his left?"

"His right hand." He was watching her intently, as if by concentrating every ounce of his energy on her he could absorb more information, help his brother more. It was somewhat disconcerting, but she reminded herself that all he was seeing was Dr. Alcott, and right now, that was who he needed to believe in.

"That is a mercy then," she said. "It would be more difficult to train him to write and eat using his weak hand. It won't be easy for him, not by a long stretch, but it will be easier this way than if he'd lost his strong hand.

"He will need you and the other members of the crew to assist him without stopping him from doing that which he is capable of doing for himself. And while it is an example pirates may not favor, remember that having one arm did not keep Lord Nelson from achieving great things."

Fletcher did not smile, but her comment lightened his features as he acknowledged her words.

"Even pirates can appreciate an able commander like Lord Nelson, Doctor," he said.

Charley realized that while they'd been speaking she was leaning against the wall, and her eyes were drifting shut. She snapped them open and straightened herself.

"Now, I need to return…" she started to say, but Captain Fletcher interrupted her.

"When was the last time you ate a full meal, Doctor? Or slept through the night?"

She couldn't remember what it felt like to sleep, but he no sooner said the words than tiredness washed over her, pulling her down like syrup oozing onto the deck. She shook herself, and forced her eyes wide open.

"I will nap in the chair in—"

"No, you will sleep in a real bunk, Doctor. I had the men scrub down the sick bay and arrange quarters for you there. It will do for now, until better quarters can be arranged."

"I do not intend to stay aboard this vessel long enough for that to be a necessity, Captain."

"You do not want to have that discussion with me now, Doctor, not when you are so weary you're swaying on your feet. I will sit with Henry, and promise to get you when he awakens. That is an order. You are no good to him or anyone else as exhausted as you are."

She wanted to argue further with him, but the lure of sleep was a siren call to her weary bones. She nodded, and when he hailed a passing sailor, followed the man back to sick bay. The *Lady Jane* had been far from commodious, but this pirate ship was crowded with more men and gear—as well as purloined cargo—crammed into its nooks and crannies 'tween decks, and she fretted for a moment about how she would preserve her disguise.

But that would have to wait for when her mind was clearer. In the meantime, the sailor directed her to the hastily constructed sick bay. The cabin reeked of vinegar and soap with a whiff of coppery blood. She feared the lingering dampness from its scrubbing would give her an ague, but it was still better than sleeping on her feet. When the door closed behind her she used the covered pot kept on hand for sailors too ill to walk. She almost fell asleep there, which would have made a pretty picture in the morning, she chuckled to herself. Instead, she got up one more time and made it to her bunk, which was reasonably dry. Dry enough, anyway. She pried her boots off her tired and swollen feet and fell into the bunk fully clothed, her eyes closing as her head hit the pillow.

A knock at her cabin door brought Charley sitting straight up, blinking at the light coming in through the small window set high in the stern. She pulled her father's watch from her pocket and swore, thrusting her feet back into her boots and running her fingers through her short hair.

"One moment!" she called out, checking herself to make sure her breast bindings and the padding in her trousers was in place before opening the door.

She was stunned to see the deck lined with sailors, some gossiping, some carving at pieces of wood, some braiding macramé like the sailors aboard the *Lady Jane*.

"Wha—?"

"Good morning, Doctor," said Lewis, the steward. "The captain's compliments, and would you please come to Mr. Fletcher's cabin? He is awake."

"Yes, I will be right there. But who are all these men?"

Lewis glanced over his shoulder at the sailors watching the doctor with interest.

"Oh, the men wanted a real sick call, now that we have a doctor aboard. They will wait for you."

Charley looked out over the crew of men watching her expectantly.

"Are any of you bleeding, or have broken bones?"

They looked at each other and shook their heads, some with a muttered, "No, Doctor."

"Then you can all wait until after I have seen Mr. Fletcher and had my breakfast and seen to myself. If Captain Fletcher is agreeable, I will hold sick call then."

Some of the men grumbled, but they accepted her words as law and dispersed back to their various tasks. It looked like Lewis was having trouble keeping a grin off his narrow face, but she grabbed her satchel and followed the steward, his bald pate catching the gleam of the lanterns.

Lewis knocked softly at Henry Fletcher's cabin door, and it was opened by the captain, who looked relieved when he saw Charley.

"My brother is awake."

She nodded. "Step out of the cabin, please, and I will examine him. Oh, and if someone could find me some breakfast for afterward I would very much appreciate it."

This last was punctuated by a loud growl from her belly, and a smile twitched at Captain Fletcher's firm lips.

"Lewis will have it for you in my cabin, Doctor. If you need me, send him."

"Thank you, Captain," she said, and waited for him to

leave. He looked back at his brother one more time, then sighed and exited the cabin, heading back to his duties.

Charley stepped in and smiled at Henry Fletcher.

"Good morning, Mr. Fletcher. How are you today?"

"Maimed," the young man said sullenly, and waived his bandaged arm at her, then winced as the movement brought fresh pain.

"Stop that," Charley snapped. "Of course you are maimed, to pretend otherwise is foolish! But self-pity will only cause others to treat you like a cripple instead of a whole man. Is that what you want?"

This wasn't what she'd planned to say, but it seemed to be the only thing she could say. Perhaps in time she would develop skills to soothe patients, but for now she had to work on getting Henry Fletcher to accept that his life would be different, but not ended.

Her harsh words took the young man aback, and he stared at her. "You do not coddle your patients, do you, Doctor?"

"Not unless they need coddling. Is that what you need?"

"No, Doctor," he said meekly.

She made that "hmph" noise her father and other doctors she knew used when they didn't want to waste words in idle chit-chat, then sat alongside him on the bunk and felt his forehead and neck for fever. His temperature was slightly elevated, but not enough to be alarming. She took his pulse and listened to his lungs with her ear on his chest.

"I need to examine you, Mr. Fletcher. Did you pass water today?"

He nodded.

"Good. I will be as careful as I can, but it will hurt. You can take laudanum afterward."

"I will not need it," he said, but sweat was springing out

on his forehead as even the small stresses of the examination caused him pain.

"You will," Charley said, as she undid the bandages and checked the site for suppuration and excessive bleeding, then bandaged him back up.

"We will fashion a sling for protection for your limb while it heals. I strongly encourage you to return to normal duties as quickly as possible, while keeping your arm immobilized."

"What use is a one-armed sailor aboard a privateer?"

"Privateer? I thought you were pirates. At least, that's what Captain Fletcher said when he kidnapped me."

Henry looked surprised. His was a softer version of his brother's face, its youthful lines edging into manhood, but the resemblance was strong.

"David told you we were pirates? You did not come willingly?"

"Why would I leave a perfectly good English merchantman to come aboard an enemy American ship?"

Now Henry looked angry.

"He did it for me, the fool! He swore he would find a doctor, but taking one as a prisoner—"

He looked fretful and he had enough on his mind, so she tried to reassure him. "Pirate or privateer, I am sure Captain Fletcher and I can work this out. And I am glad he took me aboard the ship to help you. What is the name of this vessel, anyway?"

"You are aboard the *Fancy*, Doctor, the finest schooner to ever sail out of Baltimore."

"The *Fancy*, eh? It does not look very fancy to me."

"That is because you have not seen her in action," said a deep voice.

Charley jumped and looked behind her. She hadn't heard David Fletcher enter the cabin, not surprising since he was barefoot and moved with a cat's sinewy grace. She wrenched her thoughts away from those dangerous waters and frowned at him.

"We must talk, Captain," she said sternly, but turned back to Henry.

"As I said, I am glad I could be of assistance to you, Mr. Fletcher. Right now, that is what is most important. Captain," she said, without looking at him as she finished up her examination, "I need a piece of sturdy cloth suitable for a sling. When Mr. Fletcher returns to duty, he needs to minimize any further trauma to his arm until I take the sutures out."

"How long do the sutures stay in?" Henry asked.

"Ideally, they should stay in at least a month if you are healing well. You will have them removed and the stump examined by another doctor when I am gone from this vessel."

He looked over her shoulder at his older brother, then back at her. Whatever he saw on his brother's face led him to keep further questions inside.

"Drink as much water and tea as you like, but no strong drink. I want your head clear and your balance unaffected as you learn to adjust to your new circumstances. Rest and eat lightly for two days, and if you have no problems, we will return you to a normal diet. You will be in pain, and that is to be expected. But if all goes well you will soon be on your feet and back on duty."

Behind her she heard Captain Fletcher give the orders for suitable cloth to be found for a sling. Inside she was fuming. American privateers were the bane of British shipping, but they still operated under a code of conduct that set them apart from pirates—at least in theory. She knew from dinner conversation aboard the *Lady Jane* that privateers didn't keep prisoners longer than it took to get them to port, and she certainly wasn't a military threat to them to be kept prisoner indefinitely!

Her thoughts were interrupted by Captain Fletcher handing her some sturdy calico that she fashioned into a sling and adjusted it around Henry's neck, easing his arm inside.

"Excellent," she said, studying her handiwork, then took it off him. "Later today we will put this on and you can walk about some. For now, you will take your medicine and rest. Your body has a great deal of healing ahead of it."

She mixed the opiate and watched as, grimacing, Henry Fletcher drank it down.

"I will check on you later, but you send for me if you need me."

"Aye, Doctor," Henry said, his words already slightly slurred as the medicine began its work.

When she closed the cabin door behind her, Captain Fletcher was talking to Mr. Lewis and she waited, trying not to tap her toe impatiently on the deck.

"We need to talk, Captain."

Fletcher turned and scowled down at her. He was wearing a blue linen shirt open at the collar and the loose trousers favored by sailors. It did not matter that he was dressed the same as any of his crew, there was no mistaking who was captain of the *Fancy*, a point he brought home to her.

"It may have escaped your notice, but I have a ship to command. Go eat your breakfast, hold your sick call, and we will speak later."

"I do not want to wait until later, I want to talk—"

"Later, Doctor. And do not argue with me again."

He turned on his heel and left. When she turned toward the captain's cabin, Lewis was watching her with something like awe on his face.

"Not many men brave enough to go up against Black Davy Fletcher."

Charley almost smiled at the idea of "Black Davy Fletcher," but realized Lewis was completely serious.

"Oh? Captain Fletcher has a reputation?"

"It's not for me to talk, Doctor, but there's not a fiercer privateer afloat, nor one as canny."

She wisely kept her opinions to herself and entered the captain's cabin. Lewis left to fetch her breakfast, so she studied the quarters, trying to get a feel for her captor. They were spartan accommodations, and she felt a twinge of disappointment that the notorious "Black Davy" Fletcher didn't have the heads of his enemies mounted on the wall, or the swag and booty of his raids festooning the space. The cabin had a bunk, larger than hers but not decadently so, with a quilted cover neatly tucked in. The desk was bare, but the railed shelf above it contained a grouping of framed miniatures. One was of an older woman with jet black hair and Henry Fletcher's eyes, and alongside it, a man whose face, had it not been covered by a flowing white beard, might bear a strong resemblance to David Fletcher. He looked stern and weathered, his skin sun-darkened to the shade of the oak of the shelf. The other minia-ture made her pause, and she picked it up and angled it to the light coming in from the stern window.

It was a young woman, a breathtakingly beautiful blonde. Artists sometimes exaggerated the good qualities of their subjects for a flattering portrayal, but she suspected this woman needed no additional help beyond Nature's gifts. The hair curling around her head looked like golden floss, falling in lush ringlets over her shoulder. Her neck was a graceful column and her pert nose was balanced by two rosy cheeks and a delicate little chin. Charley had no doubt the rest of her was equally lovely.

She set aside her curiosity and the miniature when she heard a noise outside the cabin, and the door opened to Lewis carrying a tray for her. There were eggs and ham, biscuits that gave her teeth a workout, and her cup was kept filled with strong coffee by Lewis, who waited on her with skill and dexterity.

"You have nimble hands, Mr. Lewis. Would you like to assist me in sick bay?"

Lewis's nimble hands fumbled the coffeepot. "Oh no, Doctor, I am not suited to that work! Blood makes me queasy. When someone throws up, it makes me throw up, too. Besides which," he pointed out with relief, "the captain needs me here and helping Mr. Fletcher."

"Tending Mr. Fletcher does not bother you? The blood on his bandages doesn't make you queasy?"

"That's odd, but you're right." A gleam of a smile split his thin face. "Maybe it's because I have known the Fletcher boys since they were lads. That is why I followed them to sea rather than stay ashore in Baltimore."

"Is it usual for brothers to go privateering together?"

"Well, it's not *unusual*, Doctor. After all, a privateer— whether British or American—is a businessman, and shipping is a family business. The *Fancy* was re-fitted for privateering after the Embargo Act for this very task, fighting for America."

Charley said nothing as she sipped her coffee, mulling over the steward's words. She suspected Captain Fletcher had more of the pirate in him than his loyal crew was willing to acknowledge, and knew he would play fast and loose with the truth when it suited him.

And right now she feared having a doctor aboard until it pleased him to let her go suited him just fine.

The question was, should she reveal herself, and see if

he'd put her ashore? Or should she maintain her disguise and hope for the best?

First, do no harm...

Henry Fletcher needed her. Leaving now would harm him, and she could not do that with a clear conscience.

Having resolved at least part of her dilemma, whether or not to reveal her sex, Charley's mind moved ahead to sick call and she attacked her breakfast with renewed appetite. Nothing stirred her quite like being able to tackle the mysteries of diagnosis and treatment, and who knew? Perhaps a crew of privateers would offer some new and exotic indispositions not seen aboard the *Lady Jane*.

"The men like having a sawbones aboard. Gives them hope of help if they're sick or hurt. Is he staying with us?"

Joseph Bryant was serving as mate with Henry injured, and his question was a valid one. David Fletcher looked at the boatswain, who'd sailed with his father and filled in the gaps in David's seafaring education after Robert Fletcher died.

"He will stay," David said grimly.

"Willingly?"

"Does it matter?"

Bryant looked at his captain, and shook his head. "Not if you say the doctor is staying, will he or nil he. But do you want a man doctoring us against his will? What if he tries to harm one of us?"

A grim smile touched David's lips as he looked at the older man. "The good doctor is a victim of his own ethical nature, Mr. Bryant. I have observed him enough to believe he could never willingly harm someone he was caring for, whether it's an enemy American or a Frenchman or anyone else."

His expression eased as he remembered how the doctor had cared for Henry following his surgery, wanting to forgo his own comfort and spend the night beside his bunk.

"He's just a lad, Joseph. Given time aboard the *Fancy*, he may decide that a better fate awaits him in the United States. We should coax the doctor to the side of 'fair trade and sailors' rights.' He's a bright fellow and enough time with us may change his loyalties."

"You know best, Captain. As I said, it's good for the men to have a surgeon aboard. Knowing he saved Henry's life will help the men accept him as part of the crew."

David, too, had heard the men chatting this morning at their tasks, discussing what ailments they wanted the young doctor to treat while he was aboard.

Bryant hesitated, then spoke again.

"Will Mr. Fletcher be returning to duty?"

"The doctor thinks so. Or perhaps he's saying that to help Henry recover. Regardless, I want to continue this voyage as long as Henry is recovering, and when we return to Baltimore he can decide for himself."

"Aye, Captain. Are we going to head for St. Mary's or Savannah to sell this cargo?"

David tapped his fingers against his spyglass as he thought. "No," he said slowly, "I do believe we will continue cruising for prizes, Mr. Bryant. These waters are rich with British shipping grown lazy and careless now that the French are driven out. I know people who will give us a good price here in the Indies, who would buy from us so they can avoid King George's tariffs.

"And," he said, looking directly at his boatswain, "I do not want Dr. Alcott in an American port where he can demand his parole or exchange. For now it suits me to have a surgeon aboard the *Fancy*, and this is where he'll stay."

∽

Later that day, Charley was prepared to acknowledge that if you have seen one sailor's genitals, you have pretty much seen them all.

And she'd seen a lot of men's parts today. At least seeing Stern's circumcised privates was a novelty, but all the others —same equipment, same problems and a sick man was a sick man, no matter what the setting.

The only instance in which the crew of the *Fancy* differed from the crew of the *Lady Jane*, she reflected as she washed her hands, was the higher incidence of venereal disease she'd been called on to treat today. Clearly, these men had never heard that "A moment with Venus may mean a lifetime with Mercury," and she would have to lay in more supplies of mercury salts and guaiacum for whoever would follow her in treating the men of the *Fancy*.

She was still thinking about it when Captain Fletcher entered sick bay. "I believe I have seen almost every privateer's privates today, Captain."

"Can you say 'privateer's privates' three times, fast?"

"No," but she was smiling. And then she frowned. She did not need to be getting friendly with her captor.

"You won't be seeing mine, Doctor," the captain said matter-of-factly.

Now, that piqued her curiosity. For purely academic reasons. "Really? And why would that be? Do you not engage in the same activities as your men?"

"I trust you are asking this in your professional capacity, Dr. Alcott. The reason is, I always use a French letter."

"I have heard of such devices, but I have never seen one used!"

"I am not going to demonstrate for you."

Charley tried not to be disappointed. She was only asking in the name of research. "You always use one?"

He looked at her as if gauging how far he wished to continue this conversation regarding his leisure time activities.

"Yes, always, unless I am with widows I know very well. Seeing men pissing blood and pus is more effective than a parson's best hellfire-and-damnation sermon to keep me from boarding the fireships in port."

"That is an extremely prudent attitude, Captain. My workload would be lessened considerably if that way of thinking infected the men."

Fletcher shrugged. "Life is short. Most of these men would rather visit the school of Venus whenever they can than worry about the possibility of a disease. Odds are a fall from the yards or a piece of shot will finish them off sooner."

"Speaking of my workload—"

But Captain Fletcher wasn't paying attention to her, he was walking around the sick bay, looking at how she'd arranged her tools and her chest, the neatly rolled bandages, the texts she'd brought with her lined up on the small desk attached to the wall. Her journal where she kept daily records of the men she'd treated and problems she'd encountered was still open, the ink drying.

"You write a neat hand, Doctor," the captain said as he picked up her journal. She would have snatched it from him because it was private information about the men, but they were his crew. And there was no personal information in her journal that could give away her identity.

Nonetheless, she said, "I would appreciate it if you would not read my journal."

He looked at her, and seemed about to argue about what he could or couldn't do aboard his own ship, but instead he gave her a small nod, pulled out the chair from the desk and sat, then motioned her to take a seat on the bunk.

She almost smiled at how she'd gotten used to men sitting in her presence, taking her masculine status for granted, but composed her features and sat across from him, legs apart in the pose that was now second nature to her.

"What kind of game are you playing, pretending to be a pirate, Captain Fletcher?"

Captain Fletcher's expression made it clear he was not used to being addressed in such a fashion, but Charley would not allow herself to be intimidated by the brash American. She must establish herself as an equal player in this game or he would stomp all over her.

"I am perfectly within my rights to take prisoners, so do not take that high-handed approach with me, you insolent puppy! I had my reasons, and they are not your concern."

"I would say they are very much my concern!" she plowed ahead. "If I am a prisoner of a privateer, then I demand you take me to shore so my freedom can be negotiated!"

Fletcher just gave her a smile that sent a chill down her spine. "And if you are believed to be in the hands of pirates, then your freedom is not as negotiable, is it?" he said softly. "Nor, might I add, are your status and safety as assured."

"You do not plan to release me, do you?" she said, stunned.

"Not until it suits my purposes to do so, and that depends on Henry's recovery. I took you off the *Lady Jane* for a reason, Doctor. I will not let you go until I am sure my brother is recovered. After that..."

"After that?"

Fletcher stood, and looked down at her, and he gave her a

charming smile that disordered her thoughts, but she forced herself to focus on his words, not his exceptional looks.

"Who knows, Doctor, you might enjoy your time aboard a privateer. It might be 'a sea change, into something rich and strange.' I would consider having you sign on for a share, if your medical skills prove valuable." He grew serious. "You are a young man yet, with your life ahead of you. In America there are great opportunities for a man with drive and ambition, and plenty of communities looking for skilled doctors."

Charley rose. She couldn't look him in the eye without tilting her head back, but she could stand straight.

"I am British, Captain, not American. Our countries are at war and I will not be a traitor to my king by signing on with enemy privateers. Or pirates."

He looked at her thoughtfully, then gave a small nod.

"I respect that. However, I expect you to give my men the same treatment you would give English sailors."

"You insult me by saying that, Captain."

"As long as we are clear. Now, in the meantime, if you give me your parole I have no problem with you having the run of the ship." He looked around the sick bay. "This is a good idea, having a sick bay and regular sick call for the men."

She crossed her arms over her chest, and said, with only a small amount of trepidation, "It is not enough."

"Oh?"

"You will assign someone to help clean in here, to free me to work. Also, I will make a survey of your ship. I will not work in an environment that only contributes to disease and disorder."

He waved his hand negligently. "You do what you need to, Doctor. Talk to Lewis, he will suggest someone to help you. In the meantime, I would like you to dine with me this evening, along with Mr. Bryant and Mr. Purcell. I take my luncheon alone, and you can join the men or dine in your cabin here during the day."

She thought about it, then shook her head. "Mr. Fletcher needs to be observed Captain, as fever is almost a given after a procedure of this type. If you will excuse me this evening, I will sit with him and dine with you another time."

"As you will, Dr. Alcott."

He gave her a nod and left, and Charley took the seat he'd vacated. She imagined she could smell a faint fragrance in the captain's wake, a scent that combined salt and shaving soap and something that she could whimsically term *eau de command*.

It really was not fair. Someone that handsome should have some noticeable flaws—flatulence or rotting teeth or an annoying laugh. The damned pirate even had dimples.

Well, she could not let male beauty blind her to her goal of getting off this ship and to Dr. Wilson's home in Jamaica. Daydreaming about Black Davy Fletcher was unproductive.

And it was dangerous in too many ways to count.

CHAPTER 5

The fever Charley feared hit Henry Fletcher that night. The rising warmth in his dry skin, the brightness in his eyes and his rapid pulse told an unmistakable and all too common tale.

"It is as I expected, Captain," she told the frowning commander. "Mr. Fletcher is reacting to the trauma of the surgery. His body's humors are out of balance, and that impedes the healing."

"What can you do for him?"

"I will take some blood, but I have found that oftentimes letting nature take its course and allowing the body to fight on its own without drastic interference gives the best outcome. Sweating through the fever will also help bring him back into balance, but he needs fluids to produce a good sweat."

She sighed and looked down at Henry, now sleeping fitfully in his bunk. "I will stay here with him, but when the watch changes I would appreciate it if you would have Miller or Lewis relieve me. I need to get supplies from sick bay and I will return shortly."

The expression on David Fletcher's face told its own tale, and Charley paused at the door. "He is young, and healthy before this, and his body is fighting to survive. Do not give up hope, Captain Fletcher, for I have not."

He only looked at her, and then turned back to his brother's bedside, speaking in low tones to soothe the man tossing restlessly in his fevered sleep.

She walked the passageway to sick bay with a frown that discouraged the sailors from addressing her. She was worried about her patient's agitation jarring his stump, but she did not want to lash him to the bunk unless it became absolutely necessary.

Her medical supplies were somewhat depleted, and she paused, wondering how strong her willowbark would be after weeks at sea. Charley took it anyway, along with some chamomile, and her lancet and bloodletting bowl. She now followed Dr. Murray's custom of keeping a tourniquet or two dangling from her coat pocket, and saw the sailors eye them with approval, part of the medical paraphernalia that gave them confidence that she knew what she was doing.

Keeping up appearances was half the battle in getting patients to believe in their own recovery, a mental process that she was sure aided the physical process. At the very least, it did no harm.

The door to Mr. Fletcher's cabin was open, and Captain Fletcher was talking to Lewis.

"Excellent, just the person I need."

The men turned to look at her, Lewis with a worried expression when he saw the blood bowl.

"No, Mr. Lewis, it does not involve blood, but I need your assistance."

She looked at the medications in her hand and thought about the course of a fever in a strong man. "I need clean water and cloths, and weak tea with sugar, and coffee for me."

"Who is the tea for?"

"Your brother, when he awakens. The fever will give him a thirst, but he should avoid strong drink. The sugar in the tea will help him regain his strength. If his fever stays low, I will try to get him to take some beef tea or gruel tomorrow, but he may not have any appetite and I do not believe in forcing patients to eat. Usually their own bodies know what they need and respond accordingly. The water and cloths are to wipe his face."

Captain Fletcher nodded, and his shoulders straightened a fraction. He was a man of action, and any action would be better than nothing.

"Mr. Lewis, if you would see to that, Captain Fletcher will assist me in the bloodletting."

The relief on Lewis's face at not having to help with the bleeding would have been almost comical, but Charley had already slipped into the cabin. The space was so confined they were shoulder to shoulder, and she was aware of the man next to her as much as she was aware of the patient in his bunk. Black Davy Fletcher would dominate whatever space he occupied, whether it was a small cabin or a ballroom.

She adjusted the lantern and sat next to Mr. Fletcher, taking his good arm in hers. The captain stood behind her and closed the door.

"Hold the bowl, Captain, this will not take long."

She unwrapped her fleam from the oiled rag that protected it from rust, and held it up to the light to inspect the edge. She set it aside and took her ligature, tied it around Henry Fletcher's arm and raised the vein.

"Steady the bowl now."

The lancet flashed in the light and the blood spurted into the bowl in a crimson stream. Charley watched the liquid rise, the marks inside the bowl telling her how much was being removed. Her father hadn't needed such an aid, but he said that came with years of experience, being able to tell at a glance how much blood was being let.

When she had enough to satisfy her, she closed the wound and bandaged it, then examined the blood in the bowl before setting it aside to be disposed of.

"Is that wise, bleeding a man when he's already lost so much blood?"

"I will make a bargain with you, Captain. I will practice the medicine and you will sail the ship. It works out to be far more satisfactory that way." She looked up from where she was holding Henry's wrist and measuring his pulse rate.

He was scowling at her, again. Clearly the pirate was not used to people who talked back. Charley did not even know why she was being so antagonistic—she considered herself to normally be the most easy-going of persons, but there was something about Captain Fletcher, especially when he was so near to her that she could smell the soap on his skin, that raised her hackles and made her snap at him.

She couldn't concern herself with that now, and if his presence was going to distract her from what she needed to do, he'd have to leave. Fortunately he solved her dilemma himself by rising and looking down at his brother one more time, then at her.

"Do what you can, Doctor. Call me if you need me."

"Captain."

Fletcher stopped, his hand on the door latch, and looked over his shoulder.

"It would be better for Mr. Fletcher if he could recover ashore."

"That is no doubt true, but with the British Navy controlling these waters, there are few ports where I could safely drop anchor, and none of them are nearby. Henry will stay here, and you will see to it that he recovers."

Or else…was the unspoken punctuation to that sentence, but Charley could not let his threats distract her from the task at hand, any more than she could let his beauty distract her.

He threatened her in more ways than he could imagine.

She turned back to her patient, and prepared for a long night.

The next days passed in a blur for Charley. Trying to get fluids into Henry Fletcher, using her limited pharmacopeia to lower his fever, bathing his face and chest with cool water, and snapping at poor Mr. Lewis when he asked about a blistering plaster to draw the fever out.

After an especially tense night the fever spiked, then broke, and his sleep now was the deep sleep of healing. She returned to sleeping in her own bunk, and thought David Fletcher looked at her with new respect, but that could have been the bad lighting belowdecks.

She prepared stimulating Peruvian bark tonics, and Henry Fletcher complained about the "swill" being forced on him—a good sign, to Charley's eyes. The swelling around his stump appeared to be normal for a wound of such severity, and there were no red streaks of infection or development of proud flesh around the site, for which she thanked whatever angel guided the hands of surgeons, especially unqualified ones.

It occurred to her one morning as she was preparing a

sulphur ointment for Stern's scabies that she was oddly content. While she might question herself, and feel all too often that she wasn't up to this task, the crew of the *Fancy* had faith in her, and that strengthened her resolve.

When she wasn't tending to Mr. Fletcher, she tended the rest of the ship and soon realized that the daily sick call could be a high form of entertainment for men stuck at sea with no vessels to rob. Her schedule kept her busy enough that she spent most of her time in sick bay either seeing to the men or writing up her notes, oftentimes taking her meals on a tray. The talented carpenter, Mr. Purcell, adjusted her examining table for her so that it could be raised or lowered as she needed, and when it wasn't covered with a sailor's body it was a good workspace. While she could have wished for more windows and natural lighting, there were plenty of lanterns on hand to work by. She knew her situation, at least from a professional point of view, could have been much worse.

When Charley didn't eat in her cabin, she ate with Mr. Bryant and Mr. Purcell and "Sails," the sailmaster. The captain, she discovered, preferred to spend his scarce free moments with his brother or in his own cabin.

David Fletcher was enjoying a rare moment of quiet, a moment interrupted by a peremptory knock at the cabin door. He sighed and stood, setting aside the gothic novel he'd been reading, a secret vice he kept well hidden from his crew.

"Come in, Doctor."

Alcott strode into the cabin, frowning. "How did you know it was me?"

"I suspected it from that annoying knock."

"Oh." He looked taken aback, but recovered quickly. "We need to talk, Captain Fletcher. You have been avoiding me these past days and I will not have it!"

David looked down at the feisty youngster. The doctor had balls, there was no doubt about it. It would be sad to have to chuck him over the side, but sometimes a captain did what a captain had to do.

On the other hand, there was Henry to think about. David pulled his shirt over his head and tossed it on the bunk. When he turned back, the doctor was staring at him and... Good Lord, the boy was blushing.

Alcott cleared his throat and said, "You have quite a collection of scars, Captain Fletcher."

David went to get a clean shirt from his chest, and pulled it over his head. Alcott was staring out the window, not watching him.

"Do my scars bother you, Doctor?"

He adjusted his neckcloth, then looked back at him.

"No, Captain, certainly not. I expect in your line of work they are not at all unusual. It just...startled me." A smile twitched the doctor's lips. "Usually, people do not take off their clothes in my presence until I tell them to."

"I can see how that might cramp your social life with the ladies."

Alcott frowned again and crossed his arms. "I did not come here to discuss my social life, but the state of your ship. I refuse to work in a pigsty! I do not care if you are the most ferocious pirate to ravage the shipping of the West Indies..."

"Privateer, and as a matter of fact, I am."

"...but I will not work under these conditions! You insist I doctor your men, fine! But first get them down into the bowels of this ship with more soap, vinegar, sulphur to fumigate..." He ticked off the list on his fingers. "Oh, and while you are at it, see if you can steal a cat. You have a rat population."

"All ships have a rat popul—see here, Doctor, there is something you need clarified. I am the captain, and I might add, the owner and master of this vessel. You are a doctor. And a prisoner. That means you do not give me orders. I give the orders, and you obey them."

"Or what?" Alcott sneered. "You will let me go? Have me flogged? Set me adrift in a boat? I do not think so, Captain Fletcher. You need me, and we both know it."

David fastened his shirt to keep his hands busy. Punching the doctor in the face was probably not the best way to resolve this, but it was a temptation. "You already have Miller assisting you. Talk to Mr. Bryant, and he will know which men are available."

Suddenly the doctor's face changed as a smile broke through. A thought passed through David's mind that Dr. Alcott should smile more often if he ever hoped to attract a young lady willing to take her clothes off for something other than a medical examination.

"I do not need to bother Mr. Bryant with this, Captain, because Mr. Fletcher returned to duty."

"What?" David said, then felt his own smile flow across his face. "Why didn't you tell me right away?"

Alcott looked distracted for a moment, then blinked and said, "That is what I came to tell you, but a rat the size of a curricle ran across my foot and reminded me about the disgraceful condition of your ship. Mr. Fletcher is above and, in my opinion, is capable of resuming his duties."

"He is no longer in pain?"

"He still has pain. He will always have some pain, including phantom pains from the missing hand. But resuming his duties makes him feel needed and useful, and that will help his recovery."

"He is needed, and useful. If you say he's ready, then I will defer to your judgment."

"As you should," Alcott said recklessly. He turned to leave as David reached for his coat.

"And get a cat!" was the last thing he said as he closed the cabin door behind him, but this time David only smiled.

CHAPTER 6

When he came above David saw Henry next to Mr. Bryant. His brother was standing straight and looked less drawn, though he was still too skinny and too pale from his ordeal. With Henry's left arm in a sling it was easy to fool the eye into thinking there was nothing more than a broken limb, until you looked closer and realized there was no hand coming through the other side of the cloth.

Bryant was going over some papers with the *Fancy*'s second-in-command, and David walked over to see what they were discussing. The doctor was nowhere to be found, probably stirring up trouble elsewhere. Then the wind shifted and he caught a whiff of vinegar and brimstone, and he grinned. Clearly Dr. Alcott was wasting no time in putting his demands into effect.

"High time you stopped loafing about in your bunk, you sluggard! I was beginning to suspect you and that quack were in collusion to keep you from doing your duties."

Bryant and Henry looked over at him, and Henry's wide

grin as he saw his brother was better than any medicine Dr. Alcott could have dispensed to David.

"Not at all, Captain! In fact, Dr. Alcott was just here ordering men right and left and putting them to work below."

David grunted. He was annoyed because the doctor had a way of getting on his nerves like no one else. But he knew inside that the doctor wasn't being unreasonable.

"If it keeps the men busy, then I see no problem with the doctor's demands," he acknowledged.

"And he wants a cat, too."

"I believe his exact words were we should 'steal a cat.'"

Henry chuckled, a sound that lifted David's spirits, and Mr. Bryant returned to his duties. The *Fancy* was humming like the well-tuned machine it was, each man knowing his task and his role in capturing goods and money to line their pockets and the coffers of the U.S. Treasury. It was no wonder the navy was having a difficult time getting suffi-cient sailors to man their ships, when the pickings and prizes were so much better aboard the privateers.

There was a fair wind from the southwest, and a lookout aloft kept an eye open for further opportunities for the crew to enrich itself. *And help the war effort, of course*, he thought, as he saw Dr. Alcott emerge from below.

The man was still a lubber and always would be, but David had to acknowledge, in all fairness, that the Englishman made a good faith effort to integrate himself into the crew. If the *Fancy*'s captain did not give him such a difficult time, the doctor might consider staying aboard and becoming an American.

Alcott walked around the deck of the schooner, stopping to talk with the men at their tasks and ask questions of them. The crew laughed at the doctor's landsman ways, but it was good natured laughter. Mr. Bryant had been correct that having a sawbones aboard improved morale.

As if reading his mind, Henry said, "Dr. Alcott has become part of the crew in a short time. Do you think he will stay with us, or will he insist on being put ashore?"

"It is too early to say. I would like to do whatever I can to encourage him to stay with us. He is young and by his own admission untrained, but he is better than nothing."

"Far better than some I have seen," Henry said. "You and I both know ship's surgeons whose hands shake from drink and who kill more than they save."

"I am hopeful, Henry, that even if Dr. Alcott wishes to leave the *Fancy* he will consider staying in the United States. We could use men of his talents, whether at sea or ashore. In the meantime," he said, stroking his chin thoughtfully, "let us emphasize for our good doctor the benefits of casting his lot with us. If we make his stay aboard the vessel pleasant, he may not push so hard for his release."

Alcott joined them and looked Henry over with a professional eye. "The fresh air has put some color back in your face, Mr. Fletcher. I approve."

"It is good to be back at work, Doctor. But this sling hampers me!"

"Do not take it off!" he said sternly. "You need to protect your arm until the sutures are removed. When you are in your cabin, you can stretch and move your arm carefully. You will lose strength in that limb; however, given your age and your general good health, you will regain it soon."

David did not want to make Henry feel like he was hovering over him, so he joined the doctor in strolling the deck.

"I need to do this more often," Alcott confessed. "Just as the fresh air has a salubrious effect on Mr. Fletcher, it is good for me as well. Sitting all day in the sick bay and not getting enough exercise will make me a candidate for illness."

"Do you not worry about catching a disease from those you treat?"

He looked at him with a sidelong glance, a smile quirking his lips. "When I first started studying my father's texts I was sure I was developing every disease I read about. Not the women's complaints," he added hastily, "but every time my heart seemed to skip a beat, every time I felt flushed, I was sure I was coming down with some virulent plague. But I moved beyond that, and now know that with proper prevention I can do my best to avoid those ills. Exercise like this stroll, for example, and following the example of your sailors in drinking lime juice to prevent scurvy."

They walked in companionable silence, then the doctor stopped and looked up at Jenkins in the rigging.

"Your ship…"

"Not a ship, Doctor, a schooner."

"Ship, schooner, what difference does it make?"

"Ah, when you are sailing a beauty like this, it can make all the difference in the world." David smiled and lifted his face toward the sunshine, feeling the wind as the *Fancy* soared across the water in a broad reach. A man could ask for nothing finer than being master of his own vessel, feeling every plank and line of it in his bones, always aware of the wind and its direction and how it filled the sails.

"A ship has three masts and is square-rigged. The *Fancy* is rigged for speed," he said, pointing to the raking masts. "She's fine-lined and tall, and built in Baltimore, home of the fastest vessels afloat. And that ability to maneuver quickly is necessary, because unlike your British merchants, we do not have a fleet of navy ships escorting us everywhere. We Americans have to rely most on our own wits, our seamanship, and our gunnery skills to stay free."

"Your voice when you speak of this vessel is like how some men speak of their wives."

"I hope my wife will understand how I share my affections with this lady."

The doctor looked at him. "You are married, Captain Fletcher?"

"I have plans." He frowned. He didn't want to talk about his pending marriage or what it would mean to him.

"Come, let us continue our walk. Do you realize this is the first time we have been able to engage in real conversation?"

That struck David at the same time he said it. The doctor had been aboard ship for over a week, yet they'd never shared a meal or talked about anything other than ship's business. If he was going to woo the good doctor to the cause of the United States, he would have to do better. He glanced sidelong at the young man beside him. He'd seen the possessions brought aboard and suspected he had little money. A young man of his caliber could do far better in the United States where doctors were at a premium and valued members of society, but he would need assistance, mentoring and advice.

For example, he was dressed in his usual drab clothing. The sailors and officers of the *Fancy* favored colorful garments, where he looked like he would easily blend into a stand of barren trees with his walnut-colored coat and mud-hued trousers. Even his waistcoat was a washed-out shade of mustard that if it was once a vibrant hue had left the color behind in the past.

"Is there something wrong with my coat?"

"I was just wondering why you dress yourself in such a lackluster wardrobe."

Alcott looked up at him and raised an eyebrow.

"It is true, Doctor. You dress in a, dare I say, Quakerish manner. No flair at all."

"Not everyone feels incomplete without a yellow-dotted Belcher neckerchief."

"I simply dress as befits my status. The ladies expect a certain flair from Black Davy Fletcher. But you dress as if you are trying to blend into the woodwork."

"I had no idea you were such an arbiter of fashion, Captain Fletcher," Alcott said with a smile that enhanced his unremarkable face but made him seem younger.

David wondered, not for the first time, if the lad was even shaving yet. If he was, he clearly did not need to do it daily based on the fuzz growing on his jawline.

"Don't those notions of colorful attire play havoc with your republican sensibilities in the United States?" he said, bringing the conversation back 'round.

"Doctor! Have you never heard that clothes make the man? Even in an egalitarian land such as the United States we know this. Certainly in my native Maryland a man who does not dress well—he would have a hard time being taken seriously as a successful merchant."

"My clothing is perfectly suitable to my profession."

"All that brown!"

"Hides bloodstains, and other less savory fluids."

"Well, I will give you that," David acknowledged. "But if you ever wish to attract the young ladies, Doctor, I will give you this to mull over. Girls like the man who dresses with a sense of style. Think of it this way… The butterflies go to the most colorful flowers, not the drab ones."

"I will bear that in mind if I ever wish to consider myself an attractant to butterflies."

David smiled. He enjoyed sparring with the lad. The boy made up for his lack of years with a quick wit and intelligence that made him a welcome addition to the small community of a privateer. As the captain, he had to keep a distance from his men, and having someone new to joust with was good for him as well.

"I hope this voyage will be educational for you in many ways, Doctor," David went on, sounding rather ponderous even to his own ears. "A young man of your limited experience could learn a great deal from the men of the *Fancy*. Going to sea was the making of most of them, and it will be the making of you also. By the time this voyage is finished you will be a new man!"

"Too true," Alcott murmured. "But as to the duration of this voyage..."

Whatever he was going to say was interrupted by a call from aloft.

"Captain, a sail! Off the starboard bow!"

He opened his spyglass to get a better look. Alcott shaded his eyes, trying to make the vessel out.

"Is it a British ship?"

David ignored him, focusing on the vessel coming into view.

"Mr. Fletcher!"

"Sir!"

"Call the men to quarters."

"Aye, sir!" Henry said briskly, and it warmed David to hear the excitement in his brother's voice.

"Is it a British vessel? Send me over to her, Captain!"

"Get below, Doctor. Your station is in sick bay to prepare for any wounded."

"But—"

"If you poke your head abovedecks while we are in contact with that vessel, or question my orders again, I will shoot you myself."

David took a moment to glance at the man next to him.

The doctor appeared stunned at the threat, but there was no time to deal with his bruised sensibilities.

"Do I make myself clear, Dr. Alcott?" he said softly.

"Aye, Captain Fletcher," the man gritted out, and turned to go below. David watched his stiff back leave the deck, then turned to more important matters.

~

Charley almost slammed a bottle of olive oil down on her table, but pulled her hand just in time. She would not let her temper get the better of her, and she would not, by God, allow that insufferable American pirate to cause her to damage her limited supplies!

If they were engaging another ship injuries would be likely, and her first duty was to care for the injured, not to save her own skin by escaping from this enemy vessel.

But the arrogance of that man, discussing fashion one minute, threatening her life the next, it was not to be borne.

And the alternative is...?

She sighed, and ran her hand through her hair, brushing it back from her forehead. There was no alternative. She was a prisoner here, but more importantly, right now she was needed. Even though she knew her blades were freshly sharpened, she checked them again. She took out her saws, and probes, and covered them so the injured men wouldn't see them when they were brought in. She arranged bandages and ointments, and reviewed her notes from Dr. Murray, and her Woodall, and strained her ears to hear what was happening above her head. She thought about risking that head by poking it abovedecks, but trusted Captain Fletcher to be a man of his word.

Charley was unprepared for the roar of the twelve-pounder as it fired on the other ship and she nearly lost her footing, but recovered in time to hear the answering fire from the ship being attacked by the *Fancy*, and feel the blow to the schooner as one of the missiles struck, followed by yells from above. Moments later the door to sick bay burst open and Reynolds staggered in, supported by Lewis. A piece of wood protruded from Reynolds's thigh.

"Hit by a splinter, Doctor."

"I can see that. Help him over to the table."

A whiff of gunpowder and sulphur entered with the men, and Lewis left as soon as Reynolds was settled.

"Take it out quickly, Doctor. They need me above."

"Do not tell me how to do my business," Charley said absently as she cut through the blood soaked trouser leg.

Reynolds gripped the table and swore, then apologized.

"Not necessary, Mr. Reynolds, though I assure you I have never had relations with a goat. Now, I suggest you look away and try to think of something else. Is that a British ship you are fighting?"

"Naw, some Spaniard. He must have a good cargo for him to be firing back at us. Usually they just surrender. Easier that way."

Her attention was all on the gaping gash in his leg, but much as she deplored the idea of robbing some innocent Spaniard, part of her was glad it wasn't a British ship engaged with the Americans. She removed the shards of wood from Reynolds's bloody thigh, and when she was satisfied she'd gotten them all, cleaned and bandaged the battered leg.

"Do your best to keep the bandage clean and I will check on you tomorrow. For now you should stay off that leg."

Reynolds's grin split his smoke-blackened face.

"Naw, a little scratch like this can't keep me out of the fray, Doctor. I've got to get above so I can get my share!"

And with that he hobbled out, one trouser leg flapping

after him like a crimson flag.

Charley shook her head but had no time to mull over Reynolds's folly as more men came in, presenting a variety of wounds, none of them overly serious. One man had a burned hand from mishandling the match (he came in for some ribbing for that), another had a gash on his head from a bad fall, and she set a sailor's broken arm.

The din above had been a constant noise, and she still jumped at the sound of the guns from both ships. She could also smell a great deal of smoke, and the sick bay was hazy with it, but the injured men assured her the *Fancy* was sound and had not taken any serious damage.

Finally the wounded ceased trickling in, and Charley realized how exhausted she was, and how stiff and sore. She was straightening up and wincing when the door opened again, but this time it was Captain Fletcher who stood framed there. His face was blackened from soot and he had a thread of blood oozing down his arm from beneath the sleeve rolled up to his bicep, but his grin was white and wide beneath the grime.

"It was a rout, Doctor! The damned Spanish thought they could outfight my men, but we showed them right and proper!"

"Let me tend to that wound on your arm, Captain."

He looked down and seemed to notice for the first time he that he was wounded. "Huh. I don't even remember getting that."

"Sit," she directed him, and Fletcher took the chair, holding out his arm. "Are there wounded aboard the Spanish ship?"

"If there are, that's their problem. Do not look at me that way, Doctor, you are the *Fancy*'s medical man, and I'm not about to risk you by putting you aboard their tub."

Charley didn't want to get into an argument. "Was it a

good haul for you?"

That amazing smile split his face again, and she paused from cleaning the dirt and blood off of his arm. When he smiled like that, something twisted inside her and it almost hurt.

Who was she fooling? It did hurt. It hurt because she could not respond to that smile as a woman would, and it hurt because she suspected that even if she could respond, she wouldn't be the woman he wanted.

And now she'd learned he was to be married.

She needed to get over this…this obsession she was developing regarding this man. For her own health and safety, he must never suspect that she was hoodwinking him. She lowered her gaze back down to his arm. He was talking animatedly and hadn't noticed her pause.

"…and while I would vastly have preferred a specie ship outbound for Spain, there's nothing wrong with a ship carrying fine Madeira and silks and linens for the markets of Havana! The ladies in New York and Baltimore and Boston will like them just as well, and Yankees will toast the war efforts over the wine in our hold."

He frowned. "Almost too good a haul. I need to get some of this to market myself before there's not room to turn around in the hold. Oh, and that reminds me. Are you finished there?"

"In a moment," she said, tying the bandage securely. "There, you're done."

He rose and walked to the door, then stepped outside and returned carrying a covered basket. "Here, this is for you."

She took the basket from him and the weight shifted, causing her nearly to drop it. But she got the lid open and a bewhiskered head poked out, looking at her gravely.

"I brought you a kitty. But he only speaks Spanish," Fletcher said straight-faced.

The cat pushed himself out of his confinement and jumped to the deck.

"I hope 'Rat!' is a universal call to action for felines," Charley said, studying her share of loot from the Spanish prize. The cat was a gray tom who looked like he'd seen his share of action at sea. One ear was nearly chewed off and she suspected there might be a need to dust him for fleas—did she have any pennyroyal in her chest? But he seemed to take his new surroundings in stride as he strolled through sick bay, checking into the crevices and crannies, then sat on the deck to lick one paw.

"I don't suppose you bothered to find out if the cat has a name?"

"I would not be at all surprised if they referred to him as 'cat' or more likely, '*gato*.' But if you feel it is necessary, by all means give him a name, Doctor."

"Hmmm...Hippocrates is too much of a mouthful, and doesn't seem to suit his demeanor. I believe I shall call him... Pirate. Since he was stolen at sea," she finished with a bland smile.

"A most appropriate choice," Fletcher said, rolling his sleeve down over his wounded arm. He frowned again. "You are moving stiffly, Dr. Alcott."

"It is a long afternoon in sick bay, Captain. I am not used to working under such tense conditions. Remember, I am not a trained sea surgeon."

"You are at least as good as most of the ones I've known. Drunks and derelicts, the lot of them!"

"I am glad that I am in such illustrious company."

"That is my point. You are not like most of the men who go to sea to practice medicine."

"No, I dare say I am not," Charley said dryly.

"You are younger than most, but I hope you never lose your enthusiasm and commitment to your patients," he said, looking at her with sincerity shining out of those eyes like warm topazes.

Her breath caught, and she had to clear her throat before speaking.

"Thank you, Captain Fletcher. Your regard means more to me than I can say."

"I am a plain-speaking man, but I mean what I say. Would you like me to massage your neck for you, to ease some of that stiffness? A Chinaman gunner showed me some tricks that would relax your muscles in a trice."

"No! I mean, thank you for your offer, but I must set the sick bay to rights."

"Will we see you at supper?"

"Please ask Mr. Lewis to bring me a tray. I have to write up my observations of today's events while they are still fresh in my mind. While I hope this will be the last action at sea for me, I cannot count on that."

Fletcher only nodded at this. "Is there anything I need to know about the wounded?"

"No, none of the cases are serious, assuming they don't do further injury to themselves. I do want to check on Henry though. Please send him to me."

"Then I will see you later, Dr. Alcott. Thank you for patching me up."

He opened the cabin door and Pirate scooted out to earn his keep patrolling the hold. Fletcher turned in the doorway as she spoke.

"No need to thank me, Captain, it is my job."

"Nonetheless, you are skilled at your job, and I appreciate that."

He left and she watched the empty space where he'd been standing moments before, filling her cabin with his vitality and *joie de vivre*. Then she sighed and began to put her sick bay to rights.

CHAPTER 7

"...And the fighting was fierce, and Dav—Captain Fletcher was in the midst of it, his cutlass in hand, looking for all the world like he was enjoying a day in the park. I wish you could have seen it, Doctor!"

"I have no doubt the captain fought bravely, Mr. Fletcher, but if you recall, I am the person responsible for patching up the wounded. I would just as soon as not have to deal with men injured through violence in addition to those who come to me for accident or illness. Now, hold still, I do not want to jar your arm."

"Well, it is no wonder you feel that way. But I imagine if you were a man you would feel differently."

Time stood still as the blood froze in Charley's veins. Her ears were ringing and for one mercifully brief moment thought she might swoon. Then common sense asserted itself. Surely Henry Fletcher's remark was only a reflection of her perceived youth, not her sex.

But when she looked up into his eyes he was watching her carefully.

"Are you ever going to tell him?"

"Tell whom what?" she bluffed.

"Tell my brother that you are a woman."

She continued wrapping the bandage, knowing that he was watching her. When she finished, she swallowed and looked into those eyes, so similar to his brother's, but a warmer shade of brown.

"No. I am not going to tell him. Are you going to tell Captain Fletcher?"

"What, and ruin all this fine entertainment?" Henry joked, but then he got serious. "If he does find out, it will not go well for you. If you need help, Dr. Alcott, you can turn to me."

Charley looked away, blinking the unmasculine moisture out of her eyes.

"Thank you, Mr. Fletcher."

"You do not need to thank me. I owe you my life. What kind of man would I be if I repaid you with betrayal?" He smiled a gentle smile, and she thought again on how while Mr. Fletcher may not have his brother's breathtaking good looks, he would not have difficulty attracting his own butterflies.

"Why are you doing this?" he asked curiously.

She turned away and washed her hands, and he waited patiently for her to continue.

"My father was the doctor for our town and the surrounding area. When my mother died it was just easier for him to dress me as a boy and take me with him. As I grew, he discovered I had an interest and aptitude for healing. I think…I think he tried to forget I was Charlotte, and I became 'Charley' in all but reality. He wanted an apprentice, and he had one."

"Didn't your family say anything?"

"My parents were estranged from my mother's family because they wanted her to marry better than a country doctor. And my father was an orphan. So it was just the two of us, and the housekeeper and her husband, and it suited us fine. Until my father died."

"I cannot imagine being without family," Henry said. "They are always there for you—whether you like it or not. David had most of the raising of me, first with our father at sea, and then after his death when David took over the business."

"It was a mixed blessing," Charley confessed, "being raised as a boy. I never experienced what other young ladies do, and yet I had an education that was unique. I would sit at table when my father's medical friends would come to visit, and the knowledge I picked up was invaluable, especially when combined with my father's teaching."

"But it is not a natural life for you."

She leaned against the bulkhead and crossed her arms over her chest, a deliberately masculine stance.

"On the contrary," she said, "for me it is the most natural life. To try and change now into something I am not, something I have no skill at... No, I would rather be Charley Alcott than Charlotte."

"Except that Charley cannot experience what Charlotte could," Henry said softly. "A home and a family of her own."

She shrugged. "Do you have a dream, Mr. Fletcher?"

He looked down at his bandaged stump, then back up at her. His face was drawn and tired in the lamplight, and she imagined she looked much the same. She could hear men outside sick bay, one watch heading to its meal while the other went about its business, but her eyes were all on the man in front of her.

In another setting, she could see herself attracted to someone like Henry Fletcher. He was intelligent and hand-some enough, and a gentle man despite his service aboard this privateering vessel.

But he did not make the air sharper when he entered a room, he did not make her senses come alive. With Henry Fletcher, she felt safe. When Black Davy Fletcher was about, she felt anything but safe. And yet if she had to choose this minute between the men, she knew which one she would choose.

Now Henry sighed as he considered her question. "My dream is to command a ship of my own. This voyage…David was grooming me for my own ship. See, Dr. Alcott, when David marries Miss Dixon, she will bring enough wealth into the family that we can expand our holdings, increase our ships. I, too, want to be a captain, but of a merchantman, not a privateer."

"Ah. Those must be the marriage plans Captain Fletcher mentioned."

"Yes, it has been discussed for some time. Her father is one of the wealthiest ship owners in Baltimore. With Sarah's dowry the Fletcher family will be able to expand its own business as never before." There was something in his voice when he spoke of his brother's intended that caused Charley to look at him more closely, but he said nothing more.

"Why do you think you cannot achieve your dream?"

"What?" he looked up at her.

"Why can you no longer be a ship's captain?"

"With only one hand? I am a cripple!"

"Oh for heaven's sake, Mr. Fletcher, Lord Nelson defeated Napoleon's navy with one arm and one eye! Are you telling me you cannot command a single vessel because you are short a hand?"

"Well, it is necessary to have sufficient hands to man the ship," Fletcher said expressionlessly.

She stared at him and then burst out laughing, and couldn't stop. She knew she was on the edge of hysteria, but the tension of the day magnified by the conversation of the last ten minutes brought her to the point where her laughter morphed into something much deeper from her soul.

"Here. This looks clean."

He handed her a piece of unused bandage and sat there looking uncomfortable. She waited until she could get her sobbing under control and her eyes to stop streaming, then blew her nose vigorously.

"Thank you, Mr. Fletcher. That was good medicine for the doctor."

"And I imagine that was your dream, Dr. Alcott. To become a physician."

It cheered her no end that he was still calling her "Dr. Alcott," unlike Dr. Murray's insistence on addressing her as "Miss Alcott."

"Yes, my dream is to heal the ill and keep the healthy patients healthy. Before he died my father said he did me a disservice by training me in his ways, but I cannot accept that. I am happiest when I am working, mending those who are broken. Each day is different and exciting to me because I do not know what I will encounter, what I will learn."

"You saved my life, and you have mended many aboard this ship who were broken. I would say that even if your dream may seem an impossible one, you are right not to forsake it."

"Now you have made me cry again," she scolded him.

He sat there patiently, a much more restful presence than his brother. She could see Mr. Fletcher as a ship's captain, one who would lead his men through difficult situations by infusing their spirits with his own calm and grace, rather than by rousing them with his passions.

She blew her nose again. "What gave me away?"

"You have examined my arm every day, which gives me a chance to examine you. Your hands are too small for a man, your wrists too slender even for a boy."

Charley sighed. "One cannot practice medicine while wearing gloves. I can only hope that others aboard this vessel are not as observant as you are."

"Since most of them seem to be bending over or staring at the deck above when you are ministering to them, I wouldn't worry about it overmuch," Henry said dryly, getting up from the chair.

"Dr. Alcott," he hesitated at the door, "I meant what I said. If you need a friend aboard the *Fancy*, you can count on me. Because I must warn you—you think you have seen David in a temper. You have not, not yet, and I fear for you if he finds out you are hoodwinking him."

"Then I will do my best to make sure he doesn't find out. I hope Captain Fletcher will soon drop me in Jamaica, where this will no longer be an issue."

He frowned and seemed about to say something, then shrugged. "David Fletcher will do what David Fletcher wants. He always does."

"So I am learning," she said grimly. "Good night, Mr. Fletcher."

"Good night, Dr. Alcott."

Charley busied herself straightening sick bay, wondering if she would get any sleep at all that night. She had been complacent, fully into her identity as "Dr. Alcott." Was there anything she could have done differently to disguise her sex?

Probably not. As Mr. Fletcher said, he was in a position to observe her more than the others were. Even Miller, the sailor who helped keep the sick bay neat, did his work and left—his lack of literacy would keep him from moving up to the position of assistant surgeon and he made it clear he was happy to be rated an able seaman and was not desirous of further responsibility. That left Captain Fletcher as the only other person aboard ship who saw her on a regular basis.

There was a knock at the sick bay door.

"Come in, Captain Fletcher."

"How did you know it was me?"

"No one else has that commanding knock."

"Of course not."

He walked around sick bay and the small space felt more cramped than ever with his larger-than-life presence. The captain was wearing a shirt, unbuttoned and loose over his trousers, and she could see the dark dusting of hair on his chest.

She saw a lot of hairy chests in the course of a day. Why this one should catch her notice was something to chastise herself over later. When he wasn't standing so close to her, and smelling fresh and clean, and male. She stopped herself from leaning in to take a deep breath

"What brings you here so late? Is your wound bothering you?"

He snickered. "I would hardly call that scratch a wound, Doctor. And no, it isn't bothering me, other than my annoyance that I was not fast enough to evade that Spaniard's knife."

"Well, then?"

"Well then wh—oh, why am I here? I couldn't sleep, Doctor, and wanted to ask if you would join me in my cabin for a drink. Everyone else is busy or asleep, and we hardly see each other."

That was a good thing, because the more time she spent with handsome Black Davy Fletcher, the more she found herself drawn to him. Despite his keeping her on his schooner against her will, despite her disguise, despite everything her practical and ordered mind told her about the danger of spending time with this man, she was drawn to him.

She was no different from any of the other *lepidoptera*, even if she was more moth than butterfly.

"Yes, thank you, Captain, I would be pleased to join you. Give me a few minutes and I will meet you at your cabin."

"Excellent! I have a Jamaican rum that I would be happy to prescribe to you, Doctor, as a sovereign remedy. It will put hair on your chest, I guarantee."

He winked at Charley and left, and she chewed her lip, wondering if she had just made a colossal mistake, Henry Fletcher's warning words still fresh in her mind. *In for a penny, in for a pound*, she thought, and put away journals and locked the medicine chest.

~

As she closed the door to the privy that the sailors called the head, Charley again thanked Providence and whomever had added this enhancement to the *Fancy*. It wasn't easy maintaining her disguise, but it would have been nearly impossible without this additional privacy. There'd been an enclosed stool aboard the *Lady Jane*, but it was a larger vessel, and there the head was reserved for the officers and passengers.

She was still thinking about it as she knocked and entered Captain Fletcher's cabin.

"I have to tell you, Captain, that one of the amenities aboard your ship that makes my workload easier is the ship's roundhouse being available to all the crew. Aboard the *Lady Jane* it was an ongoing problem for the men, being costive and sore from having to hang over the bow on the lifelines. Not surprisingly, they would hesitate to go in rough weather, and the results brought them to sick bay more than it should have."

Fletcher looked at her like this was an odd conversation to be having, and poured her a drink of rum. She took it from him and sniffed it cautiously before taking a small sip.

He poured himself a more substantial serving and said, "My mother traveled with my father on his voyages, and she insisted he add this amenity before she would set foot aboard the *Fancy*. Of course, Doctor, being American and full of egalitarian values regarding sailors' rights, how could I deny the crew the opportunity to sit at ease like gentlemen?"

The last was said with such fervor that she smiled. "Joke if you must, but sometimes it is the little things like a dry place to sleep and a quiet place to…mmmm…contemplate the workings of one's bowels that make the difference between a well man and a sick one."

"Your appreciation is noted."

"Your father was a ship's captain?"

He stretched himself out on his bunk, leaning up against the bulkhead, and gestured to the chair at the desk. "Sit, Doctor, and relax a spell. It is not often we have a chance at the end of a long day to appreciate some of the other amenities in life, such as a good rum."

He took some into his mouth and she could tell he was rolling it across his tongue, savoring the taste and the bite, and his eyes closed briefly in sensual enjoyment of the moment.

She swallowed, her mouth gone dry, but resisted the impulse to gulp down her rum. She knew the last thing she needed was to drink to the point where she was foolish, and the sight of Black Davy Fletcher stretched out in all his piratical glory, combined with rum, could lead her to act foolishly.

Even fatally foolishly.

"Yes, this was my father's vessel. He named it after my mother—Frances— but her friends call her Fanny. Father thought it inappropriate to name a ship Fanny, so he settled on Fancy. Mother said she preferred that name anyway."

"Where is your mother now?"

"She still lives in Baltimore." A shadow crossed his face. "I do not know how she will take the sight of Henry without his hand."

"If you bring Henry home to her alive, she will be grateful. And if she has any understanding of life aboard ship, as you say she does, then she will understand." Charley looked him in the eye. "I am sure your mother is a woman of great sense and will not hold anyone else responsible for Henry's mishap."

Some of the tension eased from his broad shoulders. "Aye, you are right, Doctor." He looked over at her. "For such a young man you have a great understanding of human nature."

"Practicing medicine with my father showed me the best and worst of human nature. I saw frail women who were brave beyond all understanding when it came to helping their loved ones, and I saw grown men faint at the idea of being vaccinated against smallpox."

"I can understand that. I am fine in the face of fire and shot, but bring a scalpel near me and I might faint at your feet."

"Ideally, we will never have to test that, Captain."

They sat in silence for a few moments, and Charley studied him surreptitiously. The more time she spent with him, the more she was struck by the sheer physical beauty of this man. She could not imagine a life where one was so attractive heads would turn as you walked into a room and admiring glances would follow you. Mr. Lewis told her in Baltimore they'd called him "Handsome Davy" from the time he started wearing long pants, and he accepted it as his due. Everything about him bespoke confidence and assurance. She was certain those qualities were necessary for a privateer, and Davy Fletcher had it in spades.

He reached over and refilled his cup, but she shook her head when he offered her more rum.

"I do not have a head for strong spirits, and if I'm needed during the night it is best I have my wits about me."

He grunted an assent, but went ahead and poured himself more rum. Her eye was caught by a glint of silver on the shelf next to him as she followed the movement of his arm.

"Is that your betrothed?"

It was the framed miniature of the young woman, and Fletcher reached for it and passed it over to Charley.

"A swan," she murmured.

"Miss Sarah Dixon," Captain Fletcher added, frowning down at the portrait when Charley passed it back to him. He drank some more.

"When are you to be wed?

"We have not set a date. We are not officially betrothed, because Miss Dixon wished to wait until I returned from my voyages. I cannot fault her. She is a popular young miss, and no doubt is enjoying her flirtations and friendships."

Charley's eyebrows rose. This did not sound like a love match to her, but these two beautiful people appeared made for one another like matched bookends.

"But enough about my life," Fletcher said, and refilled his cup. "Tell me about Charley Alcott—who is he, and what does he want?"

"I want to go to Jamaica," she said briskly. The captain's eyes were brighter, his movements looser as the rum took hold of him, and she wondered if she should excuse herself. However, he was not being aggressive or loud, and he seemed genuinely interested in her—or rather, Mr. Charles Alcott.

"Now, Charley, you are not being open to all the possibilities. A young man such as yourself could do very well in the

United States! There are fine physicians there you can apprentice to, and you could settle in a better climate than Jamaica. Has no one told you how unhealthy life in the West Indies can be?"

"Thank you for your concern. Yes, I know the Indies can be dangerous—fevers and poisonous snakes are just two of the dangers I've been warned of—but it is where I wish to go. It is part of Britain, and that makes it part of my home. The United States is an interesting experiment, but it will not last. Even now you are facing the might of the world's finest navy. I would not bet money on America in this horse race."

"Really?" He grew very still, and Charley wondered if she'd said too much, antagonizing her captor again. She needed to learn how to keep her opinions to herself or she might find herself clapped in irons. On the other hand, if he found her opinions obnoxious enough, he might let her go. Or kill her. At the moment both options seemed possible.

But he just smiled and took a drink.

"'Free trade and sailors' rights!' That is the rallying cry of America for a reason, Doctor. We will not bow to tyranny, and we have a navy that's vigorous and prepared to take on all enemies of freedom. We did not yield to Barbary pirates or the French when they encroached on us, and we will not yield to Britain."

"Nonetheless, Captain, England is my home and my country. Perhaps I will emigrate to Canada after I study with Dr. Wilson in Jamaica, if I seek a better climate."

Fletcher shook his head.

"You have no idea what a frozen wasteland Canada can be, Doctor. You think you have experienced winters in England, but I assure you, they are nothing like the winters north of the United States! No, you would be far better off seeking a more moderate climate, like that of Maryland."

"Is that your home?"

"Aye. Baltimore, Maryland. Finest seaport in the United States and home of the best crabs you ever ate."

"You miss it, don't you?"

"It is an odd thing. When I am at sea, I miss Baltimore. When I am in Baltimore, I miss being at sea." He shrugged, and grinned at her again.

He looked younger this evening. The rum combined with his relaxed attitude took some of the tension out of his frame, and his frequent smiles contributed to his attractiveness. It would be easy to stay here, looking at Handsome Davy, sharing this moment between shipmates. Too easy. Charley heard the ship's bell and sat up, listening. It took her a moment to do the calculation in her head, but she figured it out.

"Eight bells of the first watch!" she announced proudly.

"Very good, Doctor! Next we will have you box the compass and we will make a sailor of you yet."

"Perhaps," she said with a smile of her own as she rose to her feet. "But those bells tell me it's later than I thought, and should retire to my bunk."

"I hope you will join me again tomorrow evening for a game of chess."

It was a temptation, and one she knew she should reject, but Charley found herself agreeing to a chess match on the evening to come, and made her goodbyes.

As she washed in the privacy of her own space, she hummed to herself, softly. No, there was much about her new existence that was not prudent or even in her best interest, but at the same time there was a part of her that was glad she was not yet in Jamaica.

CHAPTER 8

Charley sat straight up in her bunk, gasping for air in the dark. It was the same nightmare. The one where she was stark naked, standing on the deck of the *Fancy*, and the crew was pointing and laughing at her.

Except for Captain Fletcher. He was not laughing.

She ran her hand over the cold sweat covering her face. One didn't have to be a physician to know that keeping secrets, living a life of deception, could at the very least lead to troubled nights tossing and turning.

She drew up her legs and wrapped her arms around them, leaning her head against her knees.

Would she have it any other way? Each day aboard the *Fancy* brought new interests, new challenges. The men respected her, and addressed her as "Dr. Alcott."

She would never be Dr. Alcott in England or Jamaica.

She would never have David Fletcher as a companion in England or Jamaica either.

But she had him as a companion now. They talked, long into the evening hours, about politics and war, medicine and literature. They played chess together. He was the superior player, but not so much that she couldn't give him a run for his money. She had been ready to dismiss him as a pretty pirate who cared only for booty, but there was much more to him than that, and she risked losing her heart to this American sea rover.

Who was she trying to fool? The privateer had stolen away her heart, all unbeknownst to him. Someday there would be a reckoning of some sort, or she finally would make her way to Jamaica, but for now she could enjoy his nearness, his laughter, his arguing with her and stimulating her mind.

She would study him from across the chessboard, through her lashes, his brow furrowed as he concentrated on his next move. His long fingers would hover over a chess piece, then return to rest on the table. She'd had to put her own hands beneath the table and grip them to keep from reaching across to stroke the tanned skin, the heavy bones at his wrists.

Sometimes, in the privacy of her bunk, she indulged herself in the fantasy of standing up before Davy Fletcher and disrobing, showing him who she really was. In her fantasy he would throw the table aside and pull her into his arms, and kiss her, and tell her she was all he'd ever dreamed of.

Ridiculous. He was more likely to rear back in disgust at her unfeminine form, or throw her in chains for pretending to be a man. Such a fantasy was dangerous to her peace of mind but she could not stop dwelling on what life could be like if it were not Dr. Alcott and Captain Fletcher sitting across from one another, but Charlotte and David.

He kept trying to convince her to throw in her lot with the Americans and abandon England. She knew he meant well, and genuinely had her best interests at heart. But he was inviting Dr. Charles Alcott to come to America. There was no place there, or in his life, for Charlotte Alcott."

She heard the ring of the first bell of the morning watch and she rose from her bunk, knowing she'd never get back to sleep. She smiled to herself, realizing she now automatically told time by the watches and bells, just as the sailors did.

Maybe she wasn't quite the "lubber" Captain Fletcher termed her.

At eight bells she finished up and washed her hands to go to breakfast, but when she exited the sick bay she stifled an all too girlish shriek.

There were bodies lined up before her door.

"I've been on some ships where we'd dredge those 'millers' up with flour and enjoy a feast!"

She looked up at Captain Fletcher, standing before her, admiring Pirate's trophies.

"Indeed." Charley cleared her throat. "I trust we will not be forced to substitute rats for salt pork on this voyage, Captain."

"Oh, I don't expect that to happen, but we do need to get more water. Later today we'll be dropping anchor and refilling our barrels."

"Really? Is there a town where I can get more supplies?"

"And look for rescue? Do not think you will be escaping any time soon, Dr. Alcott."

"That is not what I meant!"

He was watching her steadily.

"No? My mistake, then, based on your rather persistent demands that we free you. Santa Rosa is a Spanish island whose chief claim to fame is a freshwater spring near the beach. We will spend the night there."

"Then if there's no British garrison within hailing distance may I have your permission to leave the ship?"

"Rank has its privileges, and sarcasm is the captain's

prerogative. However," he raised a hand, forestalling further arguments, "I don't see any reason why you cannot come ashore. I think it best that you stay near the beach and not go wandering off on your own. For your own safety, of course."

"Thank you, Captain," Charley said with appropriate deference, which only made him frown at her. But she wouldn't let that spoil her mood. A day off of the ship sounded wonderful, and she intended to take full advantage of it.

"We'll be doing laundry ashore because of the fresh water. Leave yours bundled and it will be returned to you."

Now, that cheered her, the idea of clothes not laundered in saltwater! Speaking of saltwater, she looked back down at her gifts.

"Will Pirate be offended, do you think, if I drop these over the side rather than fry them up for breakfast?"

"One thing I have learned over the years, Doctor, is not to try to fathom how cats and women think."

She glanced at him quickly, but he was looking at the rats, so she only made a "Hmmm…." noise of what she hoped was masculine solidarity and agreement, then, since Captain Fletcher was still standing there, gritted her teeth and gathered the small corpses up for an informal burial at sea.

There was a festive mood aboard the *Fancy* that day, even in sick bay, as the men discussed the delights of Santa Rosa.

"We will go ashore in shifts, Doctor," Henry Fletcher said. She was seeing him now on a limited basis, and trying to help him deal with the pain from his phantom limb. His spirits were better as he resumed more of his duties, and that in and of itself was probably the best medicine for him. He'd started discussions with the carpenter on a wooden hand, the blacksmith said he could fashion a hook. Charley would not yet give permission for him to wear such devices and saw his impatience with her as a good sign—a sign he was trying to return to a normal life.

"You seem excited to be going ashore, Mr. Fletcher. Is there a particular attraction to Santa Rosa?"

"There's a small village, and a larger community on the other side of the island. Mr. Bryant will head over there and arrange to sell some of the goods in our hold."

His cheerful face dimmed as he said this last.

"Would that normally be your task?" Charley asked neutrally.

"Yes. But I'm not sure I can handle a horse and care for it with one hand on the ride across the island."

"You will. Eventually. After all, most of riding is in the legs, not the hands. But for now, it is best you continue the healing process without risking further damage to your limb. You have made excellent progress and a set-back now would not be worth it."

"Oh, I know that, but it is frustrating."

"Patience, Mr. Fletcher. I would be most angry if you undid all my good work through foolish risks, and the last person you want to anger is the doctor."

"Shows what you know about life aboard ship. The last person you want to anger is the captain, Doctor."

Charley could see the truth in that. The captain held the power of life and death aboard ship, sometimes in obvious ways, other times in less obvious. One British naval captain had gone so far as to maroon a sailor aboard the uninhabited island of Sombrero. David told her it was an incident the American press made much of in writing of the cruelty of life aboard the Royal Navy ships.

Would Captain Fletcher maroon her if he found out her ruse? She suppressed a shudder at the thought, and pushed it into the back of her mind. It was bad enough that nightmares disturbed her sleep, she couldn't afford to have them inter-fere with her duties during daylight.

"We're all done here, Mr. Fletcher," she said. "Continue to wear the sling for another week, and then see how you do."

"Thank you, Doctor," Henry's face split into a grin. "It makes me feel and look like an invalid, and I'll be glad to set it aside."

He was her last patient of the morning, so she went above to take the air. She stood at the rail and strained her eyes, but only saw a smudge of gray on the horizon that could be their destination.

"We should be able to see Santa Rosa in about an hour, Doctor."

Charley turned to the speaker.

"And how is your rash, Mr. Bryant?"

"Much better for that ointment you made up. It worked like a treat and I sleep better at night, not waking up scratching at myself." He cocked his head to the side.

"Is that how you see us, Doctor, as a variety of ailments to be treated? One man has a rash, another has a flux?"

She looked at him, and felt a touch of warmth creep into her cheeks. A rueful smile turned up the corner of her mouth. "My father warned me not to let that happen. It is too easy to fall into the habit of seeing patients as problems to be treated rather than as people."

"Living aboard the *Fancy* and seeing the same faces every day may help you avoid that trap," Bryant pointed out.

"I hope so," she said, smiling at the older man. "I appre-ciate the reminder. I understand you will be traveling tonight? Do take some of the ointment with you."

He looked surprised, but then chuckled. "I suppose I shouldn't be wondering how you knew that, Doctor. A ship is a small place, and secrets are hard to keep."

If you only knew…

But Charley suppressed that thought and nodded. "Indeed, I thought of the *Lady Jane* as being like a miniature village, with many of the same people fulfilling the same roles."

"Well, it is much like that," he acknowledged. "But we have no women in this village to round out our numbers."

"A fact for which I am eternally grateful," said a familiar, deep voice.

"Captain Fletcher, do you not miss feminine company?" Charley asked daringly, turning around to look up at the *Fancy*'s commander.

"Not aboard my ship! Women are enough of a disruptive influence ashore. I do not need them aboard and underfoot with their swoons and airs and delicate ways!"

"Aw but, Captain, aren't you longing for a little feminine company?" Bryant asked. "Maybe there will be some friendly *señoritas* in Santa Rosa."

"Good Lord," Charley said. "Should I lay in additional supplies of mercury?"

"I don't think we will be staying long enough for the men to pick up infections from the ladies ashore, but that does raise a point. How are your supplies holding up?"

Bryant saw her hesitation and excused himself while Charley thought about the best way to frame her answer.

"That all depends on how long I will be here," she finally said. "If you get another surgeon, he will want to re-supply you with the medications he favors using."

"In the meantime, I want you to make a list, Doctor, of those supplies you might run short of over the next six months. After all, if I don't find another medical man to serve aboard the *Fancy*, I could be the one dispensing the drugs to the men, and you would not want to leave me unprepared, would you?"

She couldn't argue with this, since it was all too common for merchant captains to serve as their own ship's doctor.

"Very well, I will prepare such a list. And if the opportunity presents itself, I'll restock the supplies."

She knew she shouldn't swim in dangerous waters, but Charley couldn't resist.

"So, Captain, you believe women aboard ship would harm your little village? Do you not then plan to take your wife to sea?"

Captain Fletcher put his hands behind his back and started walking, and she fell into step alongside him.

"It takes a very special woman to live at sea, Charley. Most of them don't have the fortitude to put up with the inconveniences, the squalor, the lack of society. No, far better they stay ashore, tending to home and hearth."

"But you said your own mother went to sea with your father. And Mrs. Denham seemed quite content aboard the *Lady Jane*."

He looked down at her and shrugged, then resumed walking.

"Oh, there are exceptions. But these are rare cases. Most women want to be coddled and pampered—as they should be, for they are delicate creatures."

Charley bit her tongue to keep from pointing out the women she'd seen working in Little Abbot and Plymouth, fisherwomen and farm wives and merchants. Even the women of the gentry tended to work from sunup to sundown, overseeing households and doing domestic tasks. Their labor may not involve hauling on lines like a sailor, but she'd put most of those women up against the men on this ship for sheer physical endurance.

And she knew from experience that women were not such big babies, like men were, about a visit to the doctor or coming down with a common ague.

But nothing would be gained by baiting her captor on this, so she nodded thoughtfully and strolled alongside him, her own hands clasped behind her back.

"Hang out with the crew of the *Fancy* long enough, Doctor, and you will receive an education in the ways of the fair sex that you will find invaluable in years to come!"

"Indeed," Charley agreed. "I have already learned more than I ever anticipated."

He put his hand on her shoulder and gave it a companionable squeeze, then frowned.

"Good Lord, aren't you eating enough? There's no muscle here at all, boy!"

She shrugged herself out from under his grasp, knowing that color was flooding her face from the unexpected contact. There was nothing she could do about that.

"I am built along slender lines, Captain. The men in my family resemble greyhounds more than mastiffs."

"No need to be embarrassed about it," Fletcher said, giving her a sideways glance. "But you need to build yourself up, Charley. You might find yourself having to grab a line or pull an oar, and you don't want to let your shipmates down."

"Thank you, I will take that under advisement."

David frowned to himself as he walked alongside the doctor. The youngster was so competent, so in command in his sick bay that David forgot he was a boy until it was brought back to him by incidents such as this. The lad was as scrawny as a poor man's chicken and, if nothing else, he could act in the role of mentor and help guide him toward manhood.

Aye, maybe that was the key to bringing him around to America's point of view. Young men aboard ship looked up to older, more experienced salts, those who could teach them the ropes. David would make it his goal that before the lad left the *Fancy*—if he left the *Fancy*—he would have those experiences young men need to be guided toward their place in the world.

And it could start today.

"When we go to Santa Rosa, Doctor, we will be meeting with representatives of the merchants and planters there. They will be in a position to negotiate with us for some of the goods in our hold, and I'm anxious to lighten our load."

"And make way for more booty?"

"Sarcasm?"

"No, merely a statement," the doctor said blandly.

"Wear your finest coat and shirt tomorrow. We want to put our best face forward, because these Spaniards put great store by appearances. Do you plan to stay ashore tonight?"

The doctor thought about it for a moment, lines furrowing his smooth brow.

"No, I will come back to the ship, in case I am needed here. What about you?"

"As much as I enjoy spending the day ashore," David said, "I prefer to sleep aboard ship, out on the water where the mosquitoes cannot get to me."

"I had not considered that. The miasmic air near the water may bring on fevers. I will keep an eye on the crew and do my best to keep them healthy."

He did do his best, David believed, even though he saw the Americans as his enemies. And the men were better for it. He looked at the boy walking alongside him, the sweep of his long lashes over cheeks not yet roughened by years of exposure to salt and wind. He realized how much he had come to value the friendship and services of the doctor. While Henry's injury had been a tragedy, finding Dr. Alcott was a blessing. The doctor's services, along with the nights they spent together playing chess and discussing matters of more importance than the day-to-day maintenance of the *Fancy*—David had missed that kind of conversation and it was good to have someone to share ideas with. In some ways, it was almost like having a younger brother to guide again, but Dr. Alcott's maturity and wisdom made him an even more valuable companion.

He did not want the doctor to leave the *Fancy*. Charley Alcott was a fine lad, one any man would be proud to call friend. David would mourn the loss of the friendship growing between them if the Englishman found his way home. If he could be persuaded to settle in Baltimore, perhaps they'd ship out together again. It would be good to have a companion to talk to in the dark hours of the night, someone who listened and gave the kind of advice and counsel you only got from real friends. Not always what you wanted to hear, but what you needed to hear. That was especially important for a commander, who so often was alone in his thoughts about the best actions for the men and the ship.

That afternoon the doctor shared luncheon with David, Henry and Bryant as the men discussed their upcoming visit to Santa Rosa.

"Do you speak another language, Doctor?" Henry said.

"I can speak and read Latin, and read Greek, Mr. Fletcher."

"That will be useful if we run into a troop of Roman legionnaires, or philosophers, but not much good in Santa Rosa or Havana," David said. "For example, you need to know how to say, *¡Traéme otra, esa está podrida!*'"

Bryant hid his smile in his mug of ale, while Henry pursed his lips and stared out the stern window. Alcott just looked at David suspiciously and paused in passing the peas.

"I suspect you have just said something that cannot be repeated in polite company."

"Believe me, Dr. Alcott, for the type of Spanish you need to know, polite company has nothing to do with it."

"Here's another handy phrase then, Doctor," Bryant chimed in. "'*¡Échame más ron y deja el frasco!*' which means, 'More rum, and leave the bottle!'"

"Now, that's Spanish a man can use!" David said.

"And don't forget the first Spanish you taught Henry, Captain," Bryant added, and the two men said in unison, '*¿Cobras por hora? Toda la noche, ¿cuanto?* , and then laughed and raised their mugs to each other in a toast.

"What about that first thing, what you said, Captain?" Alcott asked.

"'I want a different girl. This one is poxy!'" Henry said quickly, and David could have sworn he was blushing, which was a surprise because it usually took a story involving spinsters, molasses and donkeys to make Henry blush.

Dammit, the boy was blushing as he added, "I'm sure Dr. Alcott doesn't need to know that."

"Yes, I do," said Alcott, glaring at Henry. "If I'm going to take my place with the other men, I need to know what they know!"

"There's a good fellow!" Bryant grinned, lines creasing his weathered face as he raised his mug to the young doctor. "No die-away airs for this boy!"

When the doctor joined them at the boats that afternoon, David raised his brows at the satchel slung over his shoulder.

"Are you expecting trouble?"

"Just as you always go armed, Captain, I always go armed —with my tools. It is best to be prepared."

David was the last to enter the boat, climbing in after the doctor clumsily made his way to the stern. Most of the men rowing had stripped down in the tropical heat, and David joined them in their casual attire, wearing a white cotton shirt unfastened, but tucked loosely into his trousers. The doctor, however, was still fully attired from shoes to hat, even wearing his ugly coat. He looked hot and uncomfortable, his face flushed as he looked at the bare-chested sailors rowing them ashore, their bronzed torsos glistening in the sun.

"Doctor?"

Alcott jumped, and looked a little startled.

"I'm sorry, I was…lost in thought."

"Why don't you remove your coat and get more comfortable, like the rest of us?"

"No, thank you, Captain. I am fine as I am," the boy said stiffly.

It occurred to David that perhaps Alcott was embarrassed by his scrawniness, especially when compared to the strapping crew of the *Fancy*. He let the subject drop.

Mostly.

"Well, at least take off your shoes. You will have to jump into the surf to get ashore."

Alcott hesitated, then nodded, removing his shoes and stockings. He tucked his bare feet beneath him on the bench, and turned to watch the island they were nearing.

David watched the shore also, scanning it for any signs of trouble, but all seemed to be well. The men had brought the casks over first and were starting to fill them, while a hunting party was off in the woods, looking for fresh game for supper. He could see Henry gesturing with his hand as he supervised, and turned to see Alcott watching him.

"Your brother is making a good recovery, Captain. He will not need my services any longer."

David clamped his jaw shut, not wanting to have this discussion now, in front of the sailors who were straining their ears to hear. Instead, he changed the topic.

"Wish the hunters luck, boys, and we will dine on roast pork tonight!"

Next to their ration of rum, sailors valued their victuals the most. The thought of freshly killed wild pig roasted over an open pit set their mouths to watering and they pulled the oars with a vengeance.

~

Charley clumsily splashed her way out of the boat and hurried to get her shoes and stockings back on. She knew enough about anatomy to know that if her hands gave her away to Mr. Fletcher, the sight of her smaller-than-male feet would give her away as well.

She stood, huffing in the heat, and took her hat off to wipe her forehead. Captain Fletcher did look comfortable, damn him, and she wanted to look away, but she couldn't as he laughed at something Bryant said to him. His hair was in need of a trim, the shaggy midnight silk curling 'round his neck. She'd had to nearly sit on her hands in the boat to keep from smoothing back a stray swath falling across his forehead.

She pushed her own hair back from her forehead, slicking the short strands down close to her scalp. She'd trimmed her hair last night, trying not to think about how her hair used to curl and wisp delicately, softening her features. That was the last thing she needed now, here, where she was so careful about how she stood, how she walked, how she held her arms and cocked her head.

If she ever gave up physicking she might consider a career on the stage, playing breeches roles as so many actresses did. Acting could hardly be more disgraceful than living with pirates.

The head pirate came over as she was brushing sand off of herself.

"I seem to be unneeded, Doctor. Mr. Bryant and Henry

have everything under control. I'm going to take a walk inland. Would you care to join me?"

She knew what the right answer was. It wasn't: "Yes, I would like that, Captain."

She hoisted her satchel and slung it over her head so the broad strap rested against her shoulder. It was sturdy leather and gave her father many years of service before she took it for her own following his death. Now the battered and worn case sat against her hip, a familiar weight as she followed behind Captain Fletcher.

The view of Handsome Davy from in front, in the boat, had been enough to warm the senses. The view from behind did nothing to cool her down. The island breeze molded the Captain's thin linen trousers against his legs, outlining their length and the play of muscles beneath the surface.

He's just a man, she scolded herself, made up of the same parts as all the others.

Which was, of course, a colossal fib. The *Fancy* was made up of rugged men, some of whom any woman would term "handsome," but its captain was in a class by himself. It was like the difference between Captain Denham's brig and Captain Fletcher's Baltimore schooner. One ship was steady and reliable, and able to get the job done. The other was all rakish lines and polished surfaces, glittering in the sunlight, making others look lumbering and heavy.

She sighed.

"Having trouble keeping up? It's not much farther now."

"I can keep up, Captain. But my legs aren't used to this."

She was trying not to huff with the effort, but the combination of the heat, her woolen attire and the effort of navigating the land after months aboard ship had her staggering.

The man in front of her chuckled. "Yes, you always seem to forget that it takes a while to get your land-legs back. But look, we're here."

"Here" was a glade in the foothills of the mountainous land, a little piece of paradise with a waterfall snaking over a ridge to fill a shaded pond. Around the pond were clusters of creamy frangipani, their perfume filling the air while coconut palms rose above to search for the sun. Purple orchids peeped out from the jungle of greenery and the sound of the waterfall soothed her. The trees filtered the sunlight and softened it, making the tropical heat more bearable, and Charley heaved a sigh of relief.

But what he said next sent her pulse racing again.

"I knew you might have felt uncomfortable, taking off your clothes in front of the men. It's nothing to be ashamed of. But here, in the privacy of this glade, you can feel more at ease."

She stared at him. Did he know? Was this mild speech his response to her deception?

What he said next clarified his statement and saved her from making a terrible mistake.

"...I know young men are sometimes shy. But you don't have to worry about me, Charley. I just thought you might enjoy cooling off."

Confusion raced through her mind. If he thought her a boy, was he asking her to take her clothes off because he had designs on her? Or was everything he said to be taken on its face?

God's Teeth, she was tired of this! Tired of the tension, of always having to lie, to pretend, to wonder!

And the alternative? her inner demon whispered.

Is worse, Charley acknowledged as she glumly sweltered. Once her secret was revealed, nothing could ever be the same again. The status quo, uncomfortable as it was, was still better than the unknown future as Charlotte Alcott.

David Fletcher left Charley to make up his mind. He wasn't about to waste this opportunity to bathe in fresh water, and if young Dr. Alcott was too missish to participate, that was his problem.

He hurriedly stripped down to the skin and dove head-first into the pool. The shock of the cold water after the heat of the afternoon made his skin sizzle and brought all his senses alive. When he brushed his wet hair back from his face he saw the doctor sitting on a boulder, with a pad of paper and pencil.

"Are you sketching?"

The doctor looked up at him and he saw a flash of that grin from beneath the brim of Charley's hat.

"If I am not going to swim, I will use this opportunity to draw some of the unusual plants here. At least, they're unusual to me. They may have medicinal purposes, and I can compare notes with Dr. Wilson in Jamaica."

David merely grunted at the mention of Jamaica and eased himself onto his back, floating there as the sun drifted through the branches.

"Look, Charley, I'm a narwhale!" He laughed, pointing to himself.

"Droll, Captain, quite droll. I vow, before I set foot aboard your ship I never knew such wit was missing from my life."

David chuckled and drifted, his eyes closing. He nearly fell into a doze, letting the fresh water soak into his pores and wash away some of the salt that was always with him.

"Captain?"

"Yes, Doctor?"

"Do you like being a privateer?"

He grinned to himself as he floated, the sunlight warming his body, relaxing him and soothing the stress from his muscles.

"Who wouldn't enjoy being a privateer? Next to having a

rich old uncle name you his heir, it's one of the best schemes I know to get wealthy in a hurry. All you need is one good haul, Charley, and you could be set for life. A specie ship, a ship carrying munitions—there are many possibilities."

"Yes, but as I understand it, you need a war to be a privateer. Otherwise, you're just another pirate. Will you turn pirate when the war is over?"

He turned over and stroked through the water until he was close to where the doctor sat with his sketchpad. He rested his arms on a sunwarmed rock and studied the odd fellow who'd rather sketch than swim. Charley glanced up at him, then back at his sketchpad, lips pressed tight together as he concentrated on his drawing.

"No, much as I enjoy privateering, it being the happy marriage of commerce and warfare, I will give it up when we have peace." He treaded water as sunshine dappled the surface. It was a glorious afternoon away from his responsibilities for a few hours, and even the doctor's allusions to David as a pirate couldn't spoil his good mood.

"Despite your desire to cast me as a villain, I have no intention of being a pirate. If I am no longer a privateer, I will go back to being what I was before the war. A merchant captain."

He turned over on his back again, catching a glimpse of the doctor fumbling as he dropped his sketching pencil.

Maybe the boy was unsure of himself because he was not comfortable in his own body. David remembered those days of adolescence, and not fondly, when he would shoot up so quickly that he would see inches of wrist sticking out from his shirtsleeves, and hit his head against lintels that he'd been able to clear scant days earlier.

He knew what Charley needed, and he would have to think about the best way to bring it about where the outcome would be satisfactory to all involved.

~

Charley retrieved her pencil and watched Captain Fletcher gliding away on his back. She sighed. He was like a sleek merman, enticing her to forget her woes and join him, drowning in the sensations she was sure he could provide.

If he didn't actually drown her for lying to him every minute of the past weeks.

So even though the water looked like pure liquid delight, and she itched with heat and discomfort and wondered if she would ever be able to scrub her entire body again, she took up her pad.

At least she could get this small satisfaction out of the day's events. She hadn't quite lied when she said she was sketching the plants, but she was not totally truthful either. At the moment she was sketching Black Davy Fletcher, his sharp profile and silken hair, the muscles that bunched beneath his skin, his wonderfully long legs and buttocks that looked so firm and tight she could bounce a shilling off of them.

He was beautiful everywhere. She had seen the privates of all the men aboard ship and thought there was nothing remarkable about most of them, but Captain David Fletcher was in a class by himself. Her face felt like it would burst into flames from the heat of her blush as she sketched him standing now beneath the waterfall, brushing his hair back from his face, his penis in repose looking like a dark ivory shaft amidst the ebony hair that curled 'round it.

She acknowledged to herself that there was anatomy... and then there was anatomy. And all men were not created equal, despite what these Americans claimed.

Charley shifted on her boulder. Her breasts ached in their binding, and she suspected if she could check herself she would find she was damp, her body's natural response to the attraction of the male animal before her. He leaned down to pick up his shirt, and used it to dry off. Some moisture escaped to bead on the column of his neck. Charley watched that silver drop trickle downward, wending its way over the chiseled pectoral muscles, and she swallowed. Her mouth was so dry, and that water looked so tempting, so…lickable.

"I'm heading back down to the beach, Charley."

She blew out her breath and waited until Captain Fletcher was dressed before putting away her sketch book. With the fresh water brought aboard the *Fancy* she'd be able to lock her door and wash her entire body back in her cabin. That cheered her, even as he said, "You should have come in, Doctor. The water was wonderful."

"No doubt it is, but I got a great deal accomplished. I don't feel like I wasted an opportunity."

She smiled to herself as they started down to the beach.

"I have some memorable sketches of my visit to Santa Rosa, and I am sure they will delight me for years to come."

They feasted that night on roast pork cooked in pits on the beach. The hunting party returned with a descendent of the pigs brought by the Spanish centuries back, and the crew took full advantage of the opportunity to dine on fresh meat. Henry was in charge of the land party and would be spending the night ashore, and David issued an extra tot of rum to the crew even as Henry scheduled guards in watches to keep a look-out for trouble.

Henry was coming into his own as a leader of men, and it made him proud. He'd had most of the rearing of his brother after their father died, and while many of the lessons were punctuated with David's fist, they took hold. If the Fletchers got the funding they needed, it wouldn't be long before he had his own ship to command.

The men returning to the ship rowed David and the doctor back. The doctor leaned over the side, entranced by the silver schools of fish darting just below the moon-lit surface.

"Join me for a drink, Doctor?"

David had already made inroads into the rum when they ate the pig, but it was too early to call it a night.

The doctor paused for a moment, then said, "Allow me to put up my gear and wash up, and I'll meet you in your cabin."

When Charley entered a short time later, David gestured to the bottle, too relaxed to get up from his bunk.

"Pour yourself some. I know you're not much of a drinker, but this is an excellent rum. Smoother than the gut rotting swill we usually get."

He poured a moderate amount and sniffed it, before taking a small swallow.

"It is good, Captain. Better than the usual."

David chuckled. He was feeling mellow, and he was glad he had someone to share the evening with, even if he could have longed for a prettier companion of the opposite gender. But the doctor was pleasant company and, in the absence of Henry and Mr. Bryant, the one person he could feel comfortable around. The doctor was educated and had a sense of humor, and even smelled better than many who'd been in this cabin to see him.

Perhaps that was part of his bedside manner, not to offend the nose of his patients.

Alcott seated himself and propped his feet on a seachest. He looked over at the silver framed picture on the shelf.

"I imagine you are looking forward to seeing Miss Dixon again."

David didn't respond to this, but instead poured more

rum into his glass for himself. When he offered the doctor the bottle, the man shook his head.

"I need a wife, Charley, and I intend to make an offer to Miss Dixon when I return to Baltimore."

"She is a beautiful lady," the doctor said a bit wistfully.

Poor lad, he was thinking he'd never have a chance with a lovely girl like Sarah Dixon. And likely, he had the right of it.

Charley Alcott had a nice smile and eyes like the morning mist. If he wasn't handsome, at least he made you want to smile back at him. Right now though, he looked serious, and downcast.

"Aye. Miss Dixon is all a man would want in a wife. Lovely, plays the pianoforte, is brought up to be a good hostess and run a fine house. A man would be a fool not to marry her."

Charley was watching him, his head cocked to the side.

"But you say she is not your betrothed?"

"Not yet. When I return from this voyage her father wants me to make it official."

"Don't you want to marry her? Do you love her?"

The doctor looked surprised at his own boldness in asking this and stared down at his glass, as if wondering how it got there. Maybe the rum was affecting him more than he realized.

"What a romantic you are, Charley! Marriage is not about love. It's about…I dunno. Combining families. Merging businesses. Money. Raising children, of course, but love?" He shrugged. "That's a game for poets and silly girls with nothing to fill the empty spaces in their heads."

"I want to marry for love," he said firmly.

David took another swallow of his rum.

"You are a foolish romantic who has not seen much of the world if you believe that. Love doesn't fill the coffers or keep food on your table, gold does. I know that. Obadiah Dixon knows that. Y'see, Charley, Sarah Dixon's father is also a sea captain. A successful one. Not like me."

"Why is he more successful?"

David looked down into his glass, seeing ghosts swirling in the brown liquid. He drank to drive them away.

"Captain Dixon is a rich man because he uses his ships to bring Africans into Cuba and Florida. Aye, slave ships. That's what men tell you brings in the big dollars, importing black gold. There's a demand for Africans, and getting them into the United States is making many a man rich."

"Isn't the importation of slaves to the United States against the law?"

David snickered. Such a shocked expression on the doctor's face! The poor lamb had indeed strayed far from his little English village.

"How naive you are, Doctor. Making it illegal in the United States only made Florida and Cuba—and Captain Dixon—richer."

The doctor was watching him as he said this, gauging him. Alcott had a way of looking at you that made you feel like he could see clear past your bones and sinews to the core of you. Maybe he was seeing inside David those humors he carried on about.

"You don't want to be one of those rich men?"

"I don't want to earn my fortune that way. I'd rather face a line of battle than make the passage across the Atlantic with Africans packed in my hold like ballast. You should grimace, Doctor, even though you've never served aboard a slaver. I pray God you never do."

David shuddered, his liquor threatening to come back up as the memories churned in his mind. He had been young, and willing to do anything to earn his money, but that one voyage would haunt him for the rest of his life.

"Do you need Miss Dixon's dowry? Is that why you are marrying her?"

"Yes." He poured himself some more rum, and tossed it back. It burned going down, but it helped keep the devils at bay. The doctor watched him still, a contemplative expression on his young face.

"You should not have to marry where you do not wish to," the boy finally said. He too had been drinking, and David suspected that he was one of those drunks who would talk more than usual and then slip silently into unconsciousness. Which was better than Henry, who tended to get silly when he drank too much. And sick. Not a good combination.

"If only life were that easy, Charley m'lad. We could do what we wanted, when we wanted. An' I am not being fair to Miss Dixon. She is a fine young lady and will make any man a good wife. I will be fortunate to marry her."

"I would like to get married some day," the lad confessed, staring into his glass.

That relieved David's mind, for he had begun to suspect—well, he was just glad to hear Charley say he wanted a woman.

The boy reached for the bottle and poured himself some more, most of it getting into the glass.

"A home, someone to love you, children..." the boy said.

"And success in business, Doctor, do not forget that. It is important to be successful in this world. Sometimes, that means making the right marriage. No matter what your own desires are."

"Right you are, Captain," he said with a hollow laugh. "If I wish to be successful at my profession, I must put off thoughts of marriage for now."

"Naw, don't be so hard on y'self! Someone will want you, you being a fine physi—physic—doctor an' all."

"My dear captain, I rather think my profession will be an impediment to a good marriage."

"Nonsense," David slurred. "You have a lot to offer som'un."

He sniffed.

"Do you wear cologne, Doctor?"

"Good heavens, no! Why do you ask?"

"You smell better than most of the crew. Y'notice things like that, belowdecks. Then your nose becomes numb and you don't notice anymore when someone smells bad, but y'notice when someone smells good. Women like it when a man smells good, they tol' me so." He staggered over to the table and reached for the bottle, but it was empty. He frowned. The damned lubber had drained his rum.

"I'm for my bunk. Blow out the lamp when you leave, will you? There's a good lad."

David fell across his bunk, his pillow scratchy beneath his cheek, and the cabin tilting at an odd angle.

"G'night, Charley," he muttered as the lamp was blown out.

"Good night...David," he thought he heard the doctor say, and thought he felt a whisper brush of a hand across his brow, then thought went away as he slipped into his sodden dreams and hoped there would be no nightmares tonight.

CHAPTER 9

If Captain Fletcher looked rather wan this morning, Charley was wise enough to keep her opinions to herself as they rowed back in the morning sun to Santa Rosa. The midnight blue coat she wore was even warmer than her usual brown one, but Charley knew it was the finest she had and followed the captain's orders to look her best.

And, she had to admit to herself, where her eyes were usually a murky shade of gray, this coat made them look even brighter, and a deeper hue. She refused to think about why that mattered to her as she stood beside Black Davy Fletcher on the beach.

"All is well here, Captain, and Mr. Bryant returned about an hour ago," Henry Fletcher reported. "*Señor* Martinez should arrive soon."

"Very good," David Fletcher said, and winced at a shout from one of the men back at the camp.

"I have coffee, if you would like a cup, Captain. Doctor?" Henry added innocently.

"Coffee would be wonderful, Mr. Fletcher." She didn't

know when her morning beverage of choice had changed from proper English tea to hearty American coffee, but she found herself looking forward to the dark brew. Perhaps she was turning into one of those coffee addicts she read about. It would make for an interesting study if she had the time to do the research in Jamaica, known for its excellent coffee plantations.

Apparently, others had noticed as well.

"We will turn you into an American yet, with your love of coffee." Captain Fletcher ventured a small smile, one that looked like it didn't strain too many muscles in his head. "And might I add, Doctor, that you look your part today. Every inch the smartly turned out sawbones. Did I not tell you that clothes make the man?"

"I cannot argue with that, Captain. Ah, here's our coffee."

Henry and Bryant came over to them, carrying mugs. Charley took hers and left the three men to discuss their business. She had risen early and bathed again, luxuriating in the fresh water, and now she went to check on the status of her laundered clothes.

As she wandered among the men they greeted her cheerfully, some mentioning various ailments she'd treated for them. She paused to extract a splinter from Jenkins's foot, refilled her coffee cup and returned to Captain Fletcher, who was calling her name.

"*Señor* Martinez is coming over the hill," he said, gesturing to the east.

Charley shaded her eyes, watching a convoy of mules and porters threading their way down to the beach. In the lead was a rotund man dressed in white, a planter's hat shading his head from the sun that already promised a day heavy with heat and humidity.

"Is Mr. Martinez the mayor of the village you mentioned?"

"He's the one who controls the commerce, the 'headman.' The mayor's just the figurehead."

Her eyebrows lifted.

"It's a good arrangement. The government can't scratch its ass without approval from Havana or Madrid. This way is more effective."

Señor Martinez dismounted from his mule, grimacing at the effort, and wiped his face with a red kerchief before waddling down to the beach. David Fletcher met him halfway, and the two men shook hands and exchanged greetings in Spanish. Charley heard her name mentioned and came over. The fat man's face lit up like a full moon, and he shook her hand with enthusiasm. She looked at Captain Fletcher, even as *Señor* Martinez continued to speak animatedly while waving his hands about.

"Captain?"

"I'm not sure. He has some kind of medical issue he wants to address with you, but I can't understand all the words. I will tell him that you will meet with him after we are done with business."

He looked at her with a gleam in his eye.

"Taking you along may have been a better idea than I suspected. But if you don't mind, I'll get his money before you do anything that may prove fatal."

"I am encouraged that you have such confidence in me, Captain."

"As I said, I will get the money first."

Señor Martinez barked out an order and one of the servants rushed to a mule and brought back a folding chair, which he opened in the shade. He carefully lowered himself into it. The servant came back with a camp table that was opened, spread with a white cloth, and an array of pastries emerged like magic from a hamper.

Martinez invited the doctor and the captain to join him

in his morning snack, offering wine as well. Charley opted for more coffee, and Jenkins brought over stools for the doctor and the captain as they conducted business with the headman.

Bryant had made most of the arrangements the evening before, so it was more a matter of money exchanging hands and pleasantries exchanged over pastries. She was happy to leave them to it, and had to resist moaning in ecstasy as she bit into a chocolate filled puff that melted in her mouth.

"I have found your weakness, Doctor. You have a sweet tooth," Captain Fletcher said as *Señor* Martinez lumbered off to consult with his head muleteer.

"Guilty as charged," she said, licking rich cream off the tip of her finger. "Will you try to lure me to America with chocolate now?"

He chuckled. "It is always good to be prepared when one goes into negotiations or into battle. Be forewarned, I will keep your weakness in mind and may use it against you, especially if I capture a pastry chef!"

"Alas, I would truly be lost then," she said, smiling at him. He looked at her, an arrested expression on his face, then slightly shook his head and said something to *Señor* Martinez, who'd returned with a substantial leather pouch.

Whatever *Señor* Martinez said in reply made the captain frown.

"Trouble?"

"There are more British ships patrolling," he said, and didn't say anything more.

Martinez sat back, looking satisfied with himself, ate another cake, and gestured at Charley, asking a question.

"*Señor* Martinez has a medical problem, and since the last doctor on the island died, he would like to have you treat him."

"Of course, I will do what I can, Captain. What is the nature of his malady?"

The two men talked and the headman frowned, looking from Fletcher to Charley, then shrugged resignedly.

"He says he has to show you in private."

Martinez grunted and pushed himself to his feet, then led them off into the bushes. Before Charley could say anything, Martinez spoke to Captain Fletcher.

"As best as I can determine, he wants to show you his buttocks. I'll just step awa—"

"Oh, no you don't!" Charley grabbed his arm to keep him from fleeing. "I need you to stand right here and translate!"

"But—"

The headman dropped his trousers, turned around, and as promised, showed them his buttocks. They were hairy. And wide. Then he bent over to give them a better view.

"Good Lord!"

"Indeed, Captain. It is a wonder he was able to sit on that mule!"

"That is one of the ugliest things I have ever seen."

Charley looked at him.

"That's a bold statement. I have seen your crew, remember. But I don't blame you for saying that. Piles aren't a pretty sight, but this is a particularly severe case."

She maneuvered the hunched over official so that he presented more into the direct sunlight, and Fletcher winced and took a step away.

"Please ask him how often he moves his bowels, whether it is once a day, or less often."

"You are joking."

"Just ask him."

"You are going to owe me for this, Dr. Alcott!"

"Deduct it from my nonexistent pay!" she snapped back at

him, straightening up from her examination of the head-man's hindquarters.

He glared at her, but then turned to *Señor* Martinez, cleared his throat and asked his question, while looking off at a bunch of coconuts hanging in a cluster.

Martinez wasn't shy at all about sharing his medical information, and expounded at great length while waving his hands in the air and pausing to point at his arse. Captain Fletcher listened stoically, hardly wincing at all, then said to Charley, "Once every few days."

"That is all he said?"

"The rest is detail I will work to forget as soon as I have a bottle of rum in my hands."

Charley frowned at him. He was a worse assistant than Miller.

"Tell *Señor* Martinez I will prepare an ointment for him that he is to use twice a day, morning and night, reapplying it after he moves his bowels. Don't glare at me, just tell him! And add that he's not to strain when he sits on the stool, and that sitting in a warm—not hot!—bath with soothing salts may help."

Fletcher glared at her anyway, but then translated while Martinez nodded his head enthusiastically.

"Also tell the gentleman he is to increase the amount of fruit in his diet, especially at breakfast—papaya, guava, oranges, mango, and more juices and lemonade. That should help him. If I were staying here longer, I would use a ligature on some of those. With no one nearby to monitor his progress, we will use ointment and diet changes and hope for the best."

Again, her translator went to work, and again, Martinez nodded like a plump marionette before seizing her hand and shaking it vigorously, all the while keeping up a voluble stream of Spanish. Both Charley and Captain Fletcher did their best to pretend this wasn't happening while *Señor* Martinez's trousers were down around his ankles.

"He says he is most grateful, Doctor, and if there's anything at all you need on the island, to let him know."

She would like to have explored Santa Rosa further to see if there were plants she could use, but knew Captain Fletcher was anxious to be under weigh, and she had to prepare the ointment.

But that gave her an idea.

"Yes, please tell him I could use a few casks of good quality olive oil, if he has some."

Fletcher raised the question and *Señor* Martinez grinned while pulling up his pants and fastening them.

"Yes, he has a shipment from Spain that he would be happy to give to you as a gift."

She smiled and nodded enthusiastically herself.

"That is one of my most used items, so it will be good to replenish my supply!"

Señor Martinez peered at the doctor's smiling face and made an offhand comment to Captain Fletcher, who looked horrified and shook his head, then took a step away from Charley.

"What did he say?"

"It is of no importance!"

The Spaniard shrugged and picked up his straw hat, which had fallen to the ground during the impromptu medical exam. Charley looked at Captain Fletcher, but he said nothing further.

They stayed at Santa Rosa the rest of the day, giving her enough time to prepare her ointment and collect her olive oil. She could not be sure, but it appeared David Fletcher was avoiding her. He may have feared he would be pressed into service again as a medical translator.

That night the crew feasted again on fresh meat and

vegetables before returning to the *Fancy*, but the captain did not invite her to join him in his cabin for chess or talk or a drink. Instead she played whist with Henry, Bryant and the carpenter, Mr. Purcell.

It was Henry's turn to shuffle. He tried to steady the cards with his stump and fold them in, but that only scattered them about.

Charley moved to help him gather them up, but felt a blow against her ankle that rattled her teeth. She glared at Purcell, but he only looked at her blandly.

"Drink your coffee, Doctor."

She was going to bark at him for kicking her, but instead sat back, drank her coffee and watched the table from under her lashes. Sweat beaded on Henry's forehead as he struggled with the cards while Purcell talked with Bryant about barnacles. Henry finally rested the cards against his stump and shuffled one-handed, sliding the cards into each other in an awkward over-and-under fashion.

"All right, we're ready!" he snapped.

They played another hand and the cabin grew warm from the heat of their bodies. Henry rose to take off his coat. He was having a difficult time working his arm out and Charley started to rise to help him when she felt another blow against her ankle.

"Stop doing that, you will break my leg!" she hissed.

"Then stop being such an idiot," Purcell said, studying his cards.

She was about to say something, but her mouth snapped shut and she stayed in her seat.

When the jokes around the table deteriorated to how Henry was going to have to be careful wiping his arse while wearing a hook, the scales fell from Charley's eyes.

She *was* being an idiot. Their rough, masculine badinage

was what Henry needed. The men knew what they were about, making the first mate work with his new reality.

So she relaxed, and lost a few coins, and marveled over how the true practice of medicine, the art that involved bringing people back to wholeness, involved far more than knowing how to stitch and prescribe.

~

Being the ship's doctor had its ups and downs, but Charley Alcott had to agree she was getting an education few young ladies received.

Which was probably a good thing, she mused to herself, as Brown and Perry debated who could fart the loudest.

She leaned back against the guardrail, enjoying the tropical sunshine, while bets were made and insults flew. Sometimes she felt much like a natural philosopher watching exotic animals in their native habitat. What she had always suspected was confirmed by life aboard the *Fancy*—men were simple creatures with uncomplicated brains.

They wanted food, and drink, and fighting, and sexual congress. They were impressed with their own body's ability to make noise and odor. Their idea of humor was at best crude, at worst painful, yet even after some of the bizarre practical jokes that brought men to her sick bay they were still laughing and bragging about whatever insane thing they'd done that got them in that condition.

So today the doctor had been pressed into service as the judge of the competition over who could generate the most noise breaking wind.

"See, Doctor," Jenkins explained, "you being an expert and all about the human body, you're in the best position to judge here."

"Yeah, and this way you can't make a bet using inside information!" Perry added.

"'struth," Jenkins said, sounding slightly apologetic. "You might know things about their guts that would help you win. All we know is they've been eating beans and cabbage for three days. We want this to be fair and on the level."

"Can't argue with logic like that," Captain Fletcher said, joining her at the rail.

Suddenly the day felt a little warmer, the sun a little brighter. Charley held herself steady, to keep from relaxing her stance, from easing closer to David.

"I still think you should be judging this, Captain," she said studying him. She noticed he was cradling his right wrist. He'd been rubbing it a few nights ago when they played chess.

"Is something wrong with your arm?"

"It's not important."

"What did I say about you sailing the ship and me practicing the medicine? Come to sick bay and I will take a look at it."

"Later. We can't expect these competitors to hold it in forever."

Lewis, who had charge of the bank, said, "Last chance to place your bets, gentlemen!"

After a final flurry of money changing hands, the crowd settled down. The two contestants took their mark, faces intent and focused.

Silence settled over the deck, all eyes on the two men who stared at each other as they stood, slightly hunched over, angling their bodies for the best outcome. The crewmen who were within a few feet moved back. Charley, alas, had to stand close to judge.

"Gentlemen, you may fire when rea—"

"Sail on the starboard quarter, Captain!"

At the call from Miller in the lookout, the crew turned as one to see where he was pointing.

Charley shaded her eyes and saw a ship out on the water. Captain Fletcher climbed up into the rigging like he was born to it, pulled his spyglass out of his coat pocket and brought it up to his eye.

"A Spanish brig, riding heavy," he said. "Battle stations, Mr. Fletcher!"

"Aye, sir!" Henry cried, and the men ran to their posts and made the guns ready, while the weapons lockers were opened and cutlasses and pikes distributed.

"I ain't gonna stand behind Brown!" someone yelled, and the laughter ramped up the excitement of the coming fight.

"The call to action includes you, Doctor."

Charley looked up at the man standing again beside her, his amber eyes gleaming as he watched the brig approaching on an opposite course. The excitement in the air was palpable, especially when the crew cheered as the American colors were run up in preparation for the coming fight. Captain Black Davy Fletcher was in his element, as much a part of the Baltimore schooner as its sails and lines.

There was a part of her that longed to stay on deck, beside him, and share in what the men were experiencing. At a brief frown from the captain she went below instead, and paced the quiet sick bay, preparing her supplies while voices yelled and feet ran on the deck over her head.

She knew from her discussions with the men that most merchant vessels surrendered rather than fight, because they were underarmed compared to the privateers, and their owners put it down as the cost of doing business.

The Americans' greatest concern was not merchants, but to meet up with a patrolling enemy frigate carrying bigger guns and a heightened desire to capture American ships. The war against their wayward former colonies had not gone as smoothly as the Royal Navy expected, with American frigates hitting crushing blows against the navy that had ruled the waves for so many years.

But the *Fancy* wasn't a frigate like the *Constitution* or the *Essex*, and its beauty lay in its speed rather than its guns.

The schooner came around sharply and she cursed and held onto the table, and a moment later the big gun amidships boomed out, and she felt the deck beneath her feet shiver. The guns roared again, and she heard a cheer from above, and more yelling, and the sound of running back and forth.

Either the Spanish vessel struck its colors, or perhaps the Americans aimed Brown in their direction and achieved victory using a miasmic gas.

That brought a small smile to her face that disappeared when the door banged open and Bryant stumbled in, blood sheeting half his face.

Charley grabbed his arm and helped him to the table. He was cursing the air blue, but she quickly determined it was a torn scalp and began to clean and stitch him up. Seems some of the Spaniards had decided they couldn't give up without trying to repel the American boarding party.

"I remember the first head wound I saw, Mr. Bryant," she said cheerfully as she sewed and he gripped the edge of the table, glaring at her. "Gave new meaning to the term 'bled like a stuck pig,' but these things often look worst than they are. There. You will be fine."

She wrapped a bandage 'round him and told him to come back if he was bothered by severe headaches in the next day.

A crewman came in with a broken arm to be set, but the remaining injuries were minor ones, and the men's spirits were high. She learned the reason when Captain Fletcher came in, freshly washed and wearing a clean shirt. He looked good enough to lick, blast him.

"Doctor! You will not believe what that ship was hauling."

"Jewels? Gold?"

"Almost as good as! Ripe gold! Here, catch."

He tossed a sphere to her and she grabbed it one handed out of the air. It was a fruit, its nubby skin mottled but whole, the fragrance rising up to her nostrils even over the scent of blood and medicine.

"Oranges?"

"Casks and casks of oranges! This cargo will fetch a fortune in New York."

"Is that where we're going, New York?"

"No, not us. We put the Spaniards in boats—they'll make it to Santa Rosa unless they die of stupidity—and Henry's going to take our prize in to the United States."

Charley paused and set down the orange, carefully, on her desk.

"If Mr. Fletcher is well enough to leave, then it is time for me to leave as well."

"Do not bother me with that now! I have a prize to prepare, papers to fill out, men to assign to her— Doctor, your sense of timing is terrible."

She didn't believe a word of it. Certainly all the preparation he discussed was needed, but he had no intention of putting her off his ship.

Black Davy Fletcher wasn't going to take her to Jamaica. He wasn't going to take her to the United States for an exchange. He was going to keep her here, on the *Fancy*, forever.

She felt like chortling in glee.

But that wasn't the expected response, so she tried to look downcast and concerned. It must have succeeded for he said, "Oh, don't worry, Doctor, eventually you will get where you need to be, but we still need you here for now. That's why I came down here! You said you would look at my wrist."

"Oh yes, the sore wrist. Hop up on the table."

He looked around. "You have not added many personal touches. One would hardly know this is your cabin, as well as sick bay."

"This is only where I sleep until you see fit to release me, Captain. But I would not call it home."

He scowled at that, but sat on the table. She tried not to notice how his nearness to her affected her senses, his scent, the energy that seemed to radiate from him, the clean line of his jaw that made her want to examine it closer, running her fingers along the slight stubble that edged it.

Instead, she kept her eyes down, looking at the wrist thick with muscle, the browned hand with its long fingers, its sinews and scars. She couldn't suppress a small shiver at the thought of that hand touching her…

"Are you cold?"

"No, a goose must have stepped on my grave. Show me your arm."

"It's my wrist that concerns me."

He unfastened his shirt cuff, then rolled up his sleeve. Charley concentrated on the problem before her, tamping down any other distracting thoughts.

You want to be a doctor, she mentally scolded herself, *act like one and not a foolish ninny at her first dance!*

But it was hard, so hard, when he was so close, and she was holding his wrist and feeling the pulse that beat there, every movement of blood through his veins calling to her own pulse and heart.

"Doctor?"

"This lump on the back of your wrist," she said, feeling around, "how long has it been there?"

He shrugged. "I don't remember when I first noticed it. Is it bad?"

"Hmmmm…" she said, making an all-purpose medico noise. "Stay there, Captain. I need one of my texts."

She pulled her copy of Woodall off the shelf, then came back to stand in front of him, leafing through it.

"Hold out your wrist on the table, and leave it quite still. Do not move."

Before he could realize what she was doing, she snapped the heavy book shut and slammed it down on his wrist.

The next thing she knew she was flying backward, only to fetch up hard against the bulkhead.

"Ow!" She yelped, rubbing the back of her head. "You hit me!"

"You struck me first, you stupid bastard!" He glared at her. "You whacked me with that goddamned book!"

"I whacked you to get rid of that lump in your wrist! It's a ganglion cyst, you great looby! I had to hit it to break it up. If I told you, you would have tensed up."

He stared at her, then started to laugh.

"Looby? Such language, Doctor! And it's 'Captain Looby' to you."

She rubbed her sore jaw and pushed herself off the wall.

He was still chuckling as he cradled his wrist, and then looked down at it.

"Huh. You made the lump go away. Oh, stop glaring at me. I barely touched you, you little girl! Want me to take a look at it?"

"Leave me alone, you've done enough damage," she said, carefully working her jaw back and forth. Little girl indeed! "You sail the ship, and I will do the doctoring, Captain."

"There's a need for doctoring and a need to know the manly arts. You need to know how to fight, Doctor. A little tap like that shouldn't have laid you out, and you must learn how to block and dodge a blow. Have you never engaged in fisticuffs?"

"And risk these hands?" She picked up the fallen copy of Woodall and set it on her desk. "No, I haven't fought since I was a young. These hands heal your crew, and I would not be able to do that so well if they are bruised and swollen."

"Nonetheless, you should know how to defend yourself. I insist you take lessons with the men on fighting with a cutlass."

"No."

He stared at her and his eyes narrowed. "I seldom have people say no to me aboard my own ship. I must admit, it is a novel experience. One that I trust will not happen again."

Charley stood firm, and crossed her arms over her chest, ignoring the throbbing in her jaw. "Sometimes no is necessary, Captain. I am a healer. I will not inflict injuries on others. I will not risk myself in swordplay. If you do not like it, put me off your ship."

He frowned at her, then relaxed.

"I will let this go for now, but I encourage you to rethink your position. Knowing how to defend yourself against attackers is only good common sense."

"Maybe," she said, and turned to put her book away.

David would never admit it to anyone, but he enjoyed sparring with the doctor, even if it was only verbally sparring. He'd be damned if he would let Dr. Alcott leave just so he could go to Jamaica to cure old planters with the pox. The boy had a way to him, fresh faced and quick, with medical skills he was coming to appreciate more and more. And while the doctor might never attain the height or muscle or fighting skills of other men, there was no reason Charley couldn't do well for himself with the ladies. Look at him there, reaching up to get something out of the cabinet. His chestnut hair shone in the light coming through the porthole, his back was straight and his legs were shape—

"Hellfire!" he swore aloud, jumping off the table.

Charley looked over his slender shoulder, those large smoky eyes wide with concern, and as he looked at David a faint wash of color filled his downy cheeks.

"Captain?"

"Nothing! It's nothing, Char—Dr. Alcott! I need to go!"

He knew he was babbling, but there was nothing for it. He needed to get out of there, fast, and away from Dr. Alcott. *Far* away from Dr. Alcott. Christ, there was something seriously wrong with him when he started thinking that way about the doctor!

He ran from sick bay like the British Navy was on his arse, and as he passed his brother he grabbed him by his good arm and pulled him along.

"Wha—?"

"Don't speak," David said through his teeth.

He pulled Henry into the cabin, slammed the door behind him and poured them each a glass of rum as Henry stood rubbing his arm. His face was still streaked with grime from the fight and the work aboard the Spanish merchantman.

"Here," he said, thrusting a drink into Henry's hand. "I need to talk to someone—you," he repeated, rubbing his hand over his eyes before taking a drink.

"Henry—have you noticed anything…funny about the doctor?"

Henry froze, his drink halfway to his mouth, and some of the color left his face. David knew then he'd been right. If a dullard like his brother could see it…

"Funny? Funny how?" Henry croaked, taking a swallow of his rum.

"I'm just not sure about him. For example, he smells…I don't know, fresh. Like he is wearing cologne."

Henry relaxed a fraction. "Dr. Alcott smells like blood and medicine to me."

"And then there's this other thing..." he fumbled, looking for the right words. "Henry, I think the doctor is...I think the doctor is developing feelings for me."

"What?"

"What I just said. Feelings. An attachment. An inappropriate attachment. He blushes when I'm near him. Sometimes, I see him looking at me."

"Looking at you, how?"

"You know—*looking* at me. Just a few moments ago when he was examining my wrist... I know that lads are sometimes confused—what the hell are you laughing at? This is not amusing!"

"Oh, it is, more than you realize. I knew that pretty face of yours would get you into trouble some day!"

"Dammit, stop laughing!" He took a drink of his own rum. "Charley needs to be set on the right path."

Henry stopped laughing and looked at his brother.

"You're right, it is not funny. Not for Charley." He turned his glass toward the light, studying it as if it contained answers. David waited for him to speak. Even a blind pig could find an acorn, and sometimes Henry offered good counsel.

"You have to be careful how you deal with this situation, Captain. You like the doctor, don't you?"

"Yes," David said slowly. "Yes, Charley is my friend, as much as I can have a friend aboard ship. I can talk to him about politics without him dozing as you do, and about business, and books we've read in common. I did not think it would be like that when he first came aboard, but the lad is bright, and entertaining and smart—smarter than you by far, but then that's not much of a stretch."

"Then do not be too quick to discard a friend," Henry said

softly. "I also like the doctor and I would not want to see him hurt."

"I would never hurt Charley!"

"You might not mean to, but..." he hesitated, searching for the right words. "A friendship between you and...and someone like Dr. Alcott, it is a rare thing. There's more to Charley than you suspect, and I think you two could become close. In a good way! You are very different, but you also have a great deal in common, particularly the way you care for this ship's crew. The doctor is unique."

He shook his head and smiled, a small, private smile.

"I have to admit that I have never met anyone quite like Charley Alcott. Not at all what I expected when you told me you'd taken a surgeon off a British brig. I've become quite fond of the young doctor, and not just because he saved my life."

"He did the job he was brought here for, and did it well, didn't he? And so much more," David said, pacing back and forth. Now that the problem was out in the open, it was a relief to have Henry here to share it with him. "It doesn't matter to me anymore that Charley loves the king and I'm a good American republican. It's like he was made to be the doctor aboard this vessel."

"Exactly. We have all been fortunate to have Dr. Alcott here, whether it's the right thing to do or not, keeping him aboard the *Fancy*." Henry sighed. "Look, brother, just...be open-minded. Don't throw away your friendship with the doctor, and the good services provided, just because Charley may be different than you expect."

David stopped pacing and looked out the stern window. There were no answers there, in the clear blue skies, so he turned back to his brother and said what needed to be said aloud.

"I can only allow such 'differences' up to a point. Even

Martinez asked if the doctor was my bumboy! If an idiot like him starts assuming that, then I have to be extra careful to discourage Charley from any tendencies that...aren't right."

"You risk losing Charley if you do that," Henry said softly.

"It is a risk I have to take. I am the captain of this vessel, and its master, and the welfare of all the men is my responsibility."

Henry looked at him. He started to speak, then thought better of it.

"Say what is on your mind, brother." He valued Henry's counsel precisely because he was the only man aboard ship who he could have this conversation with, and Henry knew that.

Henry took a deep breath. "No one has said anything. Are you certain that you aren't reacting this way because you worry about your own feelings for the doctor?"

"Do not be ridiculous," David said harshly, chopping his hand through the air like a blow. "I am not like that!"

"I know you are not, it's not that, it's just..." he fumbled, but finally said, "Never mind. You will do as you think best."

He rose to leave. David realized Henry's arm was out of its sling. The doctor was correct, Henry was ready to go on with his life.

But it didn't mean David was ready for the doctor to leave the *Fancy*. He would straighten Charley out, and get beyond this, and it would all work out for the best.

CHAPTER 10

Charley didn't think much of the captain's absence from her life over the days following the attack on the Spanish vessel. The men taking the *Trinidad* to the United States kept her busy making sure they had a rudimentary medical chest in case of emergency. She also reviewed some basics of care with Miller, who was part of the prize crew.

"...and remember, Miller, go easy on the purges. I know it's entertainment for everyone else, but it can weaken the recipient and Mr. Fletcher will need all hands available to sail this ship."

"Aye, Doctor," he said. She would rather instruct Mr. Fletcher, who was captaining the *Trinidad*, but one needed two hands to bandage and splint.

After he left, Charley cleaned up and disposed of Pirate's latest gifts—why couldn't that cat find some nice pastries to bring her?— and went above to watch the preparations aboard the *Trinidad*.

Captain Fletcher was stripping the *Fancy* of two of its four-pounders to improve the firepower on the merchantman and offer some protection for the Americans.

They would have to run the British blockade to get to New York, but the oranges wouldn't keep forever, and with winter coming the haul could bring top dollar if they made it through.

"*When* they make it through, Doctor," the captain amended when she raised this point. "The ocean is vast and the Royal Navy does not own it. We have slipped by them before, and I have every confidence Henry will elude them again."

The captain had stripped down himself in the tropical heat, as had most of the crew manhandling the guns, but Charley only had eyes for their commander. It was an amazing thing, she thought, and not for the first time, that even one who knew the workings of the human body could react in the same way as the most primitive of women to the sight of sweat-sheened muscles flowing beneath a bronzed chest.

She sighed, for looking was as close as she'd ever get. Pirate was twining himself around her ankles and she stooped to pick the cat up and cradle him in her arms, grateful for the feel of warmth and cuddling, even if it came with fur and claws.

That night the *Fancy* hosted a farewell to the prize crew, with toasts to President Madison and the United States of America. While Charley did not join in those salutes, she proposed a toast to the gallant crew of the *Trinidad*, and wished them a safe voyage.

Henry paid the doctor a final visit that evening.

"You no longer need my services, Mr. Fletcher," Charley said. She'd become close to him, and not just in a patient-doctor fashion. She often wondered what it would have been like to have brothers and sisters. Having a brother like Henry Fletcher would have added joy to her life—and likely aggravation as well, based on what she saw between the two brothers aboard the *Fancy*.

"There will always be some pain, Henry. Be careful that you do not come to rely too heavily on laudanum for relief. You will have to be carefully fitted for your artificial limb, and you will want to keep making adjustments until the fit is right. Do not settle for anything that is not as comfortable as it can be."

She smiled at him with a touch of sadness. In some ways he was her only true friend, and tomorrow he would be gone from her life.

"I have done all I can and the rest is up to you. I now officially pronounce you fit and ready to captain your own vessel."

Henry put his hand on her shoulder and looked her in the eyes.

"I wish I wasn't leaving you alone here. Be careful, Doctor. My brother knows something is not as it should be."

"What do you mean?"

"Just…be careful."

Charley sighed. "I always am careful. I am careful in how I walk. I am careful in how I stand, how I hold my cup, how I angle my body during a conversation, how I laugh, how I blow my nose, how I adjust my trousers."

He looked at her sympathetically. "Is it worth it?"

Henry stood in her sick bay, his back straight. He was minus a hand, but otherwise hale and sun-browned, his eyes clear and shining with the excitement of his coming adventure. His body nearly vibrated with his desire to be at the helm of his own vessel. Something in her own chest loosened and glowed with the evidence of her capable hands, her surgical skills reflected in Henry Fletcher's zest for life. She knew without her help there was little chance he would have survived the necessary amputation. She could take comfort in that when he was gone and there would be no one here who knew Charlotte Alcott.

"Yes, Mr. Fletcher. Yes, it is most assuredly worth it. Every man whose health has improved, every cut sewn, every bone set. I cannot do everything, but I draw comfort in knowing I do what I can, and that it can make a difference."

Henry smiled at her.

"Then God bless you, Charley, and I hope you continue to be able to live your life as you wish to."

He made a motion to open his arms for a farewell hug, but a small sound made them both look up then. David Fletcher was standing in the entrance to sick bay, watching them from the shadows, no expression on his face.

She cleared her throat and took a step back, a freezing shiver racing down her spine. Had the captain come a few minutes earlier her thoughtless conversation would have given her away. It was a good reminder she could not relax her guard, not for a second.

"I swear, Captain, you are as cat-footed as Pirate. Is there something you need?"

He didn't say anything for a long, drawn-out moment, his eyes going from Charley to Henry, who was doing his best to look as expressionless as his older brother.

"No, Dr. Alcott. There is nothing I need from you." He turned to Henry. "When you are done here, come see me in my cabin. I have some papers for you."

He turned and exited, leaving the door to sick bay ajar. Henry smiled ruefully and said, "He suspects something. Be on your guard."

"Always, Mr. Fletcher," Charley said, and shook his hand goodbye.

❧

It was hard for David to avoid the doctor in the confines of his own ship. He knew Charley knew he was avoiding him. It hurt when he looked at him with a wounded expression in those soft eyes, like David had kicked his puppy. Even Mr. Bryant, who was about as sensitive as a spar, asked if the captain and the doctor had a falling out.

"Mr. Bryant, I have a ship to command and the doctor is busy with his sick bay, and that's as it ought to be," he snapped out.

"Aye, sir," Bryant said, but looked at him strangely.

The doctor only took meals with the captain when the others were present, and there were no more late night sessions in the captain's cabin.

And David missed it. Desperately. He wanted to talk about a book he was re-reading…and there was no one to talk to. He had thoughts on expansion in the United States after the war, and what would happen in France, and the future of the China trade. He never knew how alone he was until now, with Henry gone and Charley unavailable to him.

He wandered through his ship during the middle watch, unable to sleep. There was a sliver of light coming from beneath the sick bay door, and he softly pushed it open.

The doctor's bunk was occupied, but not by the doctor. And the hammock hung for his use was empty.

Dr. Alcott sat next to the bunk, wringing out a wet cloth and speaking in a soothing voice to Wells, laid low by a fever. The doctor put the cloth on the restless man's forehead while he spoke to him. The compassion and care for his patient radiated from Charley's face like an additional light in the dim cabin. David closed the door quietly and returned to his own cabin, but there was no sleep for him that night as he thought about how to deal with this problem.

～

"Doctor, we need to talk. Come with me."

Dr. Alcott pushed himself to his feet. He'd been sitting with Jenkins, watching the man knotting string for macramé.

"It is good to see the salve is helping your rheumatism. Use it each night to keep your fingers supple."

"And it's making my hands soft, too," Jenkins said with a wink. "The ladies will appreciate it."

"A better side effect than some of my other medications," Dr. Alcott acknowledged. He followed David to the stern, where they could have some privacy without David having to be in a room alone with him. The doctor squinted as his eyes adjusted to the bright sunlight after the shaded spot where Jenkins sat, and waited for David to speak.

He had had enough restless nights. He was going to take care of Charley, and put an end to his problem.

"Doctor, we are going to be stopping at the island of St. Martin soon, and there's something I want you to do there."

Alcott looked at him sharply. "That is a French island, is it not?"

"It was. French and Dutch. At one time a friendly port for Americans. Now, well, it's still friendly, we just have to be more careful because the Royal Navy has a presence there as well."

"Is there someone on the island who's ill?"

"No, not that I know of." He took a deep breath. This was more difficult than he expected it would be.

"There is a lady there I want you to visit. A Mrs. Cornelia Olifiers. You will like her," he added quickly. "She's friendly, and outgoing, and…friendly."

Alcott was watching him with a strange expression on his face.

"And I am visiting Mrs. Olifiers because…?"

In for a penny, in for a pound. Or in this case, a fee to be paid in good American dollars.

"Madame Cornelia operates an establishment where a young man like you can meet ladies and spend the evening with them."

Dr. Alcott was young, but he was not stupid. "You are taking me to a *brothel?*"

"Not so loud, or they'll all want to go!" He took off his hat and ran his hand through his hair. This should have been simple. As usual, where the doctor was involved, it was anything but.

"Madame Cornelia's house is exclusive—not like some where the whores are as common as barber chairs. You know —no sooner is one out than another one is in. Look, I have made up my mind. You will accompany me to Madame Cornelia's house."

Alcott was looking at him with something like horror on his young face, but David would not be gainsaid on this. He had a duty to his men—all of his men—to properly maintain morale aboard ship, and in his experience, nothing did more for a man's morale than an evening in a bawdy house. In Charley's case it could be damned therapeutic as well, quashing any tendencies the boy might have to look for his pleasure elsewhere.

"Do not be missish, Charley. Honestly, you are acting like a debutante being asked to part with her maidenhead! This experience will do you good. It will be educational. And close your mouth, you look like a grouper with it gaping open that way."

His teeth snapped shut. "I have no doubt it will be educational, Captain, but this is not a good idea! What is more it offends my sense of morality to pay someone for sexual congress!"

"Dr. Alcott, this is a privateer, not a monastery. I know what is best for my crew, all of my crew, and as the commanding officer of the *Fancy*, I must insist."

"I am not part of your crew. I am your prisoner! Do you insist all of your prisoners go to brothels with you? Is this some secret American plan to undermine the Royal Navy, because I have no doubt if you offer free tokens for whores some of the sailors would cheerfully desert king and country!"

"Do not take that tone with me, sir!" David said through his own teeth. Part of the problem in dealing with this young chub was he had no sense of appropriate behavior with the ship's commander. However, clapping him in irons, while personally satisfying, would not solve the problem of Charley's misplaced desires. If Charley was ever to regain David's trust, he would have to prove himself a man—in all ways.

He was still looking too much like a gaffed fish.

"I cannot talk you out of this?"

"No. And if you fear disease, Madame Cornelia will sell you a French letter for your protection."

Sweat broke out on Alcott's smooth forehead, and he stuck a finger inside his neckcloth, loosening the tight fabric. Finally he gulped and said, his voice higher than usual, "If you insist, Captain, then I suppose there is nothing I can do about it."

"That's the lad, Charley! The experience will make a new man of you!"

"Very possibly," Alcott muttered.

David left him to contemplate his future, and walked off with a lighter step. Someday the boy would thank him for this.

The more the wind drove them toward St. Martin, the more Charley fretted. Could she fake illness and miss out on the excursion ashore? It wouldn't be hard to do, as much as her nerves were stretched thin already, but she was afraid she was just putting off the inevitable. At least on an island she would have the opportunity to run. There had to be some kind of English presence there, since they'd taken the island from France, and her best hope might be in making a bid for freedom away from the Americans.

She could only imagine how her story would be received by British officials, but it beat being exposed by Captain Fletcher as a fraud, or worse.

When they neared the island Fletcher dug a Spanish flag out of the locker and ran the false colors up.

"Won't it be obvious if we're stopped that this is not a Spanish vessel?"

"There are plenty of American Loyalists who fled south to Spanish Florida, Doctor. It is an excellent ploy."

She hadn't thought about that, but their ruse wasn't put to the test as they dropped anchor at Marigot Bay. Despite her fears, Charley was intrigued by this new stop and studied the approaching land. St. Martin wasn't as green and lush as Santa Rosa, but the town of Marigot was lively, with a definite French flavor, the Fort St. Louis looming over the city like a broody hen guarding her chicks. Charley saw the crew look longingly at the town and its pleasures as the sun sank below the horizon, but the captain made it clear that with the Royal Navy looking for the *Fancy*, they would stay aboard and be prepared for action.

If there was already a British presence on St. Martin, it was minimal. Having finally defeated the French in the West Indies by taking Guadeloupe, the Royal Navy's attitude was that it owned the oceans, with only the occasional American, or pirate, or American pirate, to keep them busy.

Speaking of which...

"How do you know this woman? Other than in the biblical sense?"

"Droll, Charley. I know Cornelia from Baltimore. She married Olifiers and he took her to the islands, and when he died she established herself in business here. I bring her news of home, and she acts as, you might say, a postmistress for me. Letters can be directed here while I'm at sea."

"And it doesn't hurt that she runs the finest house in the islands," Purcell added with a wink. He was in the boat with them, rowing them ashore to the lights of the town. Captain Fletcher had explained that Purcell had a woman at Madame Olifiers with whom he maintained a steady relationship. Charley thought that was odd, but rather sweet, and she was just as glad as not that the rest of the crew stayed behind with Mr. Bryant aboard the *Fancy*.

If she was going to have to escape in the dark, it would be easier avoiding two men than a dozen.

They approached the brothel on foot up a sandy road, with Purcell holding his lantern. Charley had her medical satchel slung over her shoulder, standing firm against the captain's protests that this wasn't a business call.

"I do not go anywhere without the tools of my profession, Captain, anymore than you go out without that knife in your boot."

She came to a sudden stop, nearly tripping Purcell.

"Mr. Purcell, bring that lantern closer, please. Captain! This is a guaiac tree." Charley put her hand on it and looked up into the glossy leaves. "The guiacum powder I use to treat the pox comes from this resin!"

She turned to him with a hopeful lilt in her voice. "Surely I could do your crew more good if I stayed here and harvested some bark...?"

"Keep marching, Doctor. That's an order."

"Aye, sir," she muttered darkly and they resumed walking.

She wasn't sure what she was expecting, but the house on the quiet road outside of the city was neat and looked well-maintained and prosperous, if tropically colorful. It was wood, three stories with balconies and shuttered doors, some of the doors thrown open for the occupants of the rooms to enjoy the evening breeze. Torches placed in the front gave off a welcoming glow, illuminating the bougainvillea that rioted around the steps of the wide veranda. The fuchsia leaves battled with the red blossoms of a geranium tree for most eye-catching display, and there was a strong fragrance of jasmine as they approached their destination.

Charley's fervid imagination had conjured up images of red velvet and an overabundance of gilt, and perhaps some diaphanously clad houris, but truly, there was nothing to distinguish Madame Olifiers house from the others around it on this tropical island.

That may not have been quite accurate. Perhaps the other houses here didn't boast ladies on the veranda in low cut gowns, languidly fanning themselves and checking out the visitors with interest. When the trio came into the light there were glad cries of recognition from the ladies, and one hefty brunette dashed off the porch and threw herself into Purcell's arms, nearly causing him to drop the lantern. But he managed to catch her, set down the lantern and swing her around, bussing her soundly on her carmined lips.

"Jeanette, my lass! It's good to see you, too!"

Jeanette chuckled throatily. "It has been an age since you have visited me, Asher Purcell! I have missed you most dreadfully."

The wiry carpenter tossed a squealing Jeanette over his shoulder and slapped her on her well-padded bottom. He turned to his captain and the doctor, who watched this performance with a tinge of awe—who would have thought the carpenter could so ably tote such a substantial load, but then, he was highly motivated, wasn't he?

"Captain, I have what I came for. I will see you in the morning!" And to the cheers of the ladies on the veranda he hustled into the house.

"Well," Charley said, clearing her throat. "That was interesting."

"Ah, Charley me lad," the captain said, picking up the lantern, "I have no doubt that is only the first of many interesting things you will see tonight."

"I fear you may be correct," she muttered.

The footman at the door who'd made way for Purcell and his lady was an enormous hulk, with an ear that resembled a mass of cauliflower and a grin for the captain.

"As I live and breathe, if it ain't Black Davy Fletcher! We ain't seen you in ages, Cap'n!"

David Fletcher grinned at the doorman and handed him his hat.

"You remember how it is, Taylor, ships to stop, cargoes to rob, a privateer's work is seldom finished."

"Aye, Cap'n. You should consider taking yourself a softer berth ashore. There's much to be said for life where the ground don't move beneath your feet."

"The company here smells and looks better than the crew aboard the *Fancy*, I know. But I believe I'll stay where I am, and if you decide to come back we'll hang a hammock for you."

Taylor guffawed. "Leave the ladies for that lot of pirates? Thank ye, but no, Cap'n Fletcher."

The big man grinned again at his former captain, then spotted Charley, who was trying to look small and unobtrusive.

"Who's this sprat then?"

"I was wondering the same thing," said a soft alto voice from the doorway.

The doctor also removed his hat, and the two of them made a bow to their hostess. Madame Olifiers was well past her youth, but had a lively eye and a firm step, Charley noted. In the light coming from the house the proprietress's hair gleamed a soft chestnut threaded with silver, bound up atop her head in an elegant style. Her clothing was attractive, but not outrageous, complimenting her small, slim form. Madame's elegant gown of sea-green crepe was embellished by vandyking 'round the gold petticoat and at the short sleeve, and would have looked perfectly appropriate in a fine London or Baltimore residence.

She had to confess herself a tad disappointed. The house and its owner were anything but flamboyant, and if she was going to stand on the precipice of hell, she'd hoped for a more colorful display.

"Cornelia, I have brought you a special visitor. Dr. Charles Alcott is our ship's surgeon, and a young man in need of having his horizons broadened. And getting horizontal will broaden them considerably, I believe."

"Did you stay up all night thinking of that line?" Charley muttered to him.

He ignored her and focused instead on his hostess, who was watching Charley. Her face held only mild amusement, and she extended her hand.

"Dr. Alcott, it is a pleasure to have you in our house."

Charley bowed over her hostess's hand. Madame's smile broadened and she said, "My, but you are a pretty young man! I know my girls will be delighted to meet you."

She blushed, for how could she not? But that seemed to be an appropriate response for a young man in a bawdy house, for as she straightened her back, the captain clapped her on the shoulder, his muscled arm nearly driving her to her knees.

"We've been preparing this lad with tales of the delights to be found here, Cornelia. I know you won't disappoint."

"Oh, we can handle all kinds of requests here, Captain. I have no worries the doctor will fit right in."

"Now, nothing unusual, Connie," David Fletcher said with a frown. "This is his first time and we don't want to do anything that will frighten the boy."

"We will take care of Dr. Alcott properly. Why don't you gentlemen accompany me?"

With a swish of her skirts and a lingering fragrance of damask roses, Madame Cornelia led them into her parlor. It was decorated with framed needlework on the walls, and after ringing for refreshments Madame seated herself and picked up her latest fabric project. Charley envied her speed and dexterity as her needle flashed through the cloth.

"I would wager you could sew up a person as finely as you sew that flower."

Madame's broad smile revealed gaps where a few teeth had gone missing over the years, but the sentiment was genuine.

"Haven't I stitched up a girl or a customer a time or two? I would imagine we have some things in common, Doctor. The ladies here need doctoring on occasion, and when I cannot get someone from the town, I do for them myself."

"I would be happy to take a look at any of your ladies needing medical assistance." If she kept busy all night doctoring, she might not have to take her clothes off.

But Captain Fletcher had anticipated this and said, "We brought you here for a reason, Charley, and that's not it. You are here to relax and have fun. That's an order!"

Before she could argue, the refreshments arrived, carried in by a stately butler who could have graced a London townhouse, though his mahogany-toned skin might have made him stand out amidst the Englishmen.

"Thank you, Lasalle," Madame Olifiers said, and setting aside her work, poured them each a glass of the island's famed guavaberry cordial. "Would you fetch the parcel in my study for the captain?"

The butler bowed and exited silently, drawing the door closed behind him. Charley took a sip of her drink. It was an interesting blend, both bitter and sweet, but she set it aside, for she'd need all her wits about her tonight. Sweat was trickling down her back, and she felt her heart racing. She looked around the room, noting the location of the doors and windows if she needed to jump and run. Being nervous did not seem inappropriate for a young man's first visit to a bawdy house, and the others did not remark upon it further.

"Captain, I have some correspondence for you, and news from home. Ah, here's Lasalle with your mail. You will note some of it is marked 'urgent.'"

"There go my plans for the evening," Fletcher said with a wry smile. "But it is just as well. Tonight I want the attention to be on you, Charley Alcott."

"Just as I feared," she said under her breath. To hell with caution. She took a fortifying swallow of her drink, and coughed.

"Careful, youngster, you're not used to strong spirits. You don't want to do anything to impair your performance later," the sage elder said as he sorted through his mail.

She watched him frowning down at his letters, and was glad he would not be hiring one of Madame Cornelia's girls for the evening. She didn't question why she was glad—she knew she was jealous of the sloe-eyed beauties she'd seen languidly fanning themselves on the veranda, the ones with more bountiful charms to lure a lonely sailor to bed.

The ones who were quite obviously women. And available.

"Will you stay to supper?" Madame Olifiers asked.

He looked up from the letter he was reading, his eyes shadowed.

"I beg your pardon, it was rude of me to open my mail while I am here."

"Is the news from home bad?" Charley asked.

"It is mixed news. There was fighting near my home in Baltimore. Madame Olifiers, Doctor, I have to ask you to excuse me. I am afraid I would not be good company tonight, and I need to return to my ship to draft replies for you to send home for me, Cornelia."

"Of course. Do not fear, I will give Dr. Alcott the best of the house."

"Fortunate lad!" David rose to his feet, as did Charley.

"I will see you in the morning then, Doctor. I hope this night turns out to be everything you want it to be."

"I am sure it will be a night to remember, Captain," Charley said. She looked deeply into his eyes, memorizing his features, knowing that if she had to run, this might be the last time she would see him.

"Now, no need to look so frightened. I don't know a single man yet who's died of the experience," he said with a wink. Then with a nod to Madame Olifiers, he turned his back and walked out. The little parlor was still and silent in his absence.

Charley turned back to her hostess, whose blue eyes watched her over the rim of her glass as she took a small sip of her liqueur. She put down her glass and looked Charley over carefully, as she stood there, poised to dash out the front of the house.

"You can relax, Doctor, he is gone. Now, would you like to tell me why a young lady is pretending to be a man?"

CHAPTER 11

"Good Lord," Charley gasped, and grasped the back of her chair to support her weak limbs. "Does everyone know?"

"Based on tonight's events, I expect Captain Fletcher does not know."

"Are you going to tell him?"

"I don't see why I would. It's none of my affair. Davy Fletcher paid me for you to stay the night and receive some entertainment and an education. He did not pay me for information about you."

"Thank God," she said, and collapsing back into her chair gulped down the last of her drink.

"One of the specialties of this house is offering a relaxing evening in a variety of forms, Dr. Alcott. Should I continue calling you 'Dr. Alcott'?"

"Yes, it's safer that way, though you may call me Charley, if you wish."

Madame Olifiers gave her a small nod and continued.

"Some men come for the sexual congress, but others

simply wish for cards or conversation. I would hope I can offer you an evening of relaxation as well."

Madame Cornelia rang for her butler.

"Ah, Lasalle. Please set supper for two. Dr. Alcott will dine with me this evening. And I do not wish to be disturbed."

"*Oui*, Madame," the butler said, bowing himself out.

Charley felt both relieved and galvanized. She didn't have to run away. Her identity was safe, for now.

She could return to the *Fancy*.

"An evening of relaxation where I can let down my guard. Madame, you cannot imagine how long it has been since I have been able to do that!"

Madame Olifiers resumed her stitching, the silver needle creating art in her hands.

"Sometimes," she said gently, "people want to talk and unburden themselves. On St. Martin's they can go to church and confess to *Pere* Dupre. Or they can come here. You do not have to tell me, but I confess, I am intrigued and would like to hear your story. Ah, here is Lasalle. Will you escort me into supper, Doctor?"

"It would be my very great pleasure, Madame," Charley said, offering her hostess her arm. Madame Olifiers was smaller than Charley, but her short stature took nothing away from her air of authority as her eyes moved around the main parlor, no doubt noting every detail of the evening's activities.

"My girls come to me. I do not recruit at the dockside," said Madame Olifiers in answer to Charley's question. "My house has a reputation to maintain, and I do not want to have anyone here who is sullen, or unhappy with her lot." She glanced sideways at Charley. "I also do not expect my guests to criticize my house."

Charley looked down at her.

"I am curious, not critical, Madame. As Captain Fletcher

pointed out, this is my first visit to an establishment such as yours, and you must own that curiosity would be natural."

"I hope over supper you will satisfy my curiosity, Dr. Alcott."

"If you keep my confidences, it is the least I can do."

Now that Charley was more relaxed she saw that the house was spotlessly clean, and the ladies did not look beaten down or despondent. On the contrary, they appeared cheerful and pleasant as they chatted with the clients.

The dining parlor was intimate, with a table set with fine crystal and linen, the silver winking in the candlelight. The windows were open and the evening breezes rustled through the foliage outside the parlor, blowing in the flower scented air and keeping the mosquitoes away.

The meal would have pleased the emperor himself. St. Martin combined the finest of French cuisine with the produce of the island. No doubt some gourmands would have dismissed dishes like the hearty *pâté en pot* as "peasant food," but for Charley it was a treat after weeks of subsisting on sea rations and Cook's bland meals.

"More *crabbe de terre*, Doctor?"

They were serving themselves so that they could talk freely, and she eyed the coconut infused dish with longing, but declined.

"No, I still need to fit into my clothes, and too much will make them tight."

"And add to your womanly curves," Madame said with a smile. "I know other women who prefer to go in masculine attire, and it is easier when there is less of you to disguise."

"Oh, I do not have to worry overmuch about that," Charley said. "I have always looked like a boy."

"I can see how your appearance might fool some men, but be careful. There are others who would find your slim lines exactly to their taste."

Charley ignored this. She had heard often enough from her father that her plain looks were more suited to her boy's disguise, and after living in the company of men for so long, she knew what they liked. Their talk was all of bouncing breasts and well padded hips, or lovely swans like Miss Dixon. She'd never heard a one say, "I'd like to tup a woman who looks like a boy!"

She accepted the offer of coffee, and enjoyed the rich French brew with a new appreciation.

"Captain Fletcher has made me a convert to coffee drinking, Madame, but I vow, this is the best I have had!"

"I learned many years ago with Mr. Olifiers that if you pay attention to the small comforts, life is easier and more enjoyable. One might say that is the philosophy of this house —when a client comes here, we want him to feel comfortable. If he wants something bizarre or outrageous, there are other houses to meet his needs."

Charley was itching to ask what constituted "bizarre or outrageous," but figured she was best not going off on tangents.

All she had to do was survive this night with her identity intact and she could return to the *Fancy*.

The sensible part of her mind thought that trying to make her way to the British naval station would be more prudent. But how could she put the crew of the *Fancy* at risk? While she was aboard their vessel they were her patients, and her charges. Surely risking their capture constituted a violation of her vow to "do no harm"?

"Captain Fletcher is a beautiful man, isn't he?"

Charley fumbled her coffee cup, but fortunately it was nearly empty and none spilled.

"I suppose one could say that," she tried to recover. "To me though he is just another patient."

"Really?" Madame Olifiers raised her eyebrows. "Are you

then of the Sapphist persuasion, Doctor? Because, I vow, I have seldom seen a man as well put together as Handsome Davy, and I daresay I have seen more naked men than you have, or ever will! And I know Davy must feel something for you, because I assure you, he does not take random crew members to my house and pay for them to spend the night."

Charley hid her face behind her cup, cursing the color that bloomed too easily through her cheeks. She cleared her throat and looked up at her hostess.

"Whatever feelings I may have for Captain Fletcher can only remain feelings, and not actions. And as to your other question," she said trying to deflect the conversation, "I do not believe I am attracted to members of my own sex in that fashion."

"If you are we can accommodate you. There are a number of women on staff who would be delighted to spend the evening with a good-looking lady such as yourself."

"Really?" Charley was oddly flattered, after years of being told she was plain and unpretty, to know that someone would find her attractive.

"The evening is yours, Doctor, if you want to pursue that option. In the meantime though, would you be willing to take a look at some of the girls with medical issues?"

"Absolutely," she said, glad to be on safe ground. "If you have a well-lit room where I can examine them in privacy, I am at your disposal. However, there is one service I would like to request before I begin my examinations."

Madame Olifiers raised her brows and waited.

"May I have a bath? A real bath with hot water, and soap, and a chance to soak the salt out of my skin?"

Madame Olifiers chuckled. "Believe it or not, that isn't so unusual a request in this house. Yes, I will have a bath prepared for you. With salts and soft towels as well."

"Oh, Madame, you have made me the happiest woman

alive!" Charley said passionately. She just chuckled and rang for Lasalle, giving him orders to prepare the bath in her room.

Thirty minutes later she was soaking in a fragrant cloud of steam and blessedly fresh water, her eyes closed as she leaned back.

Madame herself washed her hair and trimmed it close to her head to enhance her disguise. Afterward, dressed and feeling cleaner than she had in ages, Charley was ushered into an empty bedroom in the upper floor of the house. Again, there were no salacious paintings or red velvet, simply a bed hung with mosquito netting, a wash basin with clean cloths stacked neatly beneath, and a small balcony that opened to the night. Charley removed her coat, rolled up her sleeves and washed at the basin.

"Come in," she said to the light rap at the door.

Madame returned with a young woman about Charley's age, black curls clustered about her head and an inquiring look in her bright eyes. Her dusky skin bespoke her mixed heritage, and she asked Madame a quick question in French.

"Claire wants to know if you need her to take off her clothes, but I hardly think that is necessary for you to examine her throat," Madame Olifiers said dryly.

"No, she may leave her clothes on. But please, have her sit over here near the lamp. And if you could stay to translate…?"

Madame spoke to Claire and motioned her to the chair. A quick examination determined that the young lady was suffering from nothing more than an inflamed throat, and was prescribed a regimen of soothing teas.

"…and remind her to avoid talking overmuch or doing anything else that will put a stress on her throat until she's healed," Charley added at the end.

After the girl left Charley said, "I do not understand. Why did she look downcast at my orders?"

Madame cleared her own throat. "Claire's particular specialty is offering oral gratification. She will earn less money while her throat heals."

"Good Lord," Charley murmured to herself. Until tonight she hadn't thought about the reality of some of the Latin terms she'd learned over the years.

Over the course of the evening her education was expanded exponentially. After treating various venereal disorders, an irritated bladder, a common sprain, and an examination of a new mother who proudly showed off her baby boy, she gratefully accepted Madame Olifiers offer of a break in the ladies' parlor. There were no clients allowed in this room, and those women whose services were not engaged or entertaining in the main parlor gathered there. The girls took her male attire in stride, and were not shocked at her masquerade. Charley worried briefly about her secret being revealed, but the *Fancy* sailed in the morning and she would be away from danger.

The girl with the baby prompted Charley's first question to the experts.

"I would imagine that preventing conception is a concern in a business such as this. What steps do you ladies take to avoid conceiving?"

"Bear in mind," Madame Olifiers said dryly, "that you have seen firsthand evidence this evening that no method is foolproof."

"That is true, Madame, but there are some methods that are better than praying nothing will occur," said Marie Denise with a smile. "Most of us use sponges, soaked in vinegar. They're subtle and hard for the gentlemen to detect."

"I like lemons," said Dawn in her husky voice.

The two girls, called "Dawn" and "Dusk" by the others, sat

together on a settee, their arms around each others' waists. Madame said they were the biggest earners in the house, and Charley could see why. Dawn was as pale as new milk, with hair like cornsilk flowing down her back to her waist. Dusk was as shiny and dark as a blackberry, her hair cropped close to her head. And yet, there was a resemblance between the two in their cat-like slanted eyes and lush mouths. Men paid a fortune to spend the night with the "twins."

"Lemons?"

Dusk chuckled. "You take a small lemon and remove the meat from it. Then you insert the lemon inside yourself and it acts as a little cap to prevent babies."

Charley blinked as she assimilated this information. "Oh my. I can see how that would work. What an astounding contraceptive, Miss Dusk!"

Dusk just smiled her sleepy smile and leaned her head against Dawn's fair shoulder. "There is much we could teach you, Doctor. If you would like more lessons, Dawn and I are at your disposal."

"No." Charley cleared her throat. "I am learning so much this evening just sitting here with you all...and that reminds me," she said, reaching into her satchel. "If you ladies are talking, I should be taking notes! Now, tell me if you will, what do you use to relieve cramping during your menses?"

And like brightly colored birds of paradise the ladies chatted and drank coffee, and compared methods, sometimes ducking out to entertain clients, with others coming in to add to their store of knowledge.

As the night lengthened and the clients went home or slept beside their partners, more guavaberry liquor was fetched and the potent drink helped ease Charley past her remaining shyness, drawing her from the medical realm into the more personal.

"What I would also like to know, ladies, while I'm here, is

if you can suggest anything that might make a man…more satisfied…when he's with a woman. Any particular skills that might be useful."

"Honey, a man would be happy sticking his cock into the knothole of a tree if it's the right height!"

"Or a sheep!"

"Or his shipmate's bum!"

"Yeah, and they all want to believe they're the greatest thing you've ever had in your bed," said American Sal.

"'Ooooh, my darling, I have never seen one that big! What an amazing lover you are!'" Marie Denise sang out in a high falsetto, and the other women fell over themselves laughing.

"A better question is, what can he do for you that will make you happy?" chimed in Laurel, an English girl. "See, a man's like flint and tinder. Show him a pair o' tits or a glimpse of cunny and it's like a striking a spark and up the fire flares! But a woman? We're more like an ember you have to coax and blow on and be careful of to get a nice blaze going."

"Which is one reason why some of us prefer each others' company," Dusk said with a kiss on Dawn's pale cheek. "We know what we would like, and we give that to our lover."

"Men aren't very bright, Doctor. A wise woman can lead a man by his cock or his stomach, and the wisest lead them by both," said Sal with a wink.

"Of course, there are exceptions," said Marie Denise. "Like Black Davy Fletcher."

Some of the ladies sighed in remembrance.

"I'm so sorry he's not staying tonight," said Sal. "All men have the same equipment, but that man knows how to use his cock for something more than taking a piss!"

Charley knew she should not feel jealous that these prostitutes had what she could never have. But telling herself she shouldn't feel that way did not drive the feelings away.

"But when all is said and done, Black Davy is just a man," Dawn said. "And as such, is prone to let his little head do all the thinking for him when he's with a woman."

"Oh, but he's considerate of his crew, and he's very funny and smart…" Charley's voice trailed off as she saw how the women looked at her, with looks ranging from mild amusement to pity.

"He wants what all men want," Dusk said. "He is no different in that regard. He will want a wife who can give him meals in a warm home, and children, and when he is away he will want a whore to ease the ache in his balls."

This gave Charley much to ponder as the sky lightened and the ladies trundled off to their beds. She stretched out in the empty room where she'd done her examinations, but sleep eluded her, so she got up and sat reviewing her notes from the night before.

~

Someone else was having a sleepless night. David Fletcher roamed the narrow spaces of the *Fancy*, the news from America keeping him from his bunk.

But it was more than that, he thought as he stood outside of the quiet and empty sick bay. He wondered how Charley was doing. Not that he had a prurient interest in the doctor's nocturnal activities, he told himself, but a natural interest in seeing the boy set on the right track.

Poor lad, he looked so nervous when they abandoned him to the tender mercies of Madame Olifiers. Likely he was wondering if he would measure up, especially when compared to older, more experienced men who'd been in the house a time or two.

He pushed open the door to sick bay, and walked over to where he knew a lantern sat, lighting the lamp and bringing the room out of the shadows. Just as he expected, everything was neat and ship-shape, for that was the doctor's habit. Even the notebooks were aligned just so on the shelf, the pens arrayed in a row that looked like they'd been ordered to toe the line.

David gave in to his restless impulse and pulled the doctor's sketchbook off the shelf. There were pictures, excellently drawn, of various wounds and diseases. Fascinated, he turned the pages, examining the finely detailed illustrations of various body parts.

There was a drawing of Henry's stump and he winced and turned quickly past that one. Stern's scabies were on display, and he grinned to see *Señor* Martinez's arse once again, drawn in far too much detail!

But when he reached the pages at the end of the book, he felt like he'd been punched in the stomach, the air knocked out of him.

"Oh, Charley," he whispered.

They were drawings of him. Drawings of him swimming nude at the pool on Santa Rosa. Drawings of him on deck. Drawings of him in his cabin.

Charley had captured him, he could see that at a glance. His expression, the way he smiled, the light falling across him through the trees—the doctor had an artist's eye, but even more disturbingly, he'd drawn Davy with a lover's eye.

And the drawings were achingly beautiful. Far more beautiful than he deserved. Far more loving than he could deal with.

He saw his hand reaching to tear the drawings from the book, shredding them before anyone had a chance to see them, before they could disturb him any further. He stopped, his hand clenching into a fist. No matter how he felt about the wrongness of Charley's feelings, he couldn't bring himself to destroy what he had created from his heart.

He closed the sketchbook and put it back on the shelf, and prayed that tonight's events would show Charley the error of his ways and set him onto the right path.

Because if not, David was going to have to put the young doctor off his ship, and out of his life, for both their sakes.

CHAPTER 12

Charley was enjoying breakfast with Mr. Purcell, who looked fresh and rested, when Captain Fletcher showed up.

"Good Lord, Captain, you look like you've been pulled through a hedge backward!" Purcell said, his normal caution dampened by his own good spirits.

"I didn't get any sleep," Fletcher snarled, looking anything but fresh or rested. "Some of us have to keep the *Fancy* afloat and out of the hands of the British, and we don't have time for restful evenings in bawdy houses!"

"No wonder you look so out of sorts," Purcell said, reaching for a cup to pass his commander.

Charley winced at this impolitic speech, and took a sip of her own coffee. Captain Fletcher was watching her, frowning, and she couldn't even begin to guess what might be going through his mind.

"You are awfully quiet this morning, Doctor."

"I didn't get any sleep last night either," Charley murmured, then wished she'd bit her tongue. Heaven knows what they'd make of that comment!

Sure enough, Purcell was looking as proud as if he'd been beside the bed offering advice to the novice, while Captain Fletcher was looking at her...oddly.

"Well?"

"Well, what, Captain?"

"How did your evening go?"

Charley cleared her throat. "A gentleman does not discuss such things."

Captain Fletcher opened his mouth to argue the point, but at that moment their hostess entered the parlor, and the gentlemen—and Charley—rose to their feet.

"Good morning, Captain Fletcher, gentlemen. Captain, will you stay and have breakfast with us?"

"No, thank you, Cornelia. I have to take these two libertines back to the ship and get under weigh."

Charley knew he wouldn't be in a mood to argue, so she grabbed her satchel, took a last sip of her excellent coffee—she'd miss that—and made her farewells.

"Madame Olifiers, I cannot thank you enough. This has been one of the most enjoyable evenings of my life."

She flashed Charley her warm smile and said, "You are welcome to return anytime, Doctor. The girls said to tell you they would be pleased to have you settle on the island and visit them regularly."

"I will bear that in mind," Charley said with a wink.

She joined her speechless shipmates and headed out into the sunshine. As they were walking away from the house, voices called out from the balcony. The trio stopped and turned around.

Dusk and Dawn were standing there, arms wrapped around each other's waists, their charms barely covered by their diaphanous nightrails.

"Do come and spend the night with us again, Charley," Dusk called out, her sleepy smile dazzling in the sunlight. "Dawn and I would be pleased to entertain you further."

Charley gave the ladies a most elegant bow. "Miss Dawn, Miss Dusk, what I learned last evening will be with me forever. I am a better man for my experience with you."

The girls laughed and clapped their hands.

"Goodbye, Doctor! Take care of yourself!"

Charley put her hat back on her head and turned to her shipmates. Purcell was staring at her, jaw agape.

Captain Fletcher said nothing, but as they walked back to where their boat waited, he kept looking at Charley with a puzzled expression on his face.

"You spent the night with the twins?" he finally asked.

"Yes."

"Both of them?"

"That is the custom of the house, is it not, Captain?"

"Damn me for a lubber," Purcell muttered to Captain Fletcher. "Who would have thought the boy had it in him?"

"Not me," the captain said, looking at her again.

For her part, Charley walked with her head high, a smile on her face. If she were a cock, she'd be crowing. Of course, it was the hens that did all the work, and that reminded her of what the ladies had said about men during their "hen party," and she chuckled to herself.

"What's so funny?" Captain Fletcher growled.

"Just thinking about something that happened last night," she said airily.

The men were silent in the boat as they rowed out to the *Fancy*. No one had died during her absence, which made Charley's morning brighter, and she got back into her routine of examinations and dealing with the crew's assorted aches and pains.

Over the midday meal Bryant and Purcell pressed her for details of her experiences at Madame Cornelia's, but she again refused to discuss the evening. She noticed that the captain continued to watch her with an expression on his face that was hard to read, and there was still a distance between them that couldn't be ignored.

So she was surprised when he stopped by sick bay that afternoon.

"I have something you need to look at, Doctor."

Charley cocked an eyebrow, waited for him to explain. The captain stood there next to her examining table, looking uncomfortable, and his hand hovered over his flies.

Oh dear. Could the captain have fallen prey to a disease of Venus?

As if reading her mind he said, "No, it's not the pox. I think I have a boil. On my arse."

"Oh! Well, that shouldn't be a problem. Drop your trousers and lie down on the table so I can take a look at it."

"Can't we do this with me standing?"

That raised an image of the discussions of the night before, and Charley saw herself kneeling at a naked David Fletcher's feet while he loomed above her in all his glory. The thought made heat rush through her veins and she remembered the women saying how much men loved that act, and techniques which would make it enjoyable for both of them.

She did not need that image in her head, not when he was here with a medical issue, not when he was dealing with Charles, not Charlotte.

"No, we cannot do this examination with you standing!" She reached for that gruff, no-nonsense doctor voice that she used to good effect with other patients. "Do not be a little baby, Captain Fletcher. Yours is not the first boil—or the first pair of buttocks—I have ever seen!"

"That is what worries me," he muttered, but he started to unbutton his flies. She turned away and fetched a lamp to increase the light on the table. When she turned back,

Captain Fletcher's trousers were on the floor and he was lying down on his belly, his shirt tails covering his hindquarters.

Charley swallowed and said, "Try to relax, I need to examine you."

"Just lance the damn thing and let me out of here!" he said harshly. His arms were crossed beneath his head, and he looked away from her to the bulkhead.

"Remember our rule captain. You sail, I doctor. Now let me take a look at you."

And what a view it was. Charley tried to stay detached and clinical as she rolled up his shirt, but the sight before her brought an involuntary sigh to her lips. After seeing countless ugly, scarred, unpleasant sights—and sadly, *Señor* Martinez could never be erased from her memory—the captain's arse was a treat. It was finely muscled and sleek, a shade lighter than the surrounding skin. When his leg moved and flexed those muscles the moisture in her mouth dried up, though she noted with a tiny part of her mind still working that the moisture seemed to have moved south to pool between her legs.

"Is it bad?" her patient asked.

Not hardly! she almost said aloud, but caught herself.

"You are correct, Captain, there is a boil here, but it is not brought to a head. We can try using warm compresses on it for a few days and see if it drains on its own."

"Warm compresses?" he turned to look at her and frowned.

"Yes. Two or three times a day you could come down here and I would put a warm cloth on the boil to raise the pus and help it drain."

"I am not spending days lying on my belly with my arse in the air for you, Doctor! Lance the damn thing and get it over with!"

"As you wish. However, you will still need to keep the area clean after I lance it. If you need assistance, you know where to find me."

Charley fetched her scalpel and a warm, wet cloth, and said, "This will sting slightly, and then I need to give it time to drain."

He uttered a sharp expletive when the knife pierced him, but closed his eyes and lay still beneath Charley's hands. She tried to focus on the purely medical aspects of what she was doing, telling herself there was nothing attractive about a body part draining pus and infection.

It didn't help much.

When she was satisfied she'd done what she could, she said, "Let me put some balm on that to prevent infection. I want to see you again tomorrow to make sure this is healing properly."

Fletcher said nothing, but shifted himself on the table as she smoothed in the healing balm, and she saw sweat on his forehead and grim lines around his mouth.

"Are you in pain?"

"No, you damn sawbones, I am not in pain! Aren't you done yet?"

She couldn't imagine why he was reacting as he was until she told him she was finished and he abruptly sat up.

"Oh." She swallowed and forced her eyes away. "Do not think anything of it, that can happen to anyone."

"It has never happened to me!" he snarled. "Not with a man touching my—turn around!"

"Yes, Captain," she said, turning her back. She could hear him cursing steadily under his breath while he got dressed, and then without a word of farewell or thanks, he stomped out of sick bay, slamming the door behind him.

Charley let out her breath in a rush.

Black Davy Fletcher at ease was a sight to behold, but

seeing him with his equipment erect, that was another sight entirely. A shiver raced over her frame, and she passed her hand across her hot face.

Prior to her evening at the brothel she might have been able to view this more clinically. But after her conversations with the whores she had new directions for her thoughts that were not going to make her job in dealing with the captain any easier.

The next afternoon Captain Fletcher told Mr. Bryant to muster the crew and Charley joined them, standing apart from the ranks of seamen.

When they were all assembled, he looked out over the assortment of Yankee privateers and their British doctor and said, "Men, I have news from home."

He waited for the murmurs to die down.

"I received correspondence on St. Martin that I wish to share with you. Last August, while we were at sea fighting for the rights of sailors and free Americans, the British burned our nation's capitol, Washington City."

Now the mutters from the men were angry as they shifted their feet and looked at one another. The Americans had burned York in Canada, and Great Britain might be justified in saying it's tit for tat to burn the Americans' capitol, but Charley just scratched her ear and wisely refrained from pointing that out.

Plus, Captain Fletcher was still speaking.

"But take heart, men, just as your countrymen did! America cannot be frightened into submission!" He waved a paper. "I have here the account of the battle of Baltimore and the glorious defense of Fort McHenry! The nation still stands strong, boys, and will never bow to tyrants! A cheer for the United States of America, and an extra ration of rum tonight for its gallant heroes!"

The men threw their hats into the air while cheering, "Huzzah for the United States!"

Charley slipped quietly back to sick bay, leaving the Americans to their celebration, and wondering again what would become of a British surgeon held on an American vessel during wartime.

CHAPTER 13

"How is your boil, Captain?"

It seemed an innocuous question, but Captain Fletcher rounded on Charley, his eyes narrowed in the sunlight.

"My arse is none of your affair, Charley Alcott! You won't be seeing me in your sick bay again!"

He stomped off and Purcell looked at his retreating back, then at Charley.

"What is going on with the captain?"

"I do not know, Mr. Purcell," Charley said slowly, watching the stiff figure talking with Bryant at the helm. "Something is wrong."

"Something between the two of you."

Charley looked at the carpenter.

"You can't keep secrets aboard ship, Doctor."

Can I not? Charley thought, but she just nodded.

"Whatever it is, the captain and I will work it out."

There was no invitation for the senior crew to join the captain in his cabin, so Charley took her luncheon in the sick bay, eating her lobscouse and flicking weevils out of her biscuit, an automatic action after months at sea. Pirate twined about her ankles, hoping for salvage rights to any food that might get jarred off the desk, and Charley leaned down to absently pet the animal and slip him a bite of what appeared to be beef from her stew.

She was going to have to do something about Captain Fletcher's changed attitude toward her, but first she would need to know what the problem was. It couldn't be issues with her performance of her duties. With no false modesty, Charley knew she was doing at least an adequate job, and had improved the lives of most of the men. Just today she'd fitted Larkin for a truss, having learned on the *Lady Jane* that hernias were common among sailors.

She sighed and pushed the uneaten stew away from her, then at an inquiring "Mrorrr?" put the tin bowl down for the cat, who sniffed at the lobscouse and then deigned to eat it.

"I know it's not a fresh rat, but it's the best I've got," Charley said to him. Pirate was the only creature aboard who could appreciate her purely for herself. She shook her head.

"No self-pity for you, Dr. Alcott," she said aloud. "There is work to be done."

It was a bleak thought though, that something had happened between her and Davy Fletcher. Where before there was camaraderie and companionship, now there was coldness and silence.

She missed her friend. She could never have a full relationship with David Fletcher, the relationship of man with a woman, but she'd come to treasure their friendship and she wanted it back. Without it, there was not enough to keep her aboard this vessel.

She sighed again. She would approach him tonight and pressure him again to release her from her captivity aboard the *Fancy*.

When she was finished with luncheon and writing up her

notes on Larkin, Charley went up on deck for some relief from the sultry November afternoon. She stood on deck next to Purcell, where she had an excellent view of Captain Fletcher hanging shirtless from a line as he examined some arcane piece of ship's equipment at the stern. He was wearing only his nankeen trousers, plastered to his body by the warm ocean water, with a knife strapped to the muscled calf of his leg. Charley climbed on the rail and leaned out farther, curious to see more of what the captain was doing down there.

"...and then Jeanette says I was the biggest and the best she'd ever had!"

She didn't remember slipping and losing her balance, but the next thing she knew she was falling, and then the shock of hitting the water.

It took her an agonizing minute of panic to orient herself, and find the light of day above her. The next minute the light was blotted out as a dark shape swam above.

Shark!

But she felt her collar grabbed and a force pulling her upward, and she bobbed up into the air like a cork, gasping and spitting out water.

It was Captain Fletcher, treading water next to her.

"Can you swim?" he yelled.

Charley's answer wasn't necessary because when he released his hold on her collar she started to sink, and a second later found herself grabbed again.

"Stop fighting me! I'll haul you in."

He pulled her along behind him and she heard shouts from the deck above them, and someone must have tossed them a line. The captain wrapped it around the two of them and said, "Hold on to me, Doctor," then yelled to the men above to haul them up.

As they rose out of the water like a pair of mullet, Captain

Fletcher clutched her closer. Then his body went very still. Charley blinked water out of her eyes and looked at him, his golden eyes inches from her own, the warm umber chest with its dusting of black hair flush against her soaked coat.

She tried to pull back, and of course couldn't, locked as she was in his embrace. He looked puzzled, then all the color leached from his face.

Rough hands grabbed the two of them and hauled them onto the deck of the *Fancy*, to much laughter from the assembled crew.

Charley pushed herself to her feet and stood on deck, wiping water off her face and trying to gain her bearings. Suddenly her arm was clamped by one large fist, the fingers digging into her muscle.

"Come with me, *Doctor*," Captain Fletcher said, and didn't wait for her to acquiesce as he hauled her along, pausing only to bark out an order to Mr. Purcell.

When they reached sick bay he thrust her in ahead of him, nearly throwing her across the room. She caught herself against the table as the door slammed, then she turned around.

Captain Fletcher stood across the room, arms crossed over his chest, dripping water onto the deck and blocking the only exit from the cabin. White lines of anger bracketed his mouth and his face looked—

Charley took a step away from him, then stopped.

"Take off your clothes," he said in a low voice.

"That is what I say to people, Captain," she tried to joke through chattering teeth.

"Take off your clothes," he said again. "That is an order. It is not a problem, is it, *Doctor*?" He advanced into the cabin and she backed up, until her back hit the bulkhead and she could retreat no farther. His amber eyes burned into hers, mesmerizing her.

"After all, we're all men here, aren't we? You have the same parts as everyone else aboard this ship, don't you? Now, take off your shirt, or I will do it for you!"

"I cannot," she whispered as ice trickled down her spine.

He reached with a fluid motion and pulled out his knife, one she knew was as sharp as her own scalpels.

She froze and could only stand there, dripping, shaking her head.

"You're all white, Doctor. Perhaps your humors are out of balance? Maybe you need a purging draft to restore them?"

It was his chilling smile that finally broke her paralysis. She burst forward and tried to make for the door, but he grabbed her shoulder and shoved her back up against the wall, pinning her there with his half naked body.

The cabin was silent except for their harsh breathing as David Fletcher's muscled form held her effortlessly against the rough wood. His face was like a granite carving, with no warmth and little humanity to it as he watched her.

He rubbed his thumb over her throat, bare from her cravat falling off in the water. Charley swallowed involuntarily.

And no Adam's Apple bobbed up and down at the motion.

"Why, *Doctor*, how very odd," he purred. "No, do not struggle. You don't want to get cut, for then who would bind you up?"

Out of the corner of her vision she saw the flash of his knife, and she closed her eyes. He took his free hand and grasped her chin hard, pulling her face up, not letting her turn away.

Her eyes popped open.

"That's better...Doctor. Such a smooth, soft face. It's a wonder I never noticed before. Look at me, Charley Alcott!"

he barked. "I do not want any confusion about what we're doing here."

"What?" she whispered.

"Consider it an experiment in natural philosophy." He ran his knuckles down her cheek and she tried not to flinch away from his touch. "You see, I have a theory I wish to explore, and I need your assistance. What, no questions? No sarcastic remarks? You disappoint me."

"Please...please don't do this," she said hoarsely, and then hated herself for showing weakness to this man, who was once again every inch the enemy who'd threatened her life when he hauled her off the *Lady Jane*.

"Save your pleas for later. You may need them."

She stood there, motionless, his body pressed up against hers and her hands fisted at her side. She couldn't fight him. She could feel the heat of his body even through her dampened clothing, and she could also feel him hard against her belly as he pinned her to the wall.

No matter what else he was feeling, David Fletcher was aroused, and she could see that was fueling his anger. She might survive this encounter alive, but she feared she would not survive it intact.

The blade disappeared from her view. She felt his fingers on her coat buttons, undoing them, and she went still, not even daring to breath.

The knife moved up to the top of her shirt and she heard the "plink" of a severed button hitting the deck.

"Breathe, Doctor. I do not want you swooning on me. Of course, a strong lad like you wouldn't swoon, would you, Charley Alcott?"

She closed her eyes, but he shook her shoulder, just enough to force her to open them again, watching him as he took her carefully constructed life and dismembered it. Slowly the knife worked its way down the front of her shirt placket, flicking off buttons that pinged against the planks of the deck.

"That's better," he said huskily when he'd finished. "You are bandaged, Doctor. Have you injured yourself?"

"No," she whispered. She licked her dry lips and his glance flicked down to her mouth before returning to her eyes. She stared at him, mesmerized like a trapped bird held in an amber net.

"If you are not injured, then you don't need this cloth binding you, do you?"

"Do not do this," she pleaded again, but he just smiled, a lethally cold baring of his teeth.

She shuddered as she felt the cool blade slip up between her skin and her bindings, not cutting her, but the cloth separating like wheat before the scythe, exposing her to his gaze.

There was no sound in the cabin but their mingled breathing, and Charley did not look away from the tiger eyes whose dark gaze burned into her brain, not even when she heard the knife clatter to the deck and felt one warm, rough hand cover her breast.

His breath drew in as his hand explored her, verifying what she knew he felt when he hauled her wet body against his. The womanly curves, disguised, hidden, but there nonetheless. His touch burned her with a heat she'd never experienced, and even in her fear and dread there was a part of her wanting to respond with a welcoming embrace.

But that would have been a welcome for a different David Fletcher. The set lines of his face brought crashing home the reality that this man holding her captive robbed and killed people for a living. That brutality and violence were part of his daily life, so different from hers, and nothing in her short life in the English countryside had prepared her for this encounter.

"Why, Charley," he purred. "You've been keeping secrets."

She shoved at him in a last, futile attempt at escape, but he pushed her back against the bulkhead. His breathing came harsh as he stared at her again. His head jerked back as if fighting himself, then he swooped his mouth down over hers.

She had never been kissed and at first she panicked, not knowing what to expect, what he wanted of her, what he could do to her. His hands gripped her shoulders as he punished her with his kiss, forced her to accept his anger and his passion.

His passion, and hers.

Charley knew she shouldn't want his kiss, not like this, not as if he hated her even as he was lusting for her, but it was too late. She was swept up in her own needs, her own desires for this man who was her enemy and whom she wanted as her lover. She had longed for his mouth on hers, dreamt of it in her lonely bunk, imagined it when she saw the whores kissing at Madame Cornelia's house. The reality was far beyond anything she could have imagined or witnessed. She was drowning in unknown waters, her senses over-loaded by her fervid fantasies brought to life, his kiss forcing them both to acknowledge that she was a woman, a woman at risk of danger physical and emotional.

His arms slipped down and wrapped around her like bands of steel and he held her prisoner as her knees weak-ened and he drank in her gasp. She wanted to push him away, and she wanted to pull him closer and never let him go. Davy was as solid as the oak of his ship, overwhelming her, his tongue slipping between her slack teeth to startle, then sensitize her with feelings she'd never experienced before.

Charley tentatively responded to his tongue's caress, touching him back, and he made a noise low in his throat before pulling her even tighter against him, his hand again moving across her chest to the breasts he'd bared in his anger. Now his touch was firm, but gentle, his fingers stroking across her nipple. She moaned and moved deeper into his touch, longing for more of the sensations stoked by their passions. There was anger, still, she felt it vibrating through him, but there was something more. She wanted to experience more, she wanted to experience it all, the consequences be damned.

He pushed his thigh between hers, spreading her, bringing him into contact with her with a groan that seemed pulled from deep within his chest.

Her hands moved up his back to his head, fisting in his hair, holding him, and she returned his kiss, her mouth blossoming open beneath his, her blood singing with the sensation of Davy Fletcher's luscious lips moving across hers, his tongue stroking between her teeth in a motion that brought a cry of need from deep within her soul.

He pulled back now and looked down at her, his eyes wide and confused before narrowing to slits, his breath coming out harshly.

"I have been blind, and played for a fool! There was no need to visit Madame Cornelia. Not when we had our own whore aboard ship!"

David's words struck her like a blow from his fist as he pushed himself away from her. Charley leaned against the wall, clutching her torn shirt closed. She wiped her hand across her bruised lips, afraid for a moment she would faint to the deck in front of him. She would not give him that satisfaction, and found the strength to pull herself upright and face him on her feet.

"Whore? How dare you call me names, you pirate!"

He raked her with his hot eyes, his lips drawing back in a sneer. "It is clear that you are no lady!"

Charley's hand fisted at her side and her anger flared like

the powder in the hold. "A *lady* could not have saved Henry Fletcher! I am this ship's *surgeon*, Captain! If it was a lady you wanted, you are doomed to disappointment!"

"You are not a surgeon! You are a woman!"

"I am doctor enough to care for you and your poxed crew of miscreants! I have healed the sick and bandaged the wounded, and this is how you respond? How *dare* you judge me?"

Charley advanced into the room, wishing now she'd taken up Davy Fletcher's offer of weapons training, because at this moment she would like nothing better than to run the scoundrel through. Then see who would stitch him up!

"You stole me off the *Lady Jane*. I did not ask to be here!"

"I would have put you off this ship at any time you revealed your sex!"

A knock at the sick bay door made them both freeze.

"Doctor? You in there? Reynolds's cut his hand and he's bleedin' all over the deck."

Charley watched the man blocking her door, but he said nothing.

"I will be right there, Jenkins."

Captain Fletcher made a small movement and she braced herself, but he turned away from her and put his hand on the door handle, pausing to look at her over his shoulder, his lips compressed with fury.

"Cover yourself, and deal with Jenkins. But do not think this conversation is finished, *Doctor*."

Her shoulders relaxed a fraction, but then he suddenly turned and strode across the room, muttering an expletive before grabbing her and hauling her up against him one more time and kissing her fiercely. Even though she knew more of what to expect, it still took her breath away and made her afraid for that future conversation.

He stared down at her, his face thunderous, before striding out, slamming the door behind him.

Charley stared at the door, then shook herself and grabbed fresh bindings for her breasts. She fastened her spare shirt and coat with shaking hands, then paused briefly to look into her mirror.

Charley—not Charlotte—Alcott looked back at her.

I can do this. I am needed.

She brushed her wet hair back away from her face, so it lay close to her head. With steady hands she reached for her satchel and went up on deck to see to the injured sailor.

CHAPTER 14

*D*avid Fletcher knew what anger felt like. But he had never felt anything like the white-hot emotion that gripped him when he realized Charley Alcott was a fraud. And he had never, ever thought about doing violence to a woman.

Until today.

He stood in the middle of his cabin, his fists clenching and unclenching as his damp clothes steamed from the rage radiating off of him.

How could he have been so blind? He pawed through his trunk looking for a dry shirt and remembered what it felt like to cut through Charley Alcott's shirt. As he yanked on his trousers he recalled every soft inch of her trouser clad belly pressed up against him, making it difficult to button up over a cock still swollen from the revelations in the doctor's cabin.

He nearly drove his fist into his desk in frustration and fury but stopped himself. If he hurt his hand, if he broke something, he'd have to go to that, that *freak*, and she would put her warm hands on him and treat him with compassion and he would have to restrain himself from kissing her and pulling off her clothing.

Again.

David liked women. Not on his ship, of course, but when he was on land he enjoyed being in their company. He liked them clothed in their fripperies and unclothed in all their glory, curved and rounded and sweet smelling. He liked the contrast of their softness to his hardness, their gentle ways and delicate natures to his life among rough men. And the ones who weren't so delicate but gave as good as they got in a game of slap and tickle, he liked them, too.

What he did not like was the thought of a female who talked like a man, and dressed like a man, and thought like a man, and spent her day examining the naked bodies of men when it was no proper place for a lady to be!

Clearly, Charley Alcott was no lady, but was a lying, deceitful hussy. And his body didn't give a tinker's damn for any of that. He could still feel that soft breast, small, hardly more than a handful, but fitting just right beneath his palm. The delicate skin of her throat, and the pulse that throbbed there, urging him to lean forward and put his lips on it.

He scrubbed his hands through his damp hair in frustration. He'd called her a whore, but if she was, she was a whore who'd never been kissed. He could tell from her naive response that she was a novice at lovemaking. She'd looked up at him, those smoky eyes wide and unsure, frozen with fear, but he knew she wanted him. He knew it from the drawings he'd discovered and the looks he'd intercepted, and he knew it from their kiss today.

And he knew he wanted her.

It was terrifying to want Charley Alcott when he'd thought him a man. Now that he knew Charley was a woman the knowledge still terrified him, but in a very different manner. He wanted to storm back down to sick bay, lock the door, strip her of all her male clothing and explore the doctor's body from the top of her head to the tips of her toes, paying special attention to those parts in the middle.

David walked to the stern window and braced his hands on the frame, staring out at the water, but not seeing it. For once he was not in communion with his vessel and the ocean. All he could think about was Charley Alcott and what he had to do. The knowledge made him ache in an entirely different way than he'd ached before.

There was no way she could stay aboard the *Fancy*, not now that he knew she was a woman.

There was no way she could stay aboard the *Fancy*, not now that Captain Fletcher knew she was a woman.

Charley sat at her desk, staring down at her journal. It was open, waiting for her to update today's entries with her treatment of Reynolds's slashed hand, but her mind was as blank as the page before her. All she could think about was how once she would have been thrilled at the possibility of being put off the *Fancy*. Now the thought of leaving the ship sent her into a black depression.

Which was still better than dwelling on what she'd experienced earlier.

Her first kiss. Her fingers reached up and touched her lips, sensitized in a way they'd never been sensitive before.

Charley knew she was a normal woman—in some ways, at least. In all the ways that mattered. As a young girl she'd imagined what her first kiss might be like. It would be in a garden, in England, and she would be wearing a pretty dress, and the faceless young man who kissed her would be respectful and attracted to her and handsome.

The only thing that had carried over from that fantasy into today's reality was "handsome."

Maybe not the only thing. Captain Fletcher was attracted to her. She'd like to think she had more to attract him than being a knothole in a tree at the right height, but he was, nonetheless, attracted to her.

Charley stood and walked over to her mirror. It was small and she had to angle her head to see her full face.

Two eyes, a nose, lips, a square face, a firm chin. Clear skin, browner now from exposure to the tropical sun. She looked like Charley Alcott, the *Fancy's* surgeon.

Even she could see a difference though from before. Her lips were still slightly swollen, and reddened from his kisses. Her cheeks had an unaccustomed brush of color.

But it was nothing to attract a man like Black Davy Fletcher, who had his pick of swans.

Was it?

The ladies in the brothel had been full of advice on how to act the coquette, what to say and do, how to flatter a man. She had listened with interest, but no real desire to go down that path. The idea of acting in an artificial fashion—

An artificial fashion? More artificial than dressing in men's clothing and pretending you had just as big a pair as the man next to you?

"Oh Lord, I've made myself insane," she groaned aloud, putting her hands over her eyes.

The knock on the sick bay door froze her in the midst of her ravings.

"Dr. Alcott?" said Lewis, the steward. "Cap'n wants all hands on deck, including you."

Charley's breath caught in her lungs, then she let it out with a rush.

"Thank you, Mr. Lewis, I will be right up."

So this was it then. She checked herself over, her clothing

neat and clean, her breasts discreetly bound once again, her hair brushed back close to her head, her cravat hiding her lack of other male characteristics.

She squared her shoulders, took a deep breath, and put on her hat and coat. Charley Alcott might not have all the same bits and pieces as the men up on deck, but she would show them she could hold her head high and face disaster as bravely as any of them.

CHAPTER 15

David stood amidst his loyal crew, arms crossed over his chest and a stony expression on his face that he knew had the crew wondering. He'd waited for them to assemble before sending Lewis for Charley Alcott. Now she climbed up on deck, and he grudgingly admitted that the girl had guts, for many a man would have quailed at facing him and his crew of privateers.

He looked around the deck. His men were more or less in facing lines, waiting on his orders. What they lacked in military smartness they made up for in sheer bravery and determination, and he wanted to lead them knowing that he made the best decisions for them.

Charley paused, then walked across deck to stand at the end of the row, facing him, shoulders back, head up. David was flanked by Mr. Bryant and Mr. Purcell, and he knew they were puzzled, but awaited his explanation.

"Gentlemen," he said, putting a particular emphasis on the word, and Alcott had the nerve to twitch a smile.

"Gentlemen," he repeated, "we are changing course and heading for Jamaica."

This announcement was greeted by a murmur from the men as they looked at one another, and then Bryant asked what they all were no doubt wondering.

"Why Jamaica, Captain? It is crawling with the Royal Navy."

David locked eyes with Charley Alcott, who met his gaze head on, not looking away or fretting. He gave her points for *savoir-faire*, but continued.

"Because, Mr. Bryant, our good doctor here has been defrauding us!" He pointed his finger at her. "Charley Alcott is not a man. Charley Alcott is a woman, playing the man, and I will not have her aboard this vessel! We are taking her to Jamaica!"

There was a moment of stunned silence, then the crew looked at one another, and turned their eyes back to Charley Alcott. She stood straight and tall, the color high on her cheeks, but she never took her eyes off of his.

"That ain't right!"

"Exactly, Reynolds—"

"No, Cap'n, I mean, that ain't right, putting our doctor off'a the ship."

Now it was David's turn to stand in stunned silence. He tore his eyes away from Charley's and looked at his men.

"What?"

"We need Dr. Alcott, Cap'n. Who'll take care of us if you put him off of the *Fancy*?"

"Didn't you hear me, I said—are you laughing, Mr. Bryant?"

Bryant was looking steadfastly out to sea, but his shoulders were shaking.

"As I value my life, no, Captain, I am not laughing!"

"See, Cap'n, this is how it is," continued Reynolds in reasonable tones, waving his bandaged hand for emphasis. "A woman can't be a doctor, right? And Alcott's a doctor. So,

Alcott can't be a woman. And he's a right fine sawbones! Look how well he stitched up my hand, and my rheumatism's never been better since I started using his ointment!"

"Yeah, my arsehole doesn't burn no more since I started doin' what the doctor said." Cook chimed in.

Bryant surrendered, walked over to the rail and braced himself against it. He was laughing so hard it was a wonder he could stand. David would deal with him later. Right now, he had to deal with the insanity at hand.

"Did you men not hear me? I said Charley Alcott—*that* Charley Alcott standing right there—is *a woman*! A woman! Aboard the *Fancy*!"

"Looks to me like it's the same Charley Alcott who bandaged my hand," Reynolds said, eyeing the ship's doctor up and down. "I ain't got complaints about that. Any of you men got complaints 'bout how the doctor's doing his job?"

The men all looked at each other and shook their heads, or shrugged.

"See? We need Dr. Alcott, Cap'n. We're all doin' better since he came aboard." Reynolds said. "We're out here fightin' for 'fair trade and sailor's rights,' ain't that so? The way I see it, one of our rights is to have a good doctor to stitch us up."

The Americans all muttered in agreement, some nodding their heads over this declaration of rights.

"But he can't wear a skirt!" Larkin yelled out from the back.

"Well, that's only fair," Reynolds acknowledged. "You don't want to wear a skirt, do you, Dr. Alcott?"

A pregnant silence hovered over the deck, only the wind in the canvas making a noise. David looked at his nemesis. Alcott had hi—*her* arms crossed over her chest and was watching him, one eyebrow cocked.

"If I stay aboard the *Fancy*, I promise not to wear a skirt."

The men relaxed and murmured their appreciation, the

doctor's low alto tones not seeming to register with even the thickest among them—and he was beginning to suspect some of them were very thick indeed—that the doctor was hiding a nice pair of tits beneath hi—her, *her*, dammit!—frock coat.

"It is your move, Captain Fletcher," she said evenly.

David gave in to the inevitable and barked orders at his men to get back to their tasks.

"Dr. Alcott."

She looked up from where she was talking to Mr. Purcell, who was laughing and shaking her hand. It was fortunate for her she wasn't looking triumphant, or he would be contemplating dunking her in the ocean again.

"You will join me in my cabin for supper. There is much we need to discuss."

Hesitation entered her face. He almost wished she would refuse, so that he would have cause to put her off the ship, to say she was not fitting in and obeying orders.

"Yes, Captain."

He stomped off to be sure Cook would not be doing anything special for the Doctor's supper tonight!

"Cook has outdone himself tonight," Charley said. "I am astounded, for I vow, I did not know he had it in him."

David muttered beneath his breath and poured himself some more claret.

"Did you say something?"

"I suppose now that Cook's arsehole isn't paining him, he's showing his appreciation. At least I know now why he was too distempered to cook like this before!"

Dr. Alcott—for truly, it was how he had to view the interloper if he was going to keep a grip on his sanity—gave him a level look.

"This is uncomfortable for both of us, Captain Fletcher, but we do not need to exacerbate the situation."

That was easy for her to say. She wasn't the one mentally undressing the person sitting across from her at the table. He felt like a randy young buck, which was ridiculous, because Charley Alcott just wasn't that attractive. Granted, she had long-lashed eyes of the softest pearl gray shading to the color of a robin's egg in the dusk, and her chestnut hair gleamed in the lamplight like maple leaves in autumn and he already knew the taste of her honeyed mouth…

He poured himself more wine and scowled, looking for answers in the liquor.

"I am not happy with these events, not happy at all! I have to respect the wishes of the men though, and will keep you aboard the *Fancy*, for now. But when we return to Baltimore I will put you off this ship and hope to God I never have to deal with you again!"

She drew back in her seat as if he'd slapped her, but she kept her countenance.

"As you wish. I see no reason why I cannot continue to perform my duties as I always have, to the best of my ability. That is what the men desire of me, and what they need me for. The less you and I have to deal together, the better it will be for us both."

His hand hovered over his glass as something clicked into place in his mind.

"Henry knew, didn't he?"

He remembered back to those times when he saw his brother and the doctor conferring together, their heads close, sharing laughter and private moments, and his hand tightened on his glass. He wanted Henry here in front of him to explain himself. Then David wanted to knock him on his arse.

She studied him, as if gauging how much to reveal.

"He did not know at first, but we spent so much time together while he was healing that Henry was able to figure it out. I asked him to keep my secret, and he agreed, though he rightly feared it would anger you. This situation is not his fault and you should not blame him."

He scowled again. He would most definitely have words with that donkey Henry the next time he saw him. One arm or no, he'd be lucky if David did not lay him out on the deck with his fists.

"I suppose, too, Henry knows your true name, because I doubt your parents christened you 'Charley.'"

"It's close." A smile flickered across her lips. "I was christened 'Charlotte' and it was a short step to 'Charley.'" She took a sip of her wine and looked into its depths. A tiny drop of wine lingered at the corner of her mouth and he gripped the arm of his chair to keep from reaching across the table and wiping it off with his finger.

Or even worse, licking it off.

"Much of what I have told you is the truth," she said softly. "When you brought me aboard, you asked about my training and I said I assisted my father for many years. That is the truth."

Charley—for he could not bring himself to think of her as Charlotte—sighed.

"My mother died when I was young, and my father..." She smiled wistfully. "I think he had no idea what to do with me, but he loved me and did the best he could. I spent my youth dressed as a boy, assisting my father in his medical practice. I spent so many years as 'Charley' that it was second nature to me to dress in breeches and men's coats. Why, I would hardly know what to do with a dress after all this time. Before he died, my father told me how much he regretted teaching me medicine and making my life... strange. The one thing I loved, the one thing that gave my life meaning—helping people heal and easing their ills, and it was only cause for regret for him."

She fell silent, lost in her memories, and he resisted the urge to put his hand across the table and cover hers where it rested there, looking so capable, yet so small to take on the burdens it had.

"You had no other family?"

"A grandfather who cut his ties to my mother and father after they ran off together against his wishes. He contacted me when my father died and said he would take me into his household, but the tone of his letter made it clear he was only doing his duty, not doing it out of love and concern. And of course, if I went to live with him there would be no more dissections to study or treating the ill. Even the people in my village who'd accepted me as Charley for so long were beginning to look askance at me after my father was no longer there as a bulwark.

"So I ran off to Plymouth, dressed as Charley Alcott, not Charlotte. I struck a bargain with Captain Denham of the *Lady Jane.* I would physic his crew and watch over his pregnant wife in exchange for passage to Jamaica. I slept in the sick bay there, too, and that preserved my disguise."

"Why were you going to Jamaica?"

"My godfather lives there. I hoped he might allow me to continue my studies with him."

"Instead, you were kidnapped by privateers."

"Indeed. An unexpected sea change, into something rich and strange."

That smile moved across her wine-reddened lips again, and sweat broke out on his brow. He shifted, trying to ease the pressure of his cock swelling in his trousers. He didn't want to be attracted to Charley Alcott, man or woman, but his prick had a mind of its own.

Some of the humor of the situation finally penetrated his own lust sodden brain, and he smiled.

"I will grant you, Dr. Alcott, it has been a rich and strange experience indeed."

At the change in his expression her own face lightened, and she cleared her throat.

"Are you going to make an effort to maintain a cordial relationship with me if I stay aboard the *Fancy?*" A wisp of color came into her cheeks and she looked down at her plate. "I know we can't have the same relationship we had before you knew my secret, but I hope we can still be friends."

Friends? She wanted to be friends when all he wanted was to pick her up, take her to his bunk and unwrap all those layers that kept the real Charley Alcott hidden from him? She wanted to be friends when he tossed and turned at night, unable to sleep for thoughts of her? He'd loathed and feared himself when he thought Charley Alcott a man he lusted after. At least then he'd been able to convince himself Charley was untouchable. Now, knowing that she was a woman, and aboard his vessel, and attracted to him, it was even worse.

"I do not know that friendship is something we can have between us, Doctor. Not now."

He looked at her in the lamplight, dressed so neatly in her blue coat and plain white shirt and cravat. She was unlike anyone he had ever met before or would be likely to meet again, a woman who was comfortable in her surroundings with men, sure of herself in her sick bay, able to hold her own amongst a crew of hardened privateers.

But now she looked rather lost, and vulnerable. It was all he could do not to go to her side of the table, pick her up and put her on his lap while he soothed her fears, preferably with his mouth, his hands, and other parts of him longing to get closer to the doctor.

He cleared his throat.

"I once talked to you about settling in the United States. It occurs to me that you might still find that a more congenial spot than Jamaica."

She looked at him steadily, once again the Dr. Alcott he knew, or thought he knew.

"Really, Captain? You think that in Baltimore, or Boston, or somewhere else in the United States I would find a community that's open to the idea of a woman practicing medicine? Performing surgeries?"

He opened his mouth to defend his country, then shut it. No. He could not say with any certainty that there was any community in the United States where Charley Alcott would be accepted.

"Will your godfather accept you and allow you to practice medicine?"

"I do not know." She clasped her hands on the table. "I have hopes that Dr. Wilson will take me on and further my education, because right now, that's the only hope I have."

"You could marry and busy yourself with your home, like other women!"

She looked at him, wide-eyed.

"Truly, Captain Fletcher? I can throw away all my dreams and be just like every other woman you know? The ones who aren't like Madame Olifiers, anyway. I have no doubt there will be men lining up at the docks to take on a wife who spends her days in the company of privateers, many of whom take off their clothes in her presence."

He scowled at that image. "The rules on sarcasm have not changed, Doctor!"

"Then do not say such patently foolish things to me, Captain!"

And then she startled him by grinning at him. She shook her head, and rose to her feet. "If our relationship was not what it was before, at least we're talking. But I believe I will leave now, and bid you good-night, while we are still on speaking terms."

She stuck out her hand, but as soon as he grasped her warm hand in his David knew it was a mistake. He would never again have the relationship with Charley Alcott that they'd had when he thought Charley was a man.

How could he, when he was so aware of her, her clean scent, her lean lines displayed by her men's clothing, even wrapped and hidden as they were, her laughter and her wit, her compassion for his crew? No, he could not go back to his old footing with Charley Alcott.

Then, against his own judgment, and knowing he'd regret it later, he tugged her closer, and putting his hand beneath her chin, tilted her face up. His lips brushed against hers, a whisper of sensation only, but he felt it down to the soles of his feet. He wanted to deepen that touch, to fist his hands in that silken hair and pull her into his arms and teach her everything she didn't know about kissing, and about men who'd been at sea too long without a woman, but he drew back into himself and gently maneuvered her out the door.

"Good night, Doctor."

When the door clicked behind her, David spent a long moment staring at the air where she'd been.

CHAPTER 16

The *Fancy* resumed its cruising for prizes as the crew took the revelation about the doctor in stride. David watched as she continued to physic and patch them, dispensing medicine and advice without them questioning her knowledge or ability. He had his own uneasy truce with the doctor, and to that end he invited Charley to resume their evening chess matches.

David debated propping his cabin door open this evening, then realized how foolish that would be, and how counterproductive. If the goal was to maintain the doctor's relations with the men on an even keel, he couldn't start treating her like a woman. Not when the crew was all sharing in a mass hallucination that Charley Alcott was a man—or at least that's how it sounded to him every time they used male pronouns regarding their ship's doctor. When he thought about it, and he was trying not to think about it more than fifty times a day, David attributed it to their insistence that she not wear a skirt. Just as a priest's or an admiral's attire caused one to respond in a certain fashion, seeing the doctor dressed as one expects a doctor to dress contributed to their perceptions of Charley Alcott.

Or was it his own sanity he wished to preserve by leaving his door open?

While there was an overwhelming relief in his heart of hearts that he wasn't a sodomite, he was being driven crazy by the realization that now Charley was available to him, even if she wasn't. Not if he wanted to treat her as just another member of the crew.

Despite his best intentions, his mind—and his cock—refused to listen to him. Charley invaded his thoughts, awake and asleep. Awake he knew immediately if she was in the vicinity. He could sense her, and his eyes would begin tracking her, his nose trying to get a whiff of her unique scent, his unruly manhood acting like the needle of the compass, pointing upward as if she were true north.

He'd given up on trying to figure out why it was her he wanted as he watched her now, concentrating on the chessboard. She wasn't pretty. He was honest enough to acknowledge that. She looked every bit as much like a young man as she had when he sent her off to the whorehouse—and someday he was going to get the true story of that evening!—but when he dreamed at night of tangled limbs and sweaty bodies and straining to bury himself inside his partner, it was her he saw. Her body, lithe and clean-lined, the curves subtle, but when seen by a discerning eye, all the more enticing. He'd had a glimpse of heaven while he had her up against the wall in her cabin. Her skin was soft and creamy, the nipples of those bound breasts a pale pink against the rest of her. They'd darken if he were to suck on them, darken like raspberries kissed by the sun, standing up like berries waiting for the right hand to pluck them and savor their sweetness.

He cursed and adjusted his trousers beneath the table, glancing anxiously at her, but she had her head lowered and her chin fisted on her hand. He needed to get his mind back on business. He'd invited Charley here for chess, nothing else. He was keeping an eagle eye on the crew, but none of them had made an inappropriate gesture or said anything that would get them better acquainted with his fists. He'd be a sorry commander if he could control his men, but not himself. He could control himself, he was not a beast, and she was not a ravishing beauty. There was no explaining why he was attracted to her.

Maybe it was like asparagus, he mused. Some people loved it, some hated it. He liked it. Very much. If Charley Alcott were a plate of asparagus, he'd pour butter over her and lick it off, starting with...

"What are you thinking about?"

"Vegetables."

She made a noise, as if this answer made perfect sense somewhere, and went back to studying the chess pieces arrayed before her.

He rose and stood behind her, refilling their glasses with rum, and he studied her as she studied the board. Her subtle scent of soap and lemons, her hair gleaming in the lamplight, the nape of her neck, looking vulnerable and kissable at the same time. A few wisps of hair curled there and he longed to touch them, to see if they felt as silken as they appeared. He saw his hand go out, hovering in the air over her head, and he had to stop himself, force himself not to lean down and put his lips on that scented skin.

"This isn't working."

She tensed at his words. She was no fool, and she knew what he meant.

"You are correct. At this rate you will lose in two moves. Maybe I should just leave now."

She stood abruptly, but he was standing behind her and he watched his arm wrap around her slim waist to hold her against him, almost as if he watched someone else do this thing that was so very dangerous. She stood there, imprisoned by his touch, frozen, and a tremor raced over her frame, like a rabbit that fears to move when it senses the wolf in the clearing.

Wise rabbit.

David lowered his head to where her neck rose over the edge of her collar and he rested his lips along that patch of skin and took a taste, the softness still surprising him. She shuddered in his embrace, not daring to move, or not caring to move, as he inhaled the scent of her clean hair, stroking his cheek against the soft curls that protected the delicate nape. Her essence filled his lungs and his mind, so different from any other woman he'd known, clean and fresh and wholly Charley.

She moved then, a fraction forward, but he pulled her back against him and at her startled reaction he knew she could feel him against her, the full length of him straining to get closer to her, to be buried inside her warmth.

He turned her in his arms, to face him.

An eternity passed as he watched her, memorizing the details of her face, the arched brows, the smooth cheek, and those eyes that held so many secrets. Around them there were the night sounds of a ship at sea, but all of it faded away as he looked into those eyes.

"Do you want to leave, Charley?"

He ran his thumb over her moist lower lip, and a noise was wrenched from her, a gasp at the sensation.

"Or do you want to be kissed?"

A shadow crossed her face and he said, "That was not a kiss, the other day, that was an assault. A kiss is something to be shared."

"Do you know how an inoculation works, Captain?"

Her voice was low, and husky, and despite her prosaic

question, made him even harder, if that were possible.

"An inoculation gives you a taste of a disease. Just enough to strengthen you against it."

"Am I a disease then, Doctor?"

"If I kiss you, I may be inoculated against you, and I can sleep easy again."

Her hand moved up to brush at the hair falling across his forehead. He took her hand in his and turned it, placing a kiss in the palm, then on the pulse at the wrist that raced beneath his lips. He looked back down into Charley's eyes, dark now, dark and wide and ringed by silver fire.

"Is that what you want? To have a taste, and then be cured?"

She swallowed.

"Sometimes, the inoculation brings on the disease. It can consume you and there is no cure. I must try it though, for it is the only way to know if I can survive this, David."

It was an invitation no sane man could resist and at the moment he was feeling far from sane. If he wasn't plagued by insanity he wouldn't be lowering his head to brush his lips against hers, savoring the softness, the small sound she made at the contact. He wouldn't be resting his mouth against hers, waiting for her untutored understanding of what it was he wanted, reveling in his victory when she parted her lips and gave him access, an invitation he seized just as he pulled her tighter into his arms, or was it she who pulled him against her? It didn't matter when all he could focus on was the taste of her mouth, the wonder as he slipped his tongue inside, her body moving against his in acceptance.

She sighed and moved her arms up until they encircled his neck, and he understood in that moment that the reason he wanted her was she felt right, fitting into his embrace as no one else ever had. Maybe that was all the explanation his attraction to her required.

When he finally came up for air, he was resolved.

"I do not feel inoculated, or cured!" he said harshly. "I cannot go on this way, Charley. Leave, or in a very short while you will be naked in my bunk!"

The last shred of sanity still lingering in his brain knew it was best if she left.

But the rest of him, the parts that came to life as blood flowed south of the equator, cheered the doctor's decision when Charley Alcott's eyes widened and she whispered, "I am going for naked, Captain."

He knew he should talk her out of it.

He'd sooner smash himself in the face with a belaying pin than talk her out of it.

He almost asked her if she was sure, but his cock over-ruled his mind again, and instead he lowered his head to kiss her.

Her mouth was sweet beneath his, sweet and innocent like no other women he'd ever kissed. Even the ones who were shy maidens willing to give a boy a quick peck were tutored in the way of being women, knew how to flirt and use their eyes and make a man feel so very masculine.

Charley was…Charley. Her responses were genuine and real. She was a novice at kissing, and he was thrilled to be the one who would teach her. He brought his hands up and cradled her head, angling his lips to guide her. The passion he felt from her as she tightened her arms around his neck and rose up on her toes to deepen the kiss touched a chord deep inside him, making him feel that more than at any time with any woman, he want to make this right. For Charley.

He broke the kiss and began unfastening her coat. When she tensed beneath his hands he said, "Do you want to do this yourself?"

"No—it is just that…"

"What?"

"I do not know what to do!"

He looked down at her for a long moment, at the bright color in her cheeks, and then he couldn't help it. He let out the grin threatening his mouth and said, "And you call your-self a doctor!"

A nervous squeak of laughter escaped from her, startling her. She didn't know yet one could have fun and laugh while making love. He wanted to teach her that also.

"No, you looby, I know the mechanics, but I do not know how we get from here"—she pointed at the deck—"to there." She pointed at his bunk. Her adorable look of uncertainty made him lean down and kiss her on the tip of her nose.

"There is no right or wrong way, Charley. Will you trust me to lead you tonight?"

She nodded without speaking and he went back to undoing her clothes. It was a novelty, undressing someone wearing men's attire, because there was no hesitation in his hands. Unlike women's clothing he knew exactly where every fastening and button was, and it made the process much smoother than it otherwise might have been.

"Stop."

David paused, his hands tightening on her lapels. If she started to head for the door, he could not be responsible for his actions.

But all Charley did was slide her hands up the front of his shirt and say, "I want to do this also."

"If you insist. But don't take long. I am anxious to see this nakedness I was promised."

He suspected it was her nerves that prompted her request, but he was willing to go along with it, for now. He put his hands on her hips beneath her coat, stroking up and down, feeling her through the thin layer of her trousers and marveling anew that the soft curves beneath his hand had never been obvious to his eyes.

Before the night was through he promised himself he would uncover all of the good doctor's secrets.

~

Charley knew her acquiescence surprised David Fletcher.

She'd surprised herself.

Being here in his cabin, again, facing him across a chessboard, it had been hard to concentrate on the game and not think instead about her opponent, the man who held her life in his hand like he held a rook.

David was in his shirtsleeves as they sparred across the chessboard, the collar open at his neck and she could see his pulse, speeding up as the night lengthened and the tension rose. His dark head was bent in concentration, and even at rest he nearly vibrated with energy and life.

He wanted her. It was evident, even to someone as inexperienced as she was, in the way he watched her and moved around her. And she wanted him tonight every bit as much as she ever had. More so. For now that she knew he wanted her as a woman, she refused to moralize or analyze or ask herself if it was simply the novelty or the proximity or something perverse in his makeup.

That didn't matter anymore. What mattered to her was that she had an opportunity to experience the passion of giving herself to Davy Fletcher, an opportunity she might never have again. Not if she was going to spend the rest of her life as Dr. Charles Alcott.

He was looking at her now in a fashion no man had ever looked at her before. Like she was worth looking at. Like there was no woman he'd rather be looking at. Like she was the only woman in the world. Tomorrow her sanity would return, but tonight belonged to her.

Now, standing with him next to the bunk that drew her

like a lighthouse in the dark, Charley reached up with hands that were almost steady to undo his buttons. Her efforts were hampered by his hands on her, stroking her, making her arch beneath his touch like Pirate the cat. She wanted to twine herself around his legs and purr, and a smile gleamed in his eyes as he seemed to divine her thoughts.

She lowered her eyes, and her head. His muscles tensed beneath her hands when she parted his shirt and leaned forward to kiss him on that sculpted chest, and he made a noise in his throat and tightened his grip on her hips. His hands were so strong and hard that they could bruise, but her body responded with a flair of heat she felt radiating out from her belly, engulfing her in new sensations as he flexed his fingers against her.

"Charley—" he rasped. "Let me—"

He couldn't finish speaking but began pulling her clothes off and tossing them to the deck, his hands and mouth roaming over her as he tugged at the fabric. When he got to the bindings around her breasts he grabbed handfuls of cloth, ripping them off with a sound that was loud in the small space, but before she could react to this her world tilted as he picked her up and carried her the few steps to his bunk.

When he was done undressing her they were both breathing hard. David loomed above her, braced on his arms, his hair falling across his forehead and veiling his eyes. Charley wanted to tell him to turn down the lamp so he wouldn't see her inadequacies, but she didn't have a chance to say anything because he was kissing her, his hands roaming over her and she could feel the soft linen of his shirt against her skin, his hand between their bodies fumbling at the buttons on his trousers and kicking them off.

"Wait," she whispered, and for a moment thought he wouldn't listen to her plea, but then he paused. His face was drawn with tension, and she pushed herself up and placed her hand on his cheek.

"I want to see all of you, David. I get to have nakedness also," she finished, which brought a gleam to his eye. He sat back on his haunches and slowly, achingly slowly, pulled his shirt over his head, not taking his eyes from hers until the cloth covered his face, and when he was finished, he threw it on the deck with a flourish, his dimples carving hollows into his cheeks.

"Well, Charley? Are you pleased with what you see?"

He was vain, her captain, but he was entitled, she thought with a sigh as she studied him, all golden and glowing in the lamplight.

She reached her hand up to stroke across his chest, down to the abdomen where the muscles stood out in sharp relief. His skin was like marble, fine-grained and smooth where no scars marred it, but marble that had been sun-kissed and warmed by the blood beating hard beneath the surface.

"Handsome Davy," she whispered, which made him smile again, but the smile disappeared as she brought her hand behind his head and threaded it through his soft hair, pulling him down for a kiss.

He braced his arms alongside her and let her take the lead, exploring his mouth, learning, experiencing, and when her other arm came up to wrap around his shoulders and cling to him, he lowered himself atop her with a groan. He was hard, and hot, and he throbbed against her. She shifted her hips, longing for more, and he froze.

"Charley! Do not move!" he gasped.

She wondered what she'd done wrong.

"Darling doctor, if you move this will be over far too quickly." He gave her a swift, hard kiss. "I have wanted this for so long, but you need to be ready."

She understood what he meant, that if her body was

relaxed and wet that it would help his entry, but she didn't know how to make that happen.

Fortunately, he did.

David leaned down and rasped his tongue across her breast, already sensitive from being bound and restricted. The sensation was like nothing else she'd ever experienced, and she wanted more.

"Do that again!"

He obliged her, and gave equal due to her other breast, fondling and suckling on parts of her that up until now had only been a hindrance, making her appreciate her body in an entirely new manner. He plucked at her nipples, standing up pert and erect, and when he blew lightly across them she shivered with heat and with cold.

She wanted to do something for him, but all she could do was clutch him, afraid that if she let go he might disappear and these sensations would end.

His hand moved between her legs to test the waters. She couldn't hold back her cry as her back arched and she rose up against him when he glided his fingers along her, circling the nub that poked out in anticipation, then slipping a finger inside her.

"So wet," he murmured. "You have the mechanics down pat, Charley. Now, let me..." His raspy voice trailed off as he fit himself to her and began easing himself in.

She knew her anatomy, knew they would fit, but it was hard to convince herself of it as she struggled to relax and loosen herself to ease his passage. After the sharp pinch of his initial entry there was no more pain, but there was a fullness that was nearly unbearable. When he was all the way in, when she could feel every hard inch of him inside her body, she blinked and whispered up at him, "This is the most amazing..." and her voice trailed off because David was braced above her on his arms.

He looked like he was in an extraordinary amount of pain, sweat standing out on his brow and trickling down his chest.

She shifted her hips up to try and make him more comfortable, but it seemed to have the opposite effect as his face grew tenser.

"No, don't move, Charl—hell!" and then he began to move.

If the experience up until this point was amazing, it now climbed into the realm of the transcendent. Her body, the flesh that up until now had been an obstacle to overcome, came alive, and she felt nerve endings fire and muscles clench and all her senses were swamped. The glide of sweat slicked skin against the skin of the other, the touch of his arms braced alongside her shoulders, the sounds of his murmured encouragement, the musky fragrance of their heated bodies, the sight of him above her, straining his muscles in a symphony of movement, and the taste of his salt when she leaned up to lick his corded neck.

He began to move faster and she hitched her hips higher to wrap her legs around his waist and relieve the pressure building inside her, growing with each of his thrusts. She indeed knew the mechanics, but she could not know the reality, the fire that engulfed her, that brought to life sensations she'd never known, could never know through studies but only through this, the touch and stroke of the man who held her now and worked her body in rhythm with his. She cried out as the sensations became too much for her, exploding outward from her belly, from her heart, from her soul. A minute later he stiffened above her and she felt the warmth increase as he emptied himself into her with a sigh.

David relaxed atop her, breathing heavily, letting his weight rest on her for a heavenly moment before easing himself out of her and propping himself up on one arm.

"Are you well?"

She looked at him, struggling to catch her breath as he looked down at her with concern. Was she well? Did he not know she would never be the same again? That this experience had changed forever what she thought about herself? How could she now contemplate an asexual future only practicing medicine when she had this new knowledge to savor?

But she would have to think about that later. Right now she had Davy Fletcher in her arms and that was good enough for the moment.

"Charley?"

"I know the Greek and Latin names for all the parts of the body, and for the acts we just performed. And I knew nothing, nothing about the reality of it. Until now. Now I understand that knowledge is not the same as knowing. That was incredible, amazing...could you possibly try to look less pleased with yourself?"

"I don't know why I should," he said smugly, relaxing his body against hers. "When you're the best around it is hard to remain humble."

She giggled, then put her hand over her mouth.

"It's all right," he said softly, stroking her hair. "Here you can be yourself, Charlotte, and not act the man."

She sighed, and closed her eyes for a moment, savoring his gentle touch. Then her eyes opened and she faced reality, even as she brought her own hand up to run her fingers across his jaw, memorizing the feel of him to remember later.

Because there *would* be a later, and it would be an empty time, without David Fletcher at her side.

"It is not a prudent thing to do, Captain, being Charlotte. I maintain myself best by always trying to be Charles Alcott."

"Well, I for one am glad to have Charlotte and not Charles in my bunk!"

Charley looked down at the coverlet David had flung over them and smoothed out a wrinkle as he propped his head on his arm, watching her. The bunk was not large enough for two, but she wouldn't have moved from that spot for ten thousand American dollars.

"I was beginning to think that we were dealing quite well together, when you believed I was Charles."

"Not like this. Never like this. Do not fool yourself! You have no idea how many nights I tossed and turned in agony in this bunk over my attraction to you," he said harshly. "You have no idea what that feels like for a man, to question who he is at his core. To wonder if everything he's ever known about himself is wrong."

"Would it have mattered so much if I was who you desired? I was always only...Charley."

"That kind of desire gets men hanged, Doctor, and brings disgrace to their families." He looked at her, then looked down at her hand nervously plucking at the linens and covered it with his own.

"That is what frightened me the most," he said in a low voice. "I was beginning not to care that you were forbidden. I just wanted to be near you, and touch you, and breathe in your scent. God help me, I don't know if ultimately it would have mattered to me...Charley."

She heard his words like a treasure handed to her, one she could keep locked inside her and take out later to remember, and enjoy when her nights were long and lonely. Davy Fletcher wanted her, Charley Alcott, and for tonight that would have to be enough.

He moved his hand up her bare arm to her hair, and he gave her a little shove, pushing her onto her back. She heard the ship's bell and knew she should get dressed and return to her cabin before the morning watch, but it was hard to think with Davy smiling at her and lightly touching her, stroking her, making her realize how starved she'd been for human contact and closeness. It also brought to life those feelings that she'd thought were over following her climax, and she remembered what the whores said about a woman being like an ember.

"What is making you smile?"

"You are. Being here with you." She sighed. "It feels so good to be held…it has been so long."

"How long?"

"Forever."

His lips curled up at the corners in that smile that captivated her so, and he leaned down to kiss her again. This time Charley was not going to be a passive participant, and she reached down to find and hold him, because she knew that would give him pleasure. She also knew it took men some time to recover after their climax, so when her exploring hand found him she was surprised, and broke off the kiss to raise the covers and look.

"You are remarkably tumescent," she said. If anything, her words made him swell larger. "Oh my. Is this normal for you?"

"Doctor, none of this is normal for me."

When she looked up at him he kissed her lightly.

"'Normal' is not a word that enters into a discussion of relations with you, Charley Alcott. But if you are done speaking, it is time to move to the next stage of your education."

And so saying he moved the covers down off of her body, and showed her how areas of her flesh she'd never considered especially sensitive, or beautiful, or even necessary could take on a whole new meaning in the captain's bunk.

CHAPTER 17

*I*f any of the officers or crew of the *Fancy* suspected their doctor and their captain were engaging in activities that went beyond the average doctor and commander relationship, they were wise enough to keep their thoughts to themselves.

She had other problems. David Fletcher seemed to be under the misapprehension that Charley Alcott was going to practice medicine differently than she'd done one month earlier, before she fell off of the *Fancy* into the water.

"I do not like it. As you pointed out, Dr. Alcott, you've seen the privates of every privateer aboard this ship!"

They were in the sick bay after morning sick call, and David was leaning against the door, his arms crossed over his broad chest. He was not wearing his coat, and his sleeves were rolled up past his forearms. She wanted to strip him bare and study his musculature, going over that fine body inch by inch.

But there were reports to be written and ruffled feelings to be soothed.

"You are correct. I have seen all the privateers' privates.

Including yours," she added with a smile. "Do not be jealous. I need to see the men to perform my duties."

"Oh, very well," he grumbled, pushing himself off the door. "But I don't like it!"

Charley stood on her toes and kissed him on the tip of his nose.

"You are still the prettiest privateer I've ever seen, Captain Pirate. But go back up on deck now. Sick call is over and I have work to do."

He bolted the door to sick bay and looked back at her. "Actually, Doctor, I did come down here for a reason. I've been plagued by a terrible swelling."

"Really? Where—"

Before she could finish, he stepped closer to her and pulled her against his muscled frame. He ran his hands down her back to her hips and wiggled himself against her.

"Oh, that swelling."

She pulled her head back and looked down at him, then put her hand over her mouth to hide her smile.

"It does not look so terrible to me, Captain."

"You are right, it does look rather splendid," he said, gazing down at himself with pride.

Charley felt her eyes roll, and cleared her throat. "I usually recommend a cold compress to deal with swelling."

He grabbed her hand and put it on his swollen parts. "I don't know, Doctor," he said huskily. "I think this swelling would benefit more from an application of wet heat than a cold compress. Wet heat, and friction. In fact, I know from experience that that's the cure for this swelling."

To illustrate the benefits of wet heat, he angled his head and put his mouth over hers, a maneuver guaranteed to bring her attention fully to focus on his swelling. In fact, it seemed to aggravate the problem and make it even more obvious.

She stroked her hand along his impressive length and broke away from his talented mouth. "You are practicing medicine again, Captain. You said you would leave that up to me."

She punctuated this sentence by grasping him firmly, which produced a noise from between his lips that did sound like he was in discomfort. He brought his head forward and nuzzled her beneath her ear, bringing a gasp from deep from within her own throat. His lips traveled along the skin of her neck, raising his own brand of heat and sparking a fever within her. The man did have a talent for throwing her humors out of balance, but he also knew how to restore her to contentment and satisfaction.

"You must take my advice on this, Doctor," he whispered against her skin. "I have seen and dealt with far more of these swelling situations than you have."

"Hmmmm...I will grant that you have more experience with this issue," her voice came out in a low rasp, despite her efforts to maintain a professional demeanor. "And I should always be willing to learn from all sources. Wet heat, you say?"

"A sovereign remedy," he murmured.

"I'll have to examine this more closely then."

Charley lowered herself to her knees and undid the buttons before her eyes. As David's trousers fell around his ankles and she saw exactly how severe his swelling was, she knew she had to take matters into her own hands. Discussions from her most educational evening in Madame Cornelia's house came back to her and she put her lessons into action, bringing her mouth down around him, to his incoherent delight. She applied the cure that he swore by, and to no one's surprise, she soon had the swelling—and the captain—completely relieved.

As he was leaving the cabin David winked at her and said, "Always a pleasure to see your expertise in action, Doctor."

"Scoundrel!" she said to the air where he'd been, as Pirate shot into the cabin before the door closed.

Charley smiled to herself after he left. This life she was living was as fantastical as Shakespeare's *Tempest*, full of adventures and voyages and hidden identities.

And the magic of loving her own prince, as Miranda loved Ferdinand.

But that story had a happy ending with the two lovers wed, and David had made no mention of love or marriage. He wanted her, she knew that well enough, but for how long? The rational part of her brain understood that he felt bound to offer for Miss Dixon, but the irrational part that brought her to his bunk at night wanted more. She wanted his love and his name and his children.

She also wanted to practice medicine.

Was she willing to settle for his passion and for the opportunity to be his ship's doctor?

"I will take what I can get, for now," she said aloud.

"Mrrrrowwwwr?" Pirate said from where he was washing himself atop her bunk.

"I said, you are too much like your namesake."

The cat did not argue the point and went back to his ablutions.

The tomcat and the master of the *Fancy* did resemble one another; both were fierce and independent, not giving up while hunting, and their eyes held the same gleam of masculine satisfaction when their prey was under their paw.

The evenings the doctor and the captain spent together were as before, and their arguing and sparring continued. With one difference—at some point during the evening they ended up naked.

"But surely you realize, Captain Fletcher, that now with

Napoleon exiled to Elba, Britain can devote its full attention to defeating the United States? How can you hope to prevail against the mightiest nation on earth when the Emperor Napoleon could not win?"

Charley was stretched out on the captain's bunk, leaning up against the bulkhead. She watched him as he moved in the confined space of his cabin. Davy was stripped down to his breeches and they hung low on his hips, his fine bones jutting out, a line of ebony hair pointing the way to what she desired. For now though, she was content to watch. She had never seen a panther, but based on what she'd read it seemed his lithe movements mimicked that of the hunting cat, elegant, no energy wasted, the lean form a delight to the eyes.

"You underestimate the will of the American people, Doctor." He poked his finger in the air for emphasis. "When you push us, we push back. Hard. John Bull cannot bully America into surrendering now any more than you could forty years ago. Have you already forgotten the lesson of Fort McHenry?"

He rummaged in his desk and pulled out a tattered newspaper, much folded and creased.

"My mother sent this to me with the letters, a newspaper from home. A Mr. Key wrote a poem about the battle, titled 'The Defence of Fort McHenry.' Look here—'the land of the free and the home of the brave.' That's America, Charley! I won't ask you to drink to an American victory, but you won't mind if I have a tot?"

David poured himself some rum while humming a tune. She listened, her head cocked to the side.

"I know that tune—I heard it in the inn where I waited to board the *Lady Jane*. It is 'To Anacreon in Heaven,' is it not? I recall the people who attempted to navigate its melody often failed miserably."

"Maybe it's a song best attempted while drinking for the

full effect. But I'm told it is now popular in Baltimore with lyrics based on Mr. Key's poem—'And the rockets' red glare...'"

Charley snickered as his voice strained through the notes. "That tune will never catch on, Captain. Certainly not the way you sing! Best you stick to sailing your ship."

"You don't like my singing? That's mutinous talk, Doctor, and you will be flogged for it!"

His "flogging" took the form of jumping on her and tickling her, which soon had his laughing victim begging for mercy.

"No quarter for mutineers!" her tormenter said, but then his actions shifted from tickling to touching, moving his hands over her body in ways designed to delight rather than torture.

Once again Charley marveled at the complexities of the human body. She knew about the major components involved in sexual stimulation, but who knew that where her shoulder met her neck would be so sensitive to touch? Who would have suspected that one's ankles could be licked, stimulating sensation in parts of the body far removed from her feet?

This was what was different about their relationship now, she thought afterward, as the sweat cooled on their bodies. Not just the sexual activity, but the touching. The closeness. She never knew how much she lacked it in her life, the joy that came from being hugged, from having contact with another human being. She picked up David's hand and ran her finger over his index finger, feeling the strength in that long digit which could bring her such delight.

"What are you doing?"

"There are twenty-seven bones in your hand. Blood vessels, tendons, ligaments. Muscles. A baby is fascinated when he discovers his hand and will watch it, moving his own fingers, turning it over." She held his hand and marveled at it before threading her fingers through his. "Such a complex mechanism, and capable of so much—for good or for evil."

David leaned over and kissed her hair, her body held close to his. Charley shifted slightly. Tonight she'd come prepared with a vinegar soaked sponge, but there was always the worry in the back of her mind that such a method wasn't a hundred percent effective, as demonstrated at Madame Cornelia's house. But she also understood better now the drives and desires that caused smart women to make foolish choices.

"Why such a big sigh?"

"Just thoughts of the future. David—"

But before she could say more he released her hand and placed a finger across her lips.

"A privateer learns to take each day as it comes, Charley. One day may bring boredom, the next day may bring a prize, the day after that—anything can happen and life at sea is chancy. We live for the day."

"It is that kind of philosophy that brings the men to sick bay with diseases of Venus, Captain," she said sharply.

"You think like a doctor, and not a sailor. Which is as it should be. I have sailors aplenty, but only one doctor. You."

He reached for her again, but she reluctantly disengaged herself. "I need to return to my quarters. It is late."

Charley shrugged her shirt over her head. When she looked at him again, David was propped up on one arm and watching her, a frown on his face.

"I wish things were different, and you could spend the night."

She wanted to spend the night. She wanted to spend this night and every night held in his arms, feeling safe and cherished, and maybe even loved.

"Not a good idea. We tread on thin ice here and we have to maintain our fiction for the crew."

"It would be different if you came with me to America."

Charley paused from where she was buttoning herself. A chill went over her frame that owed nothing to the warm air of the Caribbean night.

"Come to America? There is a woman in Baltimore expecting a proposal of marriage from you, Captain Fletcher. Have you forgotten? I have not."

"I told you, there is nothing formal between Miss Dixon and me."

"Does she know that?"

He started to speak, then had the grace to close his mouth and look uncomfortable.

"I can fool everyone but myself, Capt—David. We both know there is a strong attraction between us. And nothing can come of it. Nothing permanent. But for the moment I am willing to follow your piratical advice and seize the day."

He put out his hand, but did not stop her as she exited his cabin. Charley turned and nearly bumped into Mr. Bryant, who nodded and said, "Doctor," then knocked on the door.

"Lookout's spotted running lights, Captain."

"I will be right there, Mr. Bryant," she heard David say before she entered her dark sick bay.

Charley tossed and turned in her cold bunk, her conversation with Davy Fletcher running through her mind. She finally gave up on sleep and went up on deck. The men were bustling about with quiet excitement, taking their stations with conversations brought to a whisper and much dousing of lights.

Captain Fletcher stood with his nightglass, training it on something in the distance that to Charley looked like a glimmer of light on the water. The *Fancy* was running dark, all visible lights doused to hide them from their prey.

Pirate wound himself around her ankles and she picked the cat up, holding him close.

"What is it?"

"Quietly, Doctor. Sound carries across the water." He didn't take his eye away from his glass, and spoke in low tones to the officer at his side. "Stay with her, Mr. Bryant. We'll know more with the dawn."

He turned to Charley and added, "You should get rest while you can. Your services may be needed."

He was focused on his ship, and his potential prey, and was already turning away from her and talking to Jenkins. Charley wanted to stay above, but knew she would only be in the way and an unnecessary distraction to the crew, so she went below and dozed in her bunk, her dreams troubled and full of bloody images.

The dawn brought more noise from the crew as the light grew, and when she came back up on deck the excitement was palpable. She took some of the food hastily thrown together by Cook before he doused his fire. Charley savored her coffee, knowing it might be the last of the day.

Her eyes tracked the *Fancy*'s commander while Jenkins filled her in on the details.

"It could be a merchantman, riding low as it is, Doctor. Whatever, that ship's hold is full of something, and Black Davy aims to check it out for himself!"

"Are you expecting a fight?"

Jenkins looked at her oddly. "We always expect a fight. Being prepared is what keeps us alive, and successful."

"He's running, Captain!" Bryant shouted.

"Then let the chase begin, Mr. Bryant! Show them our true colors!"

The men cheered as the United States' colors were run up, the need for deception over now that the privateer was in full hunting mode. They hurried to their stations with the absorption of men who'd done this many times before as weapons lockers were opened and blades and guns distributed.

When they drew closer Charley saw the ship flew Spanish colors. The merchantman gamely attempted to out sail the schooner, but the Americans were not about to let their prize slip away.

Charley knew from previous encounters and tales told that most merchants gave up without a fight, but the *San Christoval* was coming about, and its guns were hauled out and readied.

Charley looked up at David, but the smiling companion of the evening before was gone, replaced by a privateer stripped down to his nankeen trousers and white shirt, his feet bare on the deck as he wrapped a bandana around his head to keep his hair out of his eyes. The sunlight glinted off the cutlass by his side and she couldn't tear her eyes away from that blade and what could happen in the next few hours.

"Doctor, I need to see you below."

Charley followed him down to sick bay and saw his eyes take it in at a glance—the brazier, the covered instruments, the bandages neatly rolled and ready, the sand on the floor for traction. Everyone aboard the *Fancy* had a job to do, and she was ready to do hers.

"What is it, Captain?"

He didn't say a word, but put his hands on her upper arms and stared down into her eyes. He didn't have to speak, for she could read what was there—in the hours to follow, he could die. She could die.

Or he might find himself on the table beneath her saw.

All that mattered now, in this moment, was that they were together and whole, and he pulled her against him as she threw her hands around his neck. David's mouth came down on hers seeking, and she gave him what he sought—the passion of the moment, a future neither of them could promise, but both were willing to fight for, and from Charley, all the love she knew she had for this rough man and his privateer ways.

She could only dream that Black Davy would be hers forever, but until then there was the reality of this kiss, and their shared longing, and a hope for tomorrow. When he pulled back, an eternity later, he looked down at her and smoothed his hand over her short cap of hair.

"Stay here. It will be dangerous up above." He put a finger beneath her chin and tilted her face up for a final, quick kiss.

"Wish me luck, Doctor."

"Always, Captain Pirate."

He grinned down at her, then turned to leave, and she could tell he was already thinking ahead to the coming battle, the excitement evident in his eagerness to find victory once again.

He was humming as he closed the door behind him, and it took her a moment to recognize the tune, and then it came to her, and she smiled to herself.

Black Davy was humming "Charlie is my Darling" as he went off to battle.

Charley paced the sick bay, nerves strained as she heard the shouting from above and the commands of the officers. But the first shot that shook the *Fancy* came not from the guns over her head, but from the Spanish ship. She heard the crash of wood above her, and then in a bubble of stillness, Captain Fletcher's firm command.

"Fire."

The force of the *Fancy*'s starboard guns rocked her and

she grabbed onto the table for support. The sick bay door slammed open and Jenkins and Bryant entered, carrying an unconscious Purcell, the lower half of his body covered in blood.

"Put him on the table and send Mr. Lewis to me to assist," Charley said, grabbing her shears.

"We cannot stay," Jenkins said, but they carefully put the carpenter on the table and helped Charley strap him down, then they rushed back to their posts.

Purcell didn't regain consciousness as Charley's hands flew over him, cutting off his clothing to expose the wound.

She sucked in her breath in dismay. A shard of splintered wood the thickness of three fingers jutted out from his thigh. Another burst shuddered through the ship, and Charley leaned over the wounded privateer to keep the dust and debris from filtering down onto him. She coughed and wiped her arm across her face to clear her vision. Purcell was still unconscious, most likely having suffered a blow to the head as well when he was wounded, but that would have to wait until she dealt with the most immediate injury. Charley reached for her forceps as another burst struck the *Fancy*, jarring the table and shifting the wood impaling Purcell's leg.

It happened in an eyeblink.

The nick at the femoral artery widened into a tear, and Purcell's life blood fountained out from his body, sluicing over her in a red tide. The gore spurted up to the deck above, and washed over the deck below. She cursed and brought all the strength in her arms and body to bear, but the pressure she applied couldn't stop the inevitable as he exsanguinated beneath her hands.

She blinked blood out of her eyes and stared at the corpse on the table, so vibrantly alive only minutes past. Her mind was an abyss through which one thought kept circling—a real doctor could have saved him.

The door slammed open again and Lewis stood there propping up a sailor with a gashed arm.

"Jesus Christ, what happened?"

Charley shook herself. Grabbing a cloth, she wiped her face and moved over to take the wounded man into the light.

"Mr. Purcell is dead. Clear him off the table, Mr. Lewis!"

Lewis stood frozen, glassy-eyed as he looked down at Purcell's corpse.

"I don't have time for this!" Charley snapped, and hauling back her bloodied hand slapped Lewis hard enough across the jaw to rock him on his feet.

"Mr. Lewis, help or get the hell out of my way!"

Lewis gulped. "Yes, sir!"

She was already reaching for her knives and needles to tend the wounded privateer's gashed arm. She tended the next man, and the next, and the one after that who came in with a badly burned face, and the one with his foot hanging by shreds, and the one who had splinters sticking out of his arm like a hedgehog.

Above her was the sound of hell, and she blinked smoke and dust out of her eyes from the blows that rocked the schooner, but she kept her focus on the task at hand, the task she'd trained for all of her life. As the shadows lengthened she moved efficiently, competently, no one knowing that in the back of her own mind she was screaming at herself, knowing she was a fraud.

When the endless day was over, and the injured were in their quarters, and the dead were taken away for burial, Charley looked around the cozy little sick bay where she'd played at being doctor. It was splattered with blood and vomit, and reeked of the feces and urine of men voiding themselves in fear and shock. She leaned back against a bulkhead and slid down to the deck, staring at her hands and arms, blood covering her up to her neck. Mr. Lewis said something to her, but she didn't respond, and he left.

It was pleasantly quiet after that.

The door opened one more time.

"Charley?"

David crouched down before her, his face grimed with powder and sweat, a nick below his ear oozing a thin line.

"You should have a doctor see to that," she whispered, then started to giggle, and couldn't stop, not even when it turned to deep, choking sobs.

David pulled her bloody body into his arms and sat on the deck with her, holding her as sobs wracked her. When she stilled, he laid her down on the filthy deck and went to the cabin door. She heard him say something to a sailor in the passageway, but she ignored it, because it was soothing to just lie there, in the gore and the red, wet sand, not thinking about anything.

CHAPTER 18

David picked Charley up in his arms. When he'd walked in and seen her covered in blood, her eyebrows and hair crusted with it, he'd stopped breathing until he realized it wasn't her blood. It was Purcell's, and Larkin's, and Stern's, and all the others she'd cared for so competently while the guns roared overhead.

He knew few men who had the nerve to do what Charley Alcott did that day.

Small tremors wracked her body as he carried her to his cabin and he held her closer, like a baby bird trembling after a fall from the nest. His orders had been followed and hot water waited alongside the narrow hip bath.

He placed her on her feet in his cabin, and held onto her shoulder to ensure she would not crumple to the deck.

"Can you stand?" he asked her gently.

She nodded, and he moved back from her, watching her, but she just looked at the deck. He poured her a glass of rum and pulling up his shirt tail to find a clean piece of cloth, dabbed at the blood at her mouth until it was clean enough for her to drink. She followed his instructions, choking on the rough liquor, then swallowing more until he pulled the glass away. He undressed her and Charley stood docilely as a child, her eyes staring straight ahead at something only she saw. When she was nude, and her blood-soaked clothes pushed outside the cabin door to be cleaned, she finally looked at him, as solemn as a statue of a medieval saint.

"Step into the water, Charley."

She obeyed, pulling her knees up to fit into the narrow container. He dipped a cloth in a bucket of water and soaped it, scrubbing the blood and fluids off of her white body, getting the gore out of her hair, and calling for fresh water when the tub became red as an island sunset from his task. She never said a word while he was doing this, allowing him to manipulate her, and rinse her, and dry her off and tuck her into his bunk while he washed himself in seawater.

"Was it a great victory then, Captain Fletcher?"

He paused from drying himself, hearing the thread of steel in her whispery voice. Anger was good. He could deal with anger. He could not deal with hopelessness and numbness. He turned and looked at her.

"Yes, Dr. Alcott, it was indeed a great victory. The *San Christoval* was full of rum. We will be wealthy men when we sell this cargo."

"Then it was all worth it, wasn't it? But tell me one thing."

Charley was propped up on her elbow, the bed cover slipping down her arms, her face as hard and set as bone.

"Is this why men thrust themselves into danger? For money? For glory? For the 'rockets' red glare'?"

He wrapped the towel around his hips and stalked over to her. Anger radiated off of her, but she was hale and whole, and that was all that mattered. He leaned over, his arms alongside hers, holding her there in the bunk. David's own voice was hoarse from shouting commands on the deck.

When he spoke it was barely above a whisper in the quiet cabin.

"We thrust ourselves into danger for all of those things. I knew Asher Purcell all of my life. If he was standing with us now he would agree with me. Yes. It was a good haul. Yes, I am glad we did it. We are men, Charley, this is what men do."

"That may be what men do, but I will tell you what men are, Captain. Men are bags of blood and bone, easily punctured and hard to put back together. And you, you throw them away. For gold. For glory. What a waste," she sneered.

His own temper began rising, fire skittering along his nerve endings. Did she think he did not care? That each man's injury and loss did not eat at his soul?

"You cannot understand because no matter how you clothe yourself, when it is stripped away you are a woman, Charlotte Alcott. Your nature is to heal, and nurture, and soothe. I am a man. It is our nature to fight." He put his hand on her throat and when she raised her hand to him he grabbed it and pinned it to the bed, holding her beneath him.

"The men know I will order them into harm's way, and yet they follow my orders. Why? Because they trust me. Because they want to be richer than when they left Baltimore. Because they want to show the British that they cannot subjugate us. Because they like to fight, and they like to win. Because they are men, Charley. My men."

Her eyes were narrowed slits and her lips compressed into a thin line, but he knew her now. His Charley was aware of him, of his body so close to hers, only a thin layer of linen separating them. He felt his own pulse pounding, his blood rushing through his veins. He was very much alive, and so was she, and that was enough for the moment.

Almost enough. He smiled down at her and he saw in her eyes and by the hitch in her breathing that she knew showing his teeth had nothing to do with laughter.

"After battle, a man wants to prove himself alive in the midst of death. You feel it, too," he said, rubbing his thumb across her neck. "I know you do. Do not deny it. I do not have to be a physician to know why your pulse is racing, why your breath is faster, why your eyes look like black storm clouds."

"You think you know me, but you do not, Captain Fletcher. You are no gentleman, you are a Yankee pirate dressed in patriot's clothing, looking for an excuse to rob and kill!"

She glared at him, tugging at his arm. He removed his hand from her throat and took her wrist, effortlessly immobilizing her. Would his men come running if she screamed for rescue from him? He did not know, nor did he care. Charley Alcott belonged to him, and he would prove it to her.

"You like to make free with that word 'pirate,' don't you?" He lowered his body onto hers and she jerked at the contact when he settled himself atop the covers, pushing her knees apart beneath him as his towel slipped down to the deck. Even through the bedding he knew she could feel his arousal.

"Get off of me," she hissed between her teeth, but she made no move to push him off, and his lips curled humorlessly.

"You are correct, Charley. I'm not a gentleman at all. I must be a pirate because right now there is nothing I want more than to pound myself into your body until you scream." He leaned down and put his mouth very close to her ear. "And you want that, too."

He ignored her noise of protest against his words, taking her mouth with his, his hands and body holding her down as he ravaged her senses, stoking the anger and the passion he knew she was feeling. He needed to show her that while they'd all be worm food someday, right now, right here, they were alive and had each other.

Charley squirmed beneath him, but when he released her she glared up at him, then cursing, kissed him back ferociously, biting his lip, clawing at him like a tigress in his arms when he yanked the covers away.

He held her, captive to his kisses as he devoured her with his mouth. He consumed her, pinning her beneath him as he took his fill of her anger, her passionate need to show that she, too, was still breathing, still feeling, whether she acknowledged it or not.

He inhaled her clean scent, storing it in his memories. Her body gleamed white in the lamplight, slender and muscled, her long fingered hands reaching for him when he released her. As he moved down her body, each kiss, each caress, each touch was a celebration of being alive and having someone to cling to, to share a connection with that even fraught with anger was genuine and real.

When did he realize Charley was necessary to his existence, was as beautiful as the dawn across an open sea? It snuck up on him like a pirate ship in the fog, hitting him with a broadside he never saw coming. The symmetry of her features, the liveliness of her eyes, her smile with its mix of innocence and wisdom, it all combined just so to make hers the face he wanted to see every morning. No other woman had ever made him feel this way. And he would ensure that no matter what the future brought, he would brand himself on Charley's memory as well.

He kissed her flat belly, the hipbones that jutted out beneath silken skin, and when she protested his kisses that moved into a new level of intimacy, he ignored her, putting his mouth on her and using his tongue, and his fingers to wrest every response from her body, to lick and stroke and ramp up her sensations. She tasted of the sea and of woman, and she tasted like life itself, her body responding to his mouth and to his hands. He wanted her to be mindless with passion and desire, to be at a point where she would think of nothing but them together.

When she cried out his name, when she begged him to enter her, using the rough language of the sailors she lived with, he moved up her body and flipped her over onto her knees, before sliding into her as easily as a fish gliding through the waters, her muscles clamping around him, holding him within her sheltering embrace.

She couldn't move beneath him, and he liked it like that, liked having her at his mercy as he took her. The sound of their heated flesh coming together was loud in the cabin, their harsh breathing shutting out the ship's noise.

"Come for me," he growled into her ear as he pumped himself into her. "Show me how alive you are."

"Damn you!" she gasped.

"That's right, Charley, I'm a damned pirate, but I'm the pirate who's fucking you, and you will never, ever forget me," he said, punctuating his words with thrusts that made her moan and claw at the bedding as she begged him for more.

He put his hand down where they were joined, the bud at the front of her sex so swollen with lust that it only took the smallest pressure of his fingers to bring it up against his pistoning shaft so she could feel him even more deeply. She whimpered and strained against him as he pushed himself deeper into her, stoking the flames that consumed them both.

She cried out when she climaxed, a cry of desperation as much as of satisfaction. It hurt him, but he could not stop, he would not stop, not when he needed so much to release himself into her body that was so alive and strong and beautiful in the midst of the day's carnage.

They lay there, afterward, panting in the close cabin that

still smelled of smoke and powder and blood, each trapped in painful thought.

"There is no future for us, David."

David turned his head to look at Charley on the pillow next to him. She was staring up at the deck overhead, but turned to look at him, her eyes wide and ash-gray and filled with sorrow.

"Do not talk like that."

"I have to leave. You are a fever in my blood, David Fletcher. A fever I cannot bleed out. For the sake of my own health, and my own sanity, I must leave. There is too much falseness in my life. Too many lies. I can lie about who Charlotte Alcott is. I cannot lie to myself about us." She sat up and looked at the water in the tub, still tinged with blood, then back at him, her face bleak and drawn.

"I love you, David. But it is not enough. You said it yourself. You are a violent man and I am a healer. I cannot lie to myself about how I feel about the waste of men's lives. I can only live with so many lies at one time, and that is one more than I can deal with. I do not belong here. Take me to Jamaica, or to St. Martin, or somewhere else. Anywhere else."

She loved him? How could she leave if she loved him? His mind raced frantically to say the right thing to make her stop this talk.

He sat up and grasped her bare shoulder. "What about your duty to these men, Doctor?"

"Do not call me 'Doctor.'" She tried to shake him off, but he held on. "The men need a real surgeon, not someone pretending to be a surgeon."

"It was a real surgeon who removed my brother's hand and saved his life! And try as you might, you cannot save them all. I am not a surgeon, but I know that much. Men die. They die before their time, and they die in unpleasant ways. And too often, there is nothing you can do about it."

He moved his hand to her chin to hold her gaze. "Do not look away. You are needed here, Dr. Alcott. The men need you." *I need you.* "You will stay here and treat this crew until I say otherwise."

"Is that an order, Captain Fletcher?"

"Yes, dammit!"

"Where are my clothes?"

He pointed to the bundle he'd fetched from her cabin and she climbed out of the bunk and dressed herself.

"You won't stay the night?"

"Is that an order?"

"Do not be like that, Charley."

She sighed and looked down at her hands, clean now, but he knew she was seeing them as they'd been before, when he found her sitting on the deck.

"No. I will not stay the night. I have my duty, Captain, and I will do it…" She looked away, and when she looked back there was a sheen of liquid in her shadowed eyes.

"I have to return to sick bay. The men need me."

"I need you," he said, speaking aloud the words he'd kept to himself.

"Not enough," she whispered, and left.

Charley numbly walked into her sick bay and stopped. The room was scrubbed clean, still damp and smelling of vinegar. She looked up. They'd missed the spot overhead where Purcell's blood splattered against the wood before dripping back down onto her.

No matter. She would leave it there, a reminder of her hubris in thinking she could save them all.

The men had returned to their hammocks, even the injured ones, and she sat with her journals, making notes, going through the motions of being the ship's surgeon because much as she hated to admit David Fletcher was correct, he was right about this. Whether or not she considered herself qualified to practice medicine, she was all they had aboard the *Fancy*. She owed it to the crew to be as professional as possible, no matter how the rest of the world and the healing fraternity might judge her.

CHAPTER 19

The skies were sullen the next morning, but the men were cheerful, even the ones recovering from their injuries. The health of a patient and that patient's recovery was strongly affected by attitude. Knowing their haul could make them all wealthy did much to improve their outlook.

It didn't hurt that some of the purloined rum had been freely distributed the evening before as the captain's reward to his hard-working crew.

But it was clear to even Charley's eyes that the *Fancy* sustained serious damage in its fight with the Spanish merchantman. After the *San Christoval* was allowed to limp away, cleared of its cargo and money, the *Fancy* was in need of repair.

"The question is," Bryant asked the captain as they examined the battered rigging, "Do we put into port and take our chances, or risk capture on a run for the United States?"

David Fletcher looked around him. Charley knew he was missing his carpenter, his face bleak with the loss he wouldn't acknowledge the night before.

"We have a hold full of rum, Mr. Bryant, making us a prize for anyone who hears of it. I would rather take my chances on a run to the United States than sit out here like a duck on the water or put in to an unfriendly port."

"We can do some work here in boats to keep the *Fancy* seaworthy, Captain. Or we can take her to Santa Rosa."

"Come with me, Mr. Bryant. You also, Doctor."

Charley followed the men to the captain's cabin. David pulled out some rolled charts and spread them on the table.

"There's an island, here." He gestured at the map. "Last time I was there no one lived there, and there was water."

"Is there game, and fruit?" Charley asked.

"Wild pigs, some fruit and vegetation I would recognize."

"The men who were injured would benefit from fresh food and water, Captain. If we went to Santa Rosa, I might be able to purchase more laudanum as well."

"No. We will not go to Santa Rosa, not with the rum. That is too much temptation to put in front of *Señor* Martinez."

He put his finger on the map.

"Keep the pumps going. If this weather holds, we will be there tomorrow and will patch what we can. After that we head for Baltimore."

His eyes met Charley's as he said this, but she said nothing. It had been a grand interlude, a fine adventure full of excitement and the passion of Black Davy Fletcher, but she knew that would end when she reached the United States.

If she were fortunate she'd find transportation back down to the Indies. If not, she would have to return home to England.

Bryant left them, and she watched David in the silence.

"Leave me here in the islands, Captain. I will make my way to Jamaica."

He looked at her, a bittersweet smile on his lips. "Give up

my most valuable prize? I think not. You will come with me to Baltimore, Dr. Alcott. I am not letting you go."

"You cannot keep me like a stolen cat!"

"Can I not?" He advanced on her and took her by the arms. "I caught you, Charley. I took you off that ship to tend my men. And by God, I am going to keep you!"

She shook her head. "Dreams and mist. That's all this is. Let us end it now, and hope that we can always be friends."

His grip tightened. "Friends? I don't want to be your damned friend. Don't you realize you have become as necessary to me as the air I breathe? As welcome as fresh water after a long voyage?"

Air. Water. So mundane and taken for granted, and so necessary to life. You couldn't live without them, but you could survive on short rations.

"What we want and what we have are not the same, David. You must let me go so that we can both get on with our lives!"

He released her and strode back to the table, his face set. "Go see to your duties, Doctor."

Charley dragged herself to her sick bay, schooling her face to hide her churning emotions from the men. She dispensed an encouraging word along with re-bandaging wounds and checking on their general well-being. Ives still had a ringing in his ears from the guns, but she told him it would fade in a day or two. Stern got salve for his burns. The stump of Larkin's leg appeared normal for now, and she gave him some of her dwindling stock of laudanum and reassured him it was healing, even though they both knew if it didn't become septic in the tropics it was as much luck and the grace of God as the doctor's skill.

Luncheon was a subdued affair for the officers and the doctor. The crew was manning the ship's pumps even as

Bryant and the captain discussed the best way to repair the *Fancy*.

"Is the ship seaworthy?" Charley asked.

Both men looked at her, almost as if they were just now remembering she was at table with them.

"Yes, Doctor," Bryant said firmly. "We wouldn't sail for home if it wasn't. But we will be doing repairs on her to keep her that way, with the men working longer hours."

"Right now though you need to assemble the crew, Mr. Bryant. We must say goodbye to Asher."

"Aye, Captain," he said, clearing his throat and excusing himself from the table. David still sat, staring down at his hands. It was so quiet that Charley could hear the snap of the canvas, the lines creaking, and the sound of the pumps.

"David."

He looked up, his face bleak.

"You did what you could yesterday for the men. Today you will do more. That is your task as the *Fancy's* commander."

He got up from the table and walked around, pulling her up from her chair and holding her hands tightly.

"Can you answer this, Charley Alcott? If you had to choose, today, to come aboard the *Fancy* or stay on the *Lady Jane*, with all that has happened between us, which would you choose?"

He waited, and she looked down at their hands clasped together, his so sun-browned and strong, her own, roughened and strong in their own way, not delicate, not soft, but hers. He took those hands that had failed some, and helped many, and raised them to his lips, putting a soft kiss on the back of one, then the other.

"If I had to do it all over again," he said, rubbing his thumb across the back of her knuckles, "I would steal you away, and keep you aboard my ship, and never let you go, Charley my darling."

She stared into his golden eyes, and she took her hand from his and brushed back a lock of hair that fell over his forehead.

"Your duty calls you, Captain,"

They went up on deck together, David carrying his prayer book. The men were assembled wearing their finest clothing. At the starboard rail a canvas length awaited them, sewn by Sails, weighted to carry its burden to the bottom of the ocean. It was on a trestle, covered with the flag of the United States that fluttered at the edges in the light breeze.

The crew was silent as their captain stepped forward, and a hurricane bird soared overhead, far from land but reminding them all that someday, they would return to their homes.

Some of them.

David cleared his throat.

"…They that go down to the sea in ships, that do business in great waters; These see the works of the Lord, and His wonders in the deep…Then they cry unto the Lord in their trouble, and He bringeth them out of their distresses. He maketh the storm a calm, so that the waves thereof are still. Then are they glad because they be quiet; so He bringeth them unto their desired haven."

He stepped next to the body where two sailors waited respectfully at attention.

"Asher Purcell was a patriot, and a good man. He will be remembered for doing his job well, for his love of life, and for his zeal in serving his country. For as much as it hath pleased Almighty God to take unto himself the soul of our dear brother here departed, we therefore commit his body to the deep in sure and certain hopes of the Resurrection to eternal life, through our Lord Jesus Christ."

David nodded to the sailors, who picked up the inboard end of the platform and tilted it. The canvas slipped out smoothly from beneath the flag to fall into the ocean's depths with the smallest of splashes, a faint ripple showing where their carpenter went to his final resting place.

"Dismissed!" Bryant told the men, who returned to their tasks, but Charley stood watching David, who was watching the men folding the flag. It would be kept safe for when the privateer ran it up, after fooling another ship into thinking they were British, or Spanish, or something other than a predator out on the water to savage enemy shipping.

She asked him once if the privateers made a difference for America. He looked at her blankly for a moment, then said, "Bear in mind, Doctor, we are not the Royal Navy with hundreds of years of ships at our beck and call. The United States is young, but we are strong because we put everything we have into the fight, especially at sea. Yes, our privateers make all the difference in this war. Every ship we capture is another blow to Britain and its allies."

Charley was thinking about that conversation later that evening, and how thin the line was between a privateer and a pirate when there was a knock at the sick bay door.

She turned from her desk, hesitating, but finally stood.

"Come in, Captain."

David entered sick bay and closed the door behind him. There was only the lantern on the bulkhead over the desk, and Charley studied him, the shadows in the cabin blending with his midnight hair and overlaying the strong planes of his face.

"What do you want?"

"You."

She looked at him in amazement, then a harsh laugh burst from her.

"Have you been in the sun too long? What make-believe

world are you living in? You will not listen to me when I say I cannot go with you to Baltimore! Do you expect me then to throw myself into your arms each night and give you what you want without any thought to the future?"

"Yes. Because it is what you want also."

"Damn you," she whispered, and she threw herself into his arms.

He caught her, and held her, and she smelled the salt on his skin, the scent of the ocean that would always make her think of Black Davy Fletcher. She would remember how his eyes darkened from amber to deepest sienna when he kissed her, the silken feel of his hair beneath her hands, the way he whispered her name, making it into a song.

His mouth hovered above hers, hesitating for the briefest instant before meeting hers, making that connection that brought her senses to life. They were silent in the dimness of the quiet cabin, not speaking, exploring each other, tasting the other, but finally, gathering strength she did not know she had, Charley pushed herself away from him.

"Leave. Now."

"Charley—"

She stood resolute beside her door, holding it open, her other hand fisted by her side. He looked at her for an endless moment, then stepped out into the night.

Charley was watching the boat returning to the *Fancy* from the unnamed island, loaded with casks of fresh water. David looked at the slender shoulders that carried an uncharacteristic slump to them. She hid it well from the crew, but he knew how unhappy she was.

He wanted to fix it, to make her world the place it should

be. A place where she could practice medicine and a place where she would stand by his side, always.

But there was a war to fight, and cargo to transport, and his first duty was not to her, but to his men and to his country. And that meant traveling up to the United States.

He turned and walked to the stern, leaning over the rail to where the men were working.

"What is your estimate on the time of those repairs, Mr. Bryant?"

Bryant looked up at the captain, shading his eyes against the light. "Another three or four hours should do it, Captain."

"Carry on then."

David went to his cabin to gather supplies, telling Lewis where he was off to and when he'd be back.

"Aye, Captain," Lewis said. "We'll have supper waiting when you return. Will the doctor be joining you?" he asked diffidently. Only the steward had an inkling of how things stood between David and Charley, but one of the reasons he valued the man's services was because he wouldn't gossip.

"I don't know yet, Mr. Lewis."

"Aye, Captain. If I may say so, sir, she's a fine young lady as well as a good doctor."

"She is that, Mr. Lewis."

David found Charley still standing at the rail, staring out over the water, her mind a million miles away.

"Charley."

He stepped closer to her, so that their conversation would remain private.

"Come with me into the boat, over to the island."

"Why?"

"So that we can spend time together before…" He hesitated and tried again. "I want you to come with me. Aboard ship I am always the captain, and you are always the doctor. On the island, we can be just Charley and David."

He put his hand on her face, cradling it, and rubbed his thumb across the fine grained skin, feeling the strong bones beneath. "We can be ourselves—for a few hours."

Her face was wary, and drawn with tension. He wanted that time back when they could laugh together, but it seemed like a distant dream. Which was why he needed her now to come with him.

"I do not know what will happen in the future, Charley, no one does. But I know that right now, today, we have each other and these moments. I do not claim to know much about love, but I know that what we have is rare. Do you want to look back at your life with regret for what you rejected?"

Her lashes lowered, veiling her thoughts from him, and she sighed.

"Those are pretty words, Davy. They are the same kind of pretty words that have charmed women into men's arms since time out of mind."

"Yes, but I mean them," he said, his lips curling up at how the wheels in her head kept turning. "If you were a woman of greater sensibility than sense you would not be analyzing my conversation this way."

"Then I would not be who I am," she said, and her own mouth blossomed into a smile. "Despite that, and try as I might, I find that there are times when my heart overrules my head. Too often."

"Is this such a time?" he said in a low voice.

Charley looked out at the land, the palm trees swaying and the bright birds flashing through the foliage.

"I fear so, Captain," she said with another sigh. "Let me gather some items and I will rejoin you shortly."

Yes! He controlled himself and nodded, schooling his expression to be serious and thoughtful rather than triumphant. He knew he could bring her around, but he needed time and opportunity, both of which were in short supply aboard the damaged *Fancy*.

The captain and the doctor sat silently in the boat as they were rowed ashore. Charley'd removed her shoes, but left her worn brown coat on and her neckcloth neatly knotted. David watched her. Someday he'd like to see her dressed in lace and silk, though he wondered if he'd recognize her. He smiled to himself at the thought.

"Pick us up at sunset, Wells."

"Aye, Captain," the sailor said.

David put his hand beneath Charley's elbow, steadying her on the sand. "Give yourself time to adjust, Doctor. You have been at sea a long time now."

She looked at him, her face burnished by the afternoon sun. "I feel sometimes like I have been at sea forever."

David glanced over his shoulder. Wells was already rowing back to the *Fancy* and was out of earshot.

"Why don't you take off your coat. No one will see you here."

Charley being Charley, looked around to confirm that they were alone on this little island, then she unfastened her coat and David took it from her, draping it over his arm. At the very least he'd like to buy her some new coats, as Dr. Alcott's wardrobe was showing the strain of life aboard the *Fancy*.

"Come with me, Charley. I'll show you something that will make you glad you came ashore."

He moved his hand down her arm, taking her hand in his and clasping it. He looked down at their joined hands.

"Such a small thing, holding a lady's hand. I took it for granted, thinking I could do it wherever and whenever."

"But not aboard ship," she said with a wry smile, looking down at their joined hands, his so brown, hers white, but strong and steady.

"Remember, today we are just ourselves, all alone here. I can hold your hand if I want."

So saying, he led her into the trees to where a stream burbled down to the shore amidst water smoothed rocks. Charley put her shoes back on and they began to climb, following the water to its source, a spring set deep in the forest.

"Oh my," she said. "This is like the pool at *Señor* Martinez's island!"

"Yes, but today is different. Today you can join me in the water."

It was indeed a pool similar to that on Santa Rosa, deep enough to swim in, shaded by trees and fragrant with the blossoms of plumeria and jasmine. Charley laughed in delight as their intrusion disturbed a flock of brightly colored parakeets, who flew through the trees like living flowers.

David was already taking off his clothes, and after a brief hesitation, she followed his lead.

"It is shallow at this end, Charley. I recall you do not swim."

She blushed, remembering how he had hauled her out of the ocean and discovered her secrets, but she gamely stepped into the water, placing her feet carefully on the sandy bottom.

"You're right, I can stand up here! Oh, please tell me you brought soap with you!"

David chuckled and rummaging through the basket Lewis put together pulled out soap and towels.

"I knew what would make you happy. Catch!"

He tossed her the soap, and she stood there and held it, looking at him. She was standing chest deep in the water, her breasts covered, then exposed by the wavelets that lapped back and forth.

"You do know what makes me happy, don't you, Davy?"

He waded into the water and joined her. "This makes me happy, Charley. To see you in the sunshine. All of you, unbound, unfettered."

He took the soap from her lax hand and turned her so that he could scrub her back, a move that made her purr like Pirate the cat.

"Here we are, the two of us, alone and naked in paradise," he said as he worked the creamy lather into her smooth shoulders.

"I recall there's a serpent in this story, and an apple."

"Of course there's a serpent…" He smiled against her neck, pulling her tight against him so she could feel for herself.

She chuckled and his heart lifted. This was the Charley he wanted, the one who laughed with him and appreciated his bad jokes, not the one who condemned him with her cold glances. But being morally sure was part of his Charley as well, the same core of dedication and resolve that drove her to treat every patient, every person, like he was deserving of her best efforts.

And he loved her for it.

"David? Why did you stop?"

"Forgive me, I was lost in thought for a minute."

He turned her back so she was facing him, and he stroked his soapy hands down her torso, loving her with his hands because he wasn't yet ready to say the words.

"You are so beautiful," he whispered.

"I know I am not pretty. You do not need to offer me false coin, Davy."

"You are correct. You are not pretty."

She looked away, in pain, and in resignation. David put his hand on her chin and brought her gaze back to his, forcing her to see the truth in his eyes as well as hear it in his words.

"You are not pretty. Pretty is a china figurine on a shelf. Pretty fades and cracks and withers away. You are *beautiful*, Charley Alcott. Your beauty flows out from you like honey from a comb, every time you comfort a wounded man, every time you heal a pain. You are beautiful here," he kissed her forehead, "and here," he said, kissing her graceful neck, "and especially inside here," he finished, putting his hand on her breastbone.

"You will always be beautiful, Charley, when pretty is only a memory, you will be beautiful because of who you are."

"If I have any beauty to speak of, it is because I see it reflected in your eyes, David." She looked up at him, her own eyes dark and wide in the shaded pool. He picked her up and carried her from the water, placing her on the blanket spread on the ground.

"Let me prove it to you. Let me show you how beautiful you are."

A frown creased between her eyes, but he put his finger over the spot and eased the lines out.

"You are thinking again. Today, we are in paradise, away from the war and our worries. Let me show you what paradise truly is."

Now that he knew she was a woman, David could not understand how he'd been so blind before. She wasn't pretty and dainty like others he'd known, but she was womanly in all the ways that counted. The curve of her cheek, her blessedly unbound breasts, why, he'd even thought she had a fine arse when he thought she was a lad! Now it tempted him every day in those trousers she wore, drawing attention to the length of her legs and how they felt wrapped around him.

Today she was all woman, and every woman, and the only

woman he wanted. He showed her, as he promised, loving her with all of the skill he possessed. She responded with a natural sensuality that still thrilled him. There was nothing studied or artificial in her responses because that kind of falseness went against her nature.

Funny, to be thinking of the honest core of someone who every day was dressed in a lie.

"What is so amusing?" she whispered.

"Us," he said, leaning back over her mouth to give her a soft kiss. She opened beneath him like a scented banquet, drawing him in deeper. He knew he should say the words in his heart, the words she wanted to hear, but that would have to wait. He owed her real answers and a real future, and that was something he couldn't offer her, not yet.

But he could offer himself. He put his hand on her breast, so delicate and finely formed, a tracery of blue showing through the skin, the small nipple standing up like a ripe raspberry.

"Perfect," he murmured, as much to himself as to her. "You are a perfect feast, Charley Alcott."

She smiled up at him, tentatively, and he knew she still did not believe she was beautiful, that she was everything he wanted in a woman. He would have to prove it to her. If he had his way he would spend the rest of his life proving it to her, but he knew he might only have this afternoon, and this shaded glen.

He put his mouth on her and licked her, and she threaded her fingers though his hair, pulling closer, asking him wordlessly to feast upon her. She stirred his senses, the sight of her in the sunlight sifting through the trees, the sounds she made as he used his mouth and his tongue and his teeth to show her, to prove to her that she was as beautiful as he claimed.

But she surprised him when he moved up to enter her.

Charley rolled them over so that she was on top, and a shaft of sunlight glinted off her hair as she positioned herself above him.

"I want to see you, Handsome Davy," she whispered, lowering herself atop him. "*You* are so beautiful. I want to see the sunlight on you, and I want to feel you inside me, like this."

Her words thrilled him, and made him swell inside her. Charley was in control now, and he was happy to let her play the commander. He followed her orders faithfully, even when they were only a sigh in his ear or a tightening of her muscles, and he held onto her for as long as he could, loving her as best he was able.

Until the words could come from him, it was all he could do.

CHAPTER 20

"Is it just me, or is it cooler today than it was yesterday?"

"Perhaps. It is February, after all," Captain Fletcher said, scanning the horizon. The tension on his face threw the lines around his eyes and the line of his jaw into harsh relief. She tried to imagine what was running through his mind. Was he thinking about the British navy? The family and the girl that awaited him in Baltimore?

Was he thinking about her?

Charley'd walked in on him in his cabin last evening, as David sat there studying his miniature of Miss Dixon. She said nothing, but instead of putting it back on the shelf, David put it inside his desk. Then he'd used those strong hands and that skilled mouth to once again make her forget their destination, at least for a few hours.

"Do we have enough water to get to Baltimore?"

"We should clear Cuba tomorrow and once we're through the Florida Straits we will stop at Key Marquez to re-provision, then move up the coast to St. Marys—"

"A sail, Captain, off the stern!"

The men on deck turned to look where Ives spotted the ship. David pulled out his spyglass and studied the ship following them, then ran up the rigging next to Ives for a better look. Charley shaded her eyes but could tell nothing except for a blur on the water.

"Mr. Bryant! Sound to quarters! It is England!"

David flew down the rigging, still barking out orders. The men hurried to their posts, and Charley stood, paralyzed. The Royal Navy had found them.

"Dr. Alcott! Come with me!"

David was already in motion and she blindly followed him into the dark as men shoved past her with no word of apology, their faces grim and focused. Charley was walking past the captain's cabin to sick bay when she was grabbed and pulled into the cabin and into David's arms, his mouth seeking hers in the dimness.

She threw her arms around his neck and kissed him back, tasting him, absorbing him into her soul.

"This is bad, isn't it?" she said when they broke apart.

"I won't lie to you. It's a frigate. The *Caeneus*."

Charley gasped. She remembered the Cannies's gunnery practice, the men moving together like a finely tuned machine. The Americans could do a great deal of harm with their twelve-pounders, but the British frigate carried more iron with a longer range, and a carronade that could tear a ship apart at close quarters.

"You've done battle with the *Caeneus* before?"

"I've *outrun* the *Caeneus* before. Captain Doyle is no fool, and he doesn't take defeat well. He will be burning to take the *Fancy* after we showed him our tail last time."

"You will fight, won't you?"

"If I must. I have come too far for us to risk capture now."

He framed her face with his hands. "Have faith in me, Charley, and we will see this through."

She looked up at him through the clouded lens of eyes awash in tears. But they had their duty, the captain to his ship, the doctor to the men. She pulled his head down for one last kiss to savor, and store up and remember.

Duty. It always came down to duty. Just for once she wished she knew nothing of medicine or death or dismemberment, and she could be an ordinary girl thinking about frocks and dancing.

But then she wouldn't be Charley Alcott, and her heart would never have been captured by Black Davy Fletcher.

He smiled tenderly down at her, and rubbed the tears from her cheeks with his thumbs.

"I will be with you after this is done, Charley Alcott." The smile faded from his face as he studied her. "Have your gear ready, just in case we have to leave the *Fancy*."

"Will it come to that?" She knew it was a foolish question as soon as the words left her lips, but what else could she say? Right now, with the sound of the men running up on deck, the commands being shouted out by Mr. Bryant, all she could cling to was hope and dreams.

"Being prepared is what life at sea is all about, Doctor."

Charley turned and reached for the door latch, then paused, looking over her shoulder at him one last time.

"I will see you soon, Captain. When you have won your victory."

David came over to her and put his hands on her slim shoulders and rested his forehead against hers.

He whispered something, then brushed past her out the door. She stood there, glued to the deck.

I love you, Charley Alcott.

But Black Davy was gone into the fight, and Charley Alcott was alone.

~

One expects that once preparations have begun for a battle the action happens quickly, but Charley knew by now that would not be the case. Sea battles were more about who had the wind, and maneuvering one's ship into the best position to flee or fight.

She lit another lantern as the sun moved toward the horizon, checked her supplies one more time, and looked at her satchel sitting on her desk, containing her journals, Dr. Murray's copy of Woodall and her few personal items. There was so little she owned. Whatever she had to offer someone was contained here, Charley thought, staring down at her hands. In her hands, and in her mind, and most of all, in her heart. She couldn't give David Fletcher family connections or wealth, but she could give him her heart.

When this was over, she would tell him what she should have told him long ago. That he would always be the pirate who captured her heart, who owned her love no matter what.

Charley brushed her hair back from her forehead and straightened her back, pulling her waistcoat down. As she exited sick bay to see if she could find something to eat she saw Lewis, leaning against a bulkhead, his face white.

"Mr. Lewis? Are you ill?"

"No, Doctor. The Captain said I should assist you, as I did last time." He shuddered. "I don't know if I can do that again."

"Of course you can," she said sternly. "You are a capable assistant when I need you to be one. Thinking about it now has your nerves on edge, but I assure you, when the action starts you will rise to the occasion."

"Is it that way for you?"

"Every single time, Mr. Lewis. That never changes. Now, do you know where I can get something to eat?"

He was about to reply when the boom of a gun across the water startled them both. Lewis looked at her.

"It has started, Doctor. The British have caught up with us."

Charley swallowed her fear. "I have faith in Captain Fletcher, Mr. Lewis. The day is not yet over."

The sound of the frigate's guns again coming to bear on the American vessel mocked her words as the *Fancy* was struck by a blow to starboard. Charley braced herself against the bulkhead and heard the shouts from above.

"Come, Mr. Lewis. It is time for us to take our stations."

"Aye, Doctor," he said, wiping his damp forehead.

They entered sick bay just ahead of the sailors who brought down Bryant, a large sliver of wood impaling his upper arm.

"Bind this up fast, Doctor. I'm needed above," he said through gritted teeth.

She didn't argue with him but with Lewis's assistance cut through the coat and removed the foreign object, cleaning the wound and knowing he'd ignore her advice not to use his wounded arm for fear of worsening the injury. There was too much to be done and Bryant was rushing out the door with the ends of his bandage still fluttering from where Charley's sure fingers tied them off.

The *Fancy's* guns returned fire now. She was used to working with the rhythm of her own ship's guns, but an answering broadside from the *Caeneus* exploded into the *Fancy,* hurling her to the deck. She lay there, dazed, coughing in the dust and smoke. When she pushed herself to her knees the deck was tilted at an odd angle and she held onto her table to pull herself to her feet. A sailor with a burned hand was helping Lewis to his own feet, blood from a cut across the back of Lewis's torn scalp pouring down his neck.

Through the ringing in her ears Charley heard an axe

pounding at the sick bay door, and Bryant calling out, "Doctor, are you in there?"

She winced as she moved her arm to push her hair out of her eyes.

"What has happened?" she yelled back.

"We're taking on water and we're going to the boats." He finished as the sailors broke the door open, and then Charley slung her satchel over her neck and gave Lewis a cloth to hold to his head to stanch the bleeding. She helped him out the tilted doorway, and was pulled through a moment later into the passageway by the sailors. Charley wanted to look over her shoulder at the room where she'd experienced so much joy and achievement and sorrow, but there was no time as she was hustled up the ladder.

Strong hands, hands she knew so well, grabbed her and pulled her up to the deck, and into his arms.

"Charley. My darling girl, I thought I'd lost you."

David was covered with soot and blood trickled down his arm. His face was grim and drawn in the red light. Smoke billowed across the deck of the *Fancy*, fires lighting the sunset as the injured vessel listed, its mainmast gone, a tangle of rigging and injured men on the deck. Her instinct was to go to the injured, but David gripped her arm tight.

"No, Doctor, you're to go to the boats, Captain's orders."

A blur of gray shot across the tilting deck.

"Pirate!" she called out to the cat, but David wouldn't stop. He took her to the rail where she could see their enemy through the smoke, the marines in the rigging taking shots at the Americans. David pushed her aside and stood there in his torn white shirt. A manic grin spread on his blackened face as he presented himself, a perfect target. He raised the speaking trumpet Bryant shoved into his hands.

"Ahoy, *Caeneus*," he called across the water, and the lieutenant directing the action ordered the marines and gunners to hold their fire.

"Will you strike your colors, Captain Fletcher?"

He ignored the question and called back, "I am returning something that belongs to you British, Lieutenant."

He gestured to Bryant, who pulled Charley alongside David. She could smell the smoke and sweat on him and wanted to throw her arms around him and cling to him and never let go, but he took her by the arm and shoved her up to the rail.

"This is an English prisoner I took off of the *Lady Jane*. I am returning Miss Alcott to you, with my compliments."

Across the water the midshipmen who'd escorted her aboard the *Caeneus* so long ago said, "Sir! That is Dr. Alcott that came from the *Lady Jane* to assist Dr. Murray!"

The English officer looked at Charley, her cropped hair, her bloodied brown coat, and he frowned, but called back, "You say Doct—Miss—that person is your prisoner?"

"Aye. I took this woman by force off of her ship." He rounded on her and stared deep into her eyes, into her soul. "Would you deny that, Miss Alcott? Or would you swear an oath before God and the courts that I took you prisoner?"

His eyes pleaded with her to do as he said, and she understood that this was a last effort by David to protect her. If she had served willingly aboard the enemy privateer, she would be called a traitor, and could even be charged as a pirate. She wanted to protest with all of her heart that no matter what circumstances brought her aboard the *Fancy*, now it was where she wanted to be, alongside him.

He would not keep her at his side though, not in the midst of this battle. She could do this one thing for him. When he joined her aboard the *Caeneus* as a prisoner of the English, Charley would do all in her power to help him.

"No," she said strongly, looking into the golden eyes that

reflected the flames of the burning schooner. "I cannot deny it. Captain Fletcher took me off the *Lady Jane* against my will and held me prisoner aboard his vessel."

"Thank you, Charley," he said for her ears alone. Then he raised his voice. "Take her to the boats, Mr. Bryant."

Charley thrust herself forward for one final kiss, a last embrace before they were separated, but Bryant had hold of her and was helping her down the ladder to the boat below. The air was loud with the sound of the fire and the shouts of men jumping into the water amidst the flaming debris that floated around them. More marines stood at the rail of the frigate, their weapons aimed on their new prisoners as they were hauled aboard.

She craned around in her seat to see David, but he was hidden in the smoke and the confusion. Surely he would grab a line and come over? If the Americans were sent to prison in England she would follow him there, she would wait for him, the war could not last forever, she would help him.

The thoughts raced through her head but still she didn't see him.

"Where's the captain?" she said, turning to Bryant as they made fast to the frigate.

"He will be the last to leave, making sure his men are safely off the ship."

"The *Fancy* is lost, isn't it?"

He started to answer but the British seamen were hustling them up the ladder to the deck of the *Caeneus*. One of the sailors helped her aboard and marines waited there to take them into custody.

"Hold there," a young voice said. The midshipman, younger even than Charley, came to them.

"Miss Alcott, I'm to take you to Dr. Murray. He will have charge of you until we get to Jamaica."

But she wasn't listening to him as she scanned the deck of

the ship across from her. The *Caeneus* was pulling away from the crippled American vessel.

"Why are we leaving? David isn't here yet!"

"It's the rum." Bryant's face was grim as he watched the *Fancy*. "Those barrels in the hold make the ship a floating bomb. That's why Captain Fletcher stayed behind, to be sure you and the men got off of it."

The smoke cleared and she saw David standing on deck, grinning at her like a madman as he waved.

"No!" she screamed, lunging forward as Bryant grabbed onto her shoulders to keep her from leaping over the side. "Jump, David!"

He blew her a kiss.

"Do not forget me, Charley!"

The explosion threw her off her feet. She scrambled back up as the *Fancy* flared into a fireball, turning the darkening sky into a vision of hell. Wood and red-hot metal rained down on the frigate as the English sailors yelled and ducked for cover. Charley stood like a pillar of salt as embers smoked around her like brimstone, watching for a movement in the water, a sign of life.

But there was nothing, nothing except wreckage floating on the ocean.

"Never," she whispered hoarsely. "I will never forget you, David Fletcher."

Bryant had hold of her arm, supporting her, but he released her when the marine tugged on his coat to take him away.

"Miss? Miss Alcott?"

The midshipman was speaking to her.

"I'm Andrews, miss, Daniel Andrews. Dr. Murray requests your assistance in the cock-pit."

"Yes, certainly," Charley said woodenly, turning away from the ashes of her dreams.

She followed Andrews down to the cock-pit, full of the injured of both nations. Dr. Murray barely glanced up from the patient on his table.

"Miss Alcott. Make yourself useful. These Yankees insist they want their doctor to treat them, which I suppose means you."

"Yes, Doctor," Charley said. She took a moment, only a moment, to press her hands over her eyes as if she could erase the image of the destroyed privateer, then sighed, put down her satchel and taking an apron off a peg, pushed up her sleeves.

The American injured came to her in an orderly fashion, some bitter, some dazed, none of them having much to say. They knew what awaited them. Detention in Jamaica, and then a transport to England. It was a new year, but they would spend 1815 at Dartmoor prison, far from home.

Some of the crew was missing, and the men confirmed her fears. She would not see Ives, or Stern, or Cook again in this world. She had no time to dwell on that now, not with the burns and the wounds and the limbs needing splinting or amputation.

She worked alongside Dr. Murray well into the night. Sometimes he assisted her with her Americans. He was still without his assistant surgeon, and the loblolly boy was glad to be relieved of duties beyond his ability and pass them onto the stranger.

Murray spoke little to her, but he watched everything she did, assessing her, correcting when necessary. It was good to be busy, to have to use all of her energies and skills on keeping the men alive. It kept her from having to think.

When the last of the men had been seen and either taken to sick bay or sent back to their hammocks, Murray looked at her for a long moment, then gestured to the basin and water waiting for them. Charley washed as best she could. She was red past her elbows.

He noted the condition of her blood-soaked clothing and said, "I should be able to cull some clothing from the midshipmen that will fit you."

He dried his own hands and cleared his throat.

"You will stay in my cabin, Miss Alcott, and I will share quarters with another officer."

She looked at him through the fog of her own senses and realized he was speaking to her.

"Pardon?"

"I said you will stay in my cabin. Come, I will take you to your quarters." She was glad he wasn't being compassionate and sympathetic. She couldn't handle that right now.

They stepped out of the cockpit into the gloom belowdecks.

"Where are the Americans being held, Doctor?"

"They are in the hold under guard. Are you hungry? You should eat something."

He was watching her, his old-young face grim. Murray had lost his share of patients today, and it told on him, despite his calm demeanor. She wondered how he dealt with it, day in, day out, and if he ever woke up, as she did, with tears on his face.

"No. I want nothing to eat."

"Eat anyway. You might be needed during the night."

"Yes, Doctor." It was easier than arguing with him. She was so drained that she would have fallen asleep on her feet if images of the exploding schooner didn't keep reverberating through her head.

He preceded her into his cabin to gather his gear. She wanted to tell him that she was grateful, for the berth and for him allowing her to assist him, but all she could do was lean against the bulkhead and stare down at her bloodied shoes.

"Miss?"

She was roused from her fog to look down at a midshipman even younger than Andrews, who was clutching a bundle of rags.

A squirming bundle of rags.

"The Yankees said this belongs to you, miss. We found him floating on a hatch."

The youngster put down his burden, and a disgruntled and wet cat came out of the bag.

"Pirate!" Charley cried.

The cat looked at her in disgust, as if his being wet and his fur even more ragged than before was somehow her fault, then sat to clean himself just as Murray emerged from his cabin.

"A prize, Mr. Higgins?"

"Not much of one, Doctor," George Higgins said, looking at the ragged tom as Charley swooped him up.

"I beg to differ, Dr. Murray," Charley said, with more life in her voice. "Pirate here is an excellent mouser and earns his keep."

"Then we will leave him with you, Miss Alcott."

"Send for me if you need me tonight," she said, and looked up to see Murray watching her. He seemed to be about to say something else, but instead just opened the door to his cabin and ushered her in.

"Good night, Miss Alcott."

"Good night, Doctor," Charley said as the door closed behind her. There was some ship's biscuit and a piece of cheese on the table, but she couldn't bring herself to eat. She stripped off her clothing and saw the clean nightshirt folded neatly on the bunk. It was Dr. Murray's and far too broad for her, but she put it on and crawled into the bunk. Pirate took advantage of her distraction to eat some of the cheese, then jumped in with her and curled up at her side.

The noises and the smells on the frigate were familiar and for a moment she could close her eyes and think herself back aboard the *Fancy*, but then she saw David again, his face alight as he waved good-bye to her.

Only the cat heard her sob into her pillow in the darkness.

CHAPTER 21

It didn't matter that she'd been on her feet in surgery all of the night before, or that she'd cried herself to sleep. When she heard four bells of the morning watch Charley's eyes popped open, her body tuned to the beat of a working ship.

She sat up on the bunk and lit her lantern, then stared down at her hands, steady now that her night of weeping was behind her. Was this what an amputation was like? The pain, the knowing that a vital part of yourself was missing and you would never be whole again?

None of that made a difference, did it? She would carry on, because that was her duty, and because that is what David Fletcher would have asked of her. He could no longer help his men, but she could. This was the last gift she could give Davy, and she would give it with all of her strength.

"Yes?" she said in response to a knock at her door.

"'Mornin', miss," George Higgins said. "There are clothes for you, just outside the cabin. And Captain Doyle's compliments, ma'am, and would you join him in his cabin at eight bells—that is—"

"Thank you, Mr. Higgins, I know when eight bells is," she said with a smile to herself. "And thank your fellow officers for the clothing."

"Yes, ma'am. Dr. Murray said he expects you in sick bay this morning also," Higgins added, unnecessarily.

What did Murray think, that she would languish in her bunk weeping all day? Not that there wasn't a certain attraction to that, but it would never happen.

Pirate, too, was ready to get to work, and Charley released him from the cabin, scooping up the clothing there. She splashed cold water on her swollen eyes and brushed off her own coat as best she could, then donned the clean trousers, which fit rather well in the length, even if they were tight through the seat. The last thing she wanted to do was call attention to her anatomy, but her coat covered her enough to keep the men from staring. She hoped.

She took her journals from her satchel, because she knew if Dr. Murray was talking, she would be expected to take notes.

Her final act before heading to sick bay was to pause and look into the small mirror that was part of Murray's gear.

She looked no different, except for her red eyes. It is amazing that one could be so devastated and yet not show more signs of it. In primitive cultures women tore their hair and gashed themselves to show grief. Aboard ship, one picked up one's tools and got to work.

Charley took a deep breath, picked up her journal, and prepared to go to work.

The *Caeneus's* sick bay was located forward on the starboard side and Murray was writing in his own journals when she entered.

"Miss Alcott."

"Dr. Murray."

They kept their voices low so as to not disturb the handful of men remaining after surgery. Most had returned to their hammocks, the Americans to the hold, but a few needed more observation and round-the-clock care. Canvas panels separated the injured from the smaller area where Murray now sat, awaiting the morning's sick call. He did not rise when she entered the room, but he motioned her to the other chair crowding the small space. Charley sat, adjusting her trousers, an unconscious gesture. He studied her for a moment as if assessing her general condition.

"You will attend me in the mornings, Miss Alcott, and during the day as needed. We will be in Jamaica soon, but until then you can be of use here."

"Thank you," Charley said. "I appreciate the opportunity to broaden my knowledge and skills."

"I cannot imagine why," he calmly said, wiping his pen. "You will not be allowed to practice medicine in Jamaica. But you might be able to assist Dr. Wilson, so I feel obliged to see that you are as prepared as possible."

He looked at his notes. "You have been busy with the Americans."

"Here?"

"Here and aboard their ship." He folded his hands together across his stomach and studied her from beneath heavy brows. His skin was rough and weathered, browned from years of exposure to the harsh sunlight on the ocean.

"I had heard you were taken off the *Lady Jane*," he said. "We looked for the privateer, but had to move on with the rest of the convoy."

"You did not tell anyone my secret?"

"It was not my secret to tell."

Charley digested this in silence. What it would have

meant if the *Caeneus* had pursued them when she was first taken? Henry Fletcher would be dead, and she would never have had the joy and the sorrow of knowing Black Davy Fletcher. She would not have been the *Fancy's* surgeon.

"Were you..." he hesitated, as if wondering the most delicate way to phrase his question. "Were you treated with courtesy by the Americans?"

Charley almost smiled. She wondered what the brusque surgeon would say if she responded that the Americans treated her so well they took her to a brothel to be entertained.

"The Americans treated me with all due courtesy. They were pleased to have someone aboard with medical skills, even as lacking as mine were. Because of that, I do have one request, Dr. Murray."

He raised his brows and waited. She cleared her throat.

"I feel responsible for my—the Americans, since I was their doctor. I would like to request that they be brought up out of the hold for regular exercise until we reach Jamaica. Staying down there in that miasmic atmosphere around the clock will contribute to disease, and create more work for both of us."

"I do not know what wild tales they may have told aboard that privateer, Miss Alcott, but we are not barbarians in the Royal Navy. Of course we will take care of our prisoners and safeguard their health. Now, we have a busy day ahead of us. Show me how you have been keeping records of your patients. Do you use the Clifton method?"

"Yes, Doctor," she said, leaning forward and placing her journals on the desk. While on one hand she was feeling demoted after being the surgeon aboard the *Fancy*—with all of the respect and approbation that status carried—she appreciated this opportunity to talk with someone who wouldn't look at her in horror as she enthusiastically waxed on about suppurating wounds.

"See, here is the record on Henry Fletcher…" and Charley showed Dr. Murray the daily log of each patient, including the climate and season where the disease occurred, urine output, pulse, respiration, localized symptoms and more.

He made no complaint but pointed out some areas where she might improve her notes, and offered his own insights into some of her more troubling cases.

"Cook will not be in need of that care now. He died aboard the *Fancy* during the fight."

"Did you kill many aboard the *Fancy*?"

Charley dropped her journal. He was looking at her as if he'd just asked her to pass the milk for tea.

"Do not stare at me like that. If you practice medicine you will kill some patients. We all do."

"I had men die because I could not save them," she whispered, and in her mind she saw Purcell, smiling at one of Mr. Bryant's quips.

"You are not God, Miss Alcott. It would be lovely if I woke up tomorrow morning able to cure pox and give every kitten in the world a good home. I cannot do that either. All we humans can do is stave off the inevitable for some men, but not for others."

His matter-of-fact voice and direct gaze was more bracing than all of the homilies and rationalizations Charley could have found on her own, and she felt a featherweight of tension ease out of her spine. She needed this, the company of someone who understood her, or at least understood what she was trying to accomplish, whether or not he approved of her as a person.

The ship's bell chimed eight times and she shook herself.

"Captain Doyle asked to see me, Dr. Murray."

"Return here when you are done. We have much to do today."

"Yes, Doctor."

❧

There were marines posted outside Captain Doyle's cabin and Charley wondered if they were a standard feature, or if they were there because of all the American prisoners. They kept their eyes forward and didn't boldly examine her in her breeches, as she had seen the Cannies do when she walked through the ship.

Captain Doyle started to rise as she entered the cabin, then hesitated, confused by her attire and status, then stood awkwardly and gestured to a chair in front of his desk.

"You are Miss Alcott?"

"Yes, Captain, I am Charlotte Alcott of Little Abbot, in Devon.

Captain Doyle's voice was raspy, and Charley saw scar tissue above the collar of his shirt. She guessed he'd been wounded in the throat at some point in his career. Certainly the rest of him that she could see bore testimony to years of service at sea. His face was browned to the shade of weathered mahogany and a scar creased his shiny scalp, running down past a battered ear.

The cabin was more commodious than Captain Fletcher's, but there were some similarities. Both had a compass mounted overhead and stern lights aft. Captain Doyle's frigate boasted a cot suspended on chains for sleeping, rather than the bunk aboard the *Fancy*. The room had charts and logs and personal items, but Captain Doyle's cabin looked more lived-in, as if he had no other place to call home, where in David Fletcher's cabin there were reminders that home was ashore in Baltimore.

"Miss Alcott, I must ask you some questions about your time aboard the American ship to determine your"—he hesitated—"status aboard the *Caeneus.*"

"I understand," she said, swallowing. If the captain thought her a traitor or a whore or an insane woman who harbored delusions she could be a doctor, it would affect her treatment here, in Jamaica, and maybe even back in England.

Doyle made no pretense of not staring at her, and she realized it was part of what was making her uncomfortable aboard the *Caeneus.* When everyone thought her a man, there were no second glances. Even when the Americans knew her sex they accepted her and treated her as one of them.

To her fellow Englishmen, she was a freak. Rather than huddle in her chair, Charley straightened her shoulders and looked Captain Doyle in the eye. She'd faced down American privateers, she would not cower before her own countryman.

Black Davy Fletcher would have expected no less from the *Fancy's* doctor.

"I am prepared to answer your questions, Captain Doyle."

He looked startled at her firm tone of voice, but he cleared his throat and glanced down at his notes.

"I spoke with Dr. Murray and also with the mate of the American vessel, Mr. Bryant. They confirmed that you were disguised as a man aboard the *Lady Jane,* acting as their surgeon, and were taken when the *Fancy* raided the merchantman. Is that correct?"

"Yes, I was making my way to Jamaica to join my godfather, Dr. Curtis Wilson."

"Dr. Murray spoke well of you, Miss Alcott, as did Mr. Bryant. Based on my conversations with them I see no reason to detain you once we get to Jamaica. In the meantime, you can continue to assist Dr. Murray." He looked down at his notes again, then at her. "I regret that we do not have women's clothing for you aboard the *Caeneus.*"

"I am comfortable in these clothes, Captain."

"It is unnatural for a woman to wear men's clothing, Miss Alcott, but this is a warship and we have no other option." He frowned at her. "Let me be perfectly clear on one point—regardless of how you comported yourself aboard that Yankee vessel, there will be no untoward behavior on my ship!"

Charley felt her lips thin into an angry line, but she gripped her temper and the chair arms. "For most of my time aboard the American vessel they were unaware of my true identity. I assure you, Captain Fletcher would not have kept me aboard had he thought me anything other than a competent surgeon forced into doctoring his crew. I will give you no cause for complaint, Captain Doyle."

"See that you don't, miss."

She shut her mouth, afraid she would say something to antagonize the man. Maybe something sarcastic. Though she was beginning to wonder if sarcasm could be the captain's prerogative if the man wasn't bright enough to use it.

Then she was afraid she'd break down and cry in front of him, because the captain in this cabin wasn't her captain.

But Captain Doyle only harumphed and rose, and Charley got to her feet as well.

"I will release you to Dr. Murray then, Miss Alcott. And one final thing—I will not have any fraternization with the Americans. If you need to see them, do so under Dr. Murray's supervision."

"Yes, Captain," Charley said through gritted teeth. As she exited his cabin she wanted to do something extremely childish, like stick out her tongue at the closed door.

David would have been amused.

That almost did bring the tears gushing out again, but she'd be damned if she would cry in front of the marines, so she went quickly to her cabin, noted the rat carcasses lined up there, and scooped Pirate up into her arms so that she could sob all over his furry back in the privacy of her quarters.

Pirate bore this damp assault with stoic endurance.

But even tears run out, eventually, and she washed her face, noted someone else had disposed of Pirate's offerings—would they be on the midshipmen's menu this evening?—and returned to the sick bay. Dr. Murray was examining one of her Americans, Perry, who gave her a small wave and a smile.

"There is some burgoo and tea left for you," Murray said.

"Thank you, I am not hungry."

"Miss Alcott, I have neither the time nor the patience for your maidenish vapors. You will eat and keep your strength up or you will be no use to me at all."

She sighed, but sat at the desk and began to eat. To her surprise, when she looked down at the bowl it was scraped clean. If she could look at herself dispassionately, as a doctor, she would acknowledge that she was young, and healthy, and life goes on even when all you care about is lying at the bottom of the ocean.

When she finished eating, Murray discussed with her Perry's burns and whether he was best treated with olive oil or simple ointment. Perry looked on with great interest as the two medicos debated. Charley knew the entire conversation would be repeated later in the hold, for discussing their individual ailments and treatments was high entertainment amongst the sailors.

Eventually Perry was sent back under guard, passing a Cannie in the passageway who was holding a reddened cloth against his forearm.

"What happened to you, Turner?" Murray looked up from his notes.

"Knife slipped while I was splicin' a line."

"Miss Alcott, will you see to it, please?"

Turner reared back and clutched the cloth to his arm, looking wide-eyed at Charley.

"Oi! That's that she-doctor the Yankees were braggin' about! I don't want her touching me! It ain't natural!"

There was complete silence as Murray looked at Turner for a long, drawn-out moment.

"Are you questioning my decisions, in my own sick bay?"

His voice was low and calm, but there was something in it that sent a chill down Charley's back.

Turner wisely said nothing.

"You will let Dr. Alcott treat you, Turner, and I will hear no more dissent."

He didn't have to ask if his instructions were clear and understood. Pirate the cat would have known better than to question it.

"Come over into the light, and let me have a look at your arm," Charley finally said.

He looked at her with apprehension, but there must have been something reassuring in her nondescript appearance and her smile. She could only imagine how the Americans' tales had turned her into a combination of Hippocrates and Athena.

She washed and stitched Turner's arm, distracting him with conversation about his home in Yorkshire. When she was done he examined it, and allowed that the stitches were neat, which wasn't a surprise seeing as how she was a woman and used to stitchery.

She held her tongue and sent him off with the usual admonitions not to strain the arm and to try and keep it clean.

"Something amuses you, Miss Alcott?" Murray said as the door closed.

"You referred to me as 'Dr. Alcott' when you were talking to Turner."

The ship's surgeon dismissed this with a grunt. "That was purely a slip of the tongue. Do not let it go to your head."

But Charley's step was just a little lighter when she left the sick bay. Just as she'd scolded Henry Fletcher, life did go on, after all, even when you were missing part of yourself and knew you would never be whole again.

CHAPTER 22

It took the *Caeneus* a week to reach Port Royal, but in that week Charley learned a great deal more about medicine, and about herself, as she accompanied Dr. Murray on his twice daily rounds. The ship's medical man was surgeon, physician and apothecary for the crew, and she appreciated that it was a rare opportunity to study with the taciturn Scotsman. She assisted him in the sick bay, but there was no further naval action to bring her into the cock-pit.

This was a relief. Any enemy ship they encountered at this point would be an American, with France cleared out by earlier action, and Spain an ally. Charley always considered herself a loyal Englishwoman, but it was harder to see the "Jonathans" as the enemy.

When you live with people, and bind their wounds, those differences fall away.

When you fall in love with an American…

She wrenched her mind away from that direction because Murray was discussing Lieutenant Huntley's bladder stones, and whether an operation would be necessary.

"May I assist?"

He looked at her, and for a moment Charley thought she saw his lips twitch toward a smile, but it must have been a trick of the light.

"I believe that if you assist with this procedure Mr. Huntley will never speak to me again. Which is not necessarily a bad thing, but no, I will wait until we are in Jamaica and then if I feel it is necessary I can have assistance from another surgeon."

"A male surgeon."

"There is no other kind, Miss Alcott."

Charley wisely held her tongue. There was no use in arguing with the man, and she felt she'd made tremendous progress in being allowed to assist him.

The busy days since she was taken aboard the *Caeneus* helped to keep her mind off the unknown fate awaiting her in Jamaica. Being mentored by Dr. Murray also put her under his protection in the eyes of the crew. Some of the midshipmen sniggered and whispered behind their hands when she passed them, but they never said anything when the doctor was about, for his memory was long and his chest of emetics was well-stocked. They knew better than to get on his bad side.

Assisting him also allowed her to care for "her" Americans, for which she would always be grateful. The *Caeneus* was every inch a Royal Navy ship, its decks holystoned and its brightwork gleaming. If Charley longed for the more relaxed attitudes of an American schooner and its crew's demands for "sailors rights," argued loudly and openly amongst themselves, then it was a revolutionary viewpoint she kept to herself. She was back amongst her countrymen now, and she helped these Americans best by being their doctor. She joined the men of the *Fancy* when they were brought abovedeck for their daily exercise, walking with them and helping to keep their spirits up. It was a treatment that worked both ways.

"Cheer up, Charley, the war cannot last forever."

"I thought I was supposed to be boosting your morale, Mr. Bryant."

She looked over at the weathered older man walking beside her, still in the stained and torn clothing from his last battle. She wore her own raggedy brown coat like a uniform, prideful that it had seen service with these brave Americans, her enemies, and her dearest friends. She would miss Mr. Bryant desperately. He was now a part of her world, and along with Mr. Lewis was a link to Davy Fletcher she didn't want to relinquish.

"The war is over for me, Mr. Bryant. I will, I hope, find a snug berth in Jamaica and put thoughts of life at sea behind me."

Bryant chuckled. "Too late for that. A snug berth? You are thinking like a sailor, not like a lubber."

Charley smiled as they strolled beneath the watchful eyes of the armed marines, their red-coats making them stand out like bright birds on the deck.

"Maybe I do have more salt in my blood than I did before, Mr. Bryant."

"You can still come to Baltimore. We would always welcome you there."

She looked away, so he would not see the moisture that suddenly made her vision hazy. She refused to shed any more tears. That part of her life was amputated, and it was time to move on.

"Thank you. That means a great deal to me. But I think you can understand," she continued gently, "why Baltimore cannot be where I would settle."

"Aye, of course I understand that," Bryant said, clearing

his throat and wiping his hand across his eyes. They kept walking, each lost in his or her own thoughts.

"I do have one request," Charley said suddenly.

Bryant looked at her.

"When you see Henry Fletcher, please tell him I asked after him, and wish him well. Now that he is the eldest Henry will be forced to take on Captain Fletcher's responsibilities to his family. I know David had every confidence in Henry."

"Indeed he did," Bryant said softly. "And David had every confidence in you as well. He would not want you to spend the rest of your life mourning him."

Charley said nothing in response to that. She did not know what the future held for her, but she knew she would always mourn her Handsome Davy. She looked over the larboard rail to the dark mass on the horizon. Jamaica was in sight, and she would say her good-byes tomorrow to her American friends.

"Try to stay off that leg as much as you can, Carville, and if it worsens, have the surgeon look at it right away."

"Aye, Dr. Alcott," Carville said, pulling on his forelock in a show of respect the Americans would normally never bother with, but they wanted to make a point to the Cannies that Charley was their doctor and they would treat her like Queen Amphitrite if it pleased them.

She turned to Murray, who was alongside her up on deck, when a commotion from the water brought them both to the gunwale. The boat was returning with a wildly waving Mr. Andrews, calling something out to those still aboard the *Caeneus*.

"It's peace, Miss Alcott, Dr. Murray, the Americans have surrendered!"

"That don't sound right," muttered Carville.

Charley suspected, too, that there was more to this than Andrews's statement, but waited until the young man came back on board.

"I just heard it from Captain Doyle," he said excitedly. "While we were cruising a treaty was signed between Britain and the Yankees!"

"America surrendered?" Charley asked.

"Well, how else would there be peace?" the youngster said.

"I suggest we wait for a full report from more experienced hands," Murray said, and Charley agreed with him.

"Oh, and I have a letter for you, Miss Alcott," Andrews said, reaching into his bag.

Charley took the letter, but before she opened it she said, "Mr. Andrews, do you know when this peace treaty was signed?"

"Back in December, the captain said, in Ghent."

She felt the blood drain from her head. The battle between the *Fancy* and the *Caeneus* was fought on February 20th.

"Miss Alcott? Are you quite all right?"

Murray was looking at her keenly.

"What a waste," Charley murmured. There had been no need for it. No need for the injuries and the amputations. No need for David's senseless death. The peace treaty was already signed, the war was over. There had been no need for men to die, or bleed, or get maimed for the glory of it and the gold and the love of their countries. No need at all.

Murray looked like he was about to say something, but Carville spoke up, saying stubbornly, "I still don't believe the United States surrendered."

"A peace treaty is not a surrender," she said. "I am certain there is more to this than we know."

Indeed, when Captain Doyle returned there was a full

report. A peace treaty had been negotiated restoring Great Britain and the United States to their antebellum status.

"But what of the prisoners?" Charley asked Captain Doyle.

"A Yankee trader from France bound for Charleston put into port a few days back. That is how we got the news. The governor is not interested in having a gang of Americans roaming through Kingston, and asked if we would 'host' them for a while longer until they can ship out with their countrymen."

It was that simple. Men who two days earlier would have run each other through or blown each other to pieces, now were up on deck toasting each other's countries with carefully rationed grog. Captain Doyle wisely put a limit on the amount of alcohol served, knowing that it wouldn't take much to re-ignite the conflict on a smaller scale.

"Captain Fletcher told me I do not understand men, Mr. Bryant," Charley said in bemusement later that night. "I have to agree with him."

He shrugged his shoulders. "They fought when they needed to fight. Now they're anxious to go home. We sailors are not complicated creatures, Doctor."

They were of an equal height and he looked over at her, putting his hand on her shoulder.

"Are you certain you will not come to the United States with us?"

Charley smiled at him in the dusk as the men sang patriotic songs of both countries, avoiding the more incendiary ones, such as that new ditty from Baltimore about Fort McHenry.

"No, Mr. Bryant, my life is here now. Dr. Wilson is sending a carriage for me tomorrow and I will be living with him."

Her godfather's letter was everything she could have

hoped for. He was thrilled to have her on the island, he wanted her to come live with him, he was anxious to introduce her to Jamaican society.

Charley had not made mention of her masquerade, thinking it a story best told in person. Then Dr. Wilson could decide if she was a suitable house guest, or if he wished her to return to England.

For tonight though she would enjoy her last evening as "Dr. Alcott," at least among the Americans. She dined with the officers of the *Caeneus*, who asked Mr. Bryant to join them as well. The Brits put on a feast, knowing they could restock in Jamaica and not wanting to stint in front of their recent foes. The ship's livestock was sacrificed for the cause, and the officers and their American guests dined on fresh chicken and roast lamb, with a pudding that all applauded as the final course. Toasts were drunk to President Madison and to the king, and Charley was pressed with invitations to visit when she returned to England.

Dr. Murray was largely silent throughout the evening, but that was not unusual. He drank sparingly, watching the other men celebrating. Charley had been laughing at one of Lieutenant Huntley's jokes about Jamaican cooking and looked up to see Murray's gaze resting upon her. The knock on her cabin door later that night as she packed also was not unusual, given that she was often enough called out to help with the sick.

"Dr. Murray!" She smiled at her mentor when she opened the cabin door. "I am glad you came by, as I have not yet had a chance to thank you for all you have done for me."

"Mmmph," he said, a sound signifying much and nothing, as Charley knew it was part of his repertoire when dealing with the ill. But he looked oddly uncomfortable.

"May I come in?"

"Is something wrong?"

He entered and stood in his cabin with his hands clasped behind his back, peering at her intently. His eyes had gold flecks in the green and brown, she thought suddenly. Odd that she was only noticing that now.

"I have come here tonight to ask you to marry me, Miss Alcott."

Charley blinked her eyes. "Did you just ask me to marry you?"

"Yes." He cleared his throat, rocking back nervously on his feet, his hands still clasped behind his broad back. She was certain she had never seen the phlegmatic surgeon so discomfited.

"Yes, Miss Alcott. I would like you to do me the honor of accepting my hand in marriage. I believe we would suit each other well, and circumstances in my life—and the end of the war—lead me to think I should take a wife now. You are not like other young ladies I have met. You are sensible and intelligent and, as I said, we would suit one another."

Charley knew she was staring, but she couldn't help herself. The gruff Scotsman never gave her any leeway in his sick bay, and his views on women practicing surgery and medicine seemed to be engraved in the granite he resembled. She had to admit that he wasn't an unhandsome man, being a couple of inches taller than her, and solid through the shoulders and arms from years of setting bones and performing amputations.

But he wasn't Black Davy Fletcher.

"You do me great honor, Dr. Murray—" she said gently, then paused. "I do not even know your given name, Doctor."

"Alexander."

"You do me great honor, Alexander, and I am touched by your offer of marriage, but I do not believe we would suit. Not in that way."

He looked at her with the intensity he brought to his

medical practice, reading signs and symptoms in her face and stance.

"There was someone aboard the *Fancy* who was special to you, wasn't there?"

"Oh yes," Charley said, swallowing. "Someone special. But he is gone now."

Murray only nodded, then said, "I suspected that was the case."

He cleared his throat again.

"If you change your mind, or find that you need my assistance, you may call upon me anytime while I am in Jamaica. However, I hope to leave for England as soon as I can book passage."

He turned to leave, but Charley stopped him with a hand on his arm. When he looked back at her, eyebrows raised, she leaned over and kissed him on his stubbled cheek.

"I will always treasure your proposal of marriage. It does mean a great deal to me."

He said nothing more, but as he was leaving she had to ask.

"Dr. Murray, how old are you?"

He looked back, and this time there was a definite twinkle in his eyes.

"I am thirty-four years old. Practicing medicine ages one before one's time, a thought you might well keep in mind."

Charley smiled at him. "Goodnight, Dr. Murray."

"Goodnight, Miss Alcott."

CHAPTER 23

Dr. Curtis Wilson was anxiously pacing as Charley climbed out of the *Caeneus's* boat at Port Royal. The face beneath the planter's hat was wrinkled and weathered from the tropical sun beating down on them. From the slightly yellow cast of his face, she suspected her godfather suffered from malaria as well. He appeared startled when one of the midshipmen disembarking pointed to Charley as the young lady he awaited.

But when he opened his arms, his soft eyes sheened with emotion, Charley felt she'd finally found that safe berth she sought.

"Oh, my dear Charlotte, you look just like your mother!"

She smiled to herself as she leaned down and was enfolded in an embrace that smelled of tobacco and chinchona bark. Dr. Wilson was being kind, for she knew from her mirror that all she'd inherited from her petite and dainty mother were her eyes. It was good though to be with someone who knew her family, even with memories dimmed by time and sentiment.

"Let me look at you," he said, holding her at arm's length. Wilson, who barely came up to Charley's shoulder, frowned up at her.

"What have they done to you, my dear? You are quite drawn and undernourished!" But then he shook his head and said, "Listen to me go on. That's not important now, my dear, what is important is taking you home, and getting you settled."

A Cannie passed Charley a fishy-smelling basket over whose rim Pirate surveyed the landscape. Another Cannie carried her satchel and the pitiful amount of worldly goods she could call her own.

Ah, but the experiences I have had are priceless!

Wilson took her arm to lead her to the open phaeton where his coachman was holding the horses, but Charley stopped him for a moment to wave back to the Americans who were watching from the rail of the *Caeneus.*

"Goodbye, Mr. Bryant! You have my direction if you need assistance in Jamaica. And, Mr. Lewis, continue the treatment of that rash and it should clear in a fortnight."

The men waved at her, and she turned back to her godfather, who was sitting facing the rear and watching her with his eyebrows raised.

"I imagine you have quite a story to tell me, Charlotte Alcott, but it will wait until luncheon."

"Yes, Dr. Wilson."

"Oh, please call me Uncle Curtis as you did when you were a child!"

"Yes, Uncle Curtis."

The older man smiled and patted her hand. "You always were a sweet girl, Charlotte, following your father and me around the house and asking so many questions! I miss those times, and I miss Horatio."

"I miss him also," she said, "but finding you here, waiting for me, gives me great comfort in his absence, Uncle Curtis."

"I never married, Charlotte, so my friends' children are the closest I have come to having a family of my own. I do believe having a young lady in the house will be an invigorating tonic for this old man."

The phaeton was richly appointed and Charley realized her godfather must be quite well off, which eased her conscience. She did not want to be a burden to him, and judging from his finely tailored clothing and the carriage with matched pair, he appeared able to handle another mouth at his supper table. Her godfather entertained her on the drive around the harbor to Kingston, pointing out sights of interest along the way.

"….and tomorrow I will take you to Mrs. Norton, the dressmaker. She can outfit you for all the social occasions coming up, Charlotte. It will be a great pleasure to attend the routs and assemblies with such a lovely young lady on my arm!"

"I wish you would call me Charley, Uncle Curtis," she said.

"I could never do that!" He stared at her, looking nearly as scandalized as when she'd climbed out of the boat in her trousers. "Charlotte is such a pretty name! If you like, I will call you Lottie, but I could not bring myself to call my darling goddaughter by a boy's name."

She sighed as she felt part of herself slipping away, but in all fairness to her godfather, he was warm and welcoming where he might have shown her the door after her adventures at sea.

"I understand, Uncle. It may be best if we stick with Charlotte then."

Dr. Wilson's house was an airy enclave behind high walls

covered with bougainvillea, the misty Blue Mountains hovering in the background.

A Jamaican woman with dusky skin splattered with freckles across her wide face met them at the door and introduced herself as Mrs. Mansfield, the housekeeper.

"Annabelle, do you have a frock Charlotte might borrow to wear to the dressmaker's tomorrow?"

Mrs. Mansfield looked at Charley and they both started to laugh while Dr. Wilson stood there, confused.

"Men!" the housekeeper said, shaking her head. "Dr. Wilson, this young lady is two heads taller than me and my dresses would be wide enough to fit two of her inside!"

"Oh dear," he said, realizing what the problem was. "But how can I take Charlotte to the dressmaker then?"

"Dr. Wilson, you are an important man in this town. Send Mrs. Norton a note, sir, and ask her to come here. I am sure she will be delighted to do that. In the meantime," Mrs. Mansfield said in her softly accented voice, "I imagine Miss Charlotte would like some luncheon and a chance to settle in."

"Luncheon sounds lovely, Mrs. Mansfield," Charley said, and the housekeeper smiled, showing an impressive array of white teeth. Dr. Wilson escorted Charley upstairs to her room, an open spot that had shutters cast wide to let in the air and light, and a veranda for sitting outside. The bed was hung with mosquito netting, and there was a dressing table with a brush set, and a separate bathing room. All was painted in a buttery yellow with white trim, and it looked warm and inviting.

"I hope you like your accommodations," he said with a touch of shyness. Charley put her hand on his arm.

"It is everything a young lady could desire, Uncle Curtis. You have made me feel most welcome."

"You are family now, Charlotte. I want you to think of this as your home."

That would be difficult, she thought, after he left her to freshen up before luncheon. She was overwhelmed by the amount of space that was to be hers. After months aboard ship, living in cramped quarters where every inch of room was precious, it was almost frightening to think about sleeping where the ceiling was so high, the walls so wide apart, the bed so soft.

She sat on the bed, and leaned down to sniff the pillow. It smelled of lavender and fresh air. She was used to her pillow smelling of salt, with a slight tang of mildew, and wondered if she could sleep in such a strange environment.

"Oh well, I'll adjust." Charley sighed, looking around at the luxurious appointments.

For luncheon there was fish brought to market fresh that morning, served with ackee fruit fried with oil and spices. It resembled scrambled eggs, but Charley pronounced it deli-cious. The bountiful fruits available, the bananas, mangoes, papaya and more, delighted her after the sea rations of the *Caeneus*. As they ate a young boy sat in a corner, pulling a rope which rotated a fan stirring the air around the diners, and the strong light coming in through the open doors was filtered through wooden shutters to make the room inviting and comfortable.

After luncheon Charley broached the subject of why she had thrown herself on the hospitality of her godfather. She gave him an abbreviated and highly edited version of her life over the past months, and watched in dismay as his face grew redder in the telling.

"This is a shocking tale, Charlotte Alcott! You should have stayed in England and written to me immediately. I would have fetched you myself!"

She took a sip of the light wine, feeling the need for fortification.

"I no longer had a home, Uncle Curtis. My father's illness left me with very little and we did not own our house. Where would I have lived while waiting for you?"

He looked ready to explode, but she plowed ahead.

"You have not seen me for years, Uncle, and you do not know the life I was living. I could not stay in Little Abbott, not without my father. It was a good life, but it had its difficulties and I would have been lost waiting there for someone to rescue me."

She brushed the hair back off of her forehead, an automatic gesture for someone who could not look as if there was a feminine fringe of curls framing "his" face.

"My father raised me as best he could after my mother died, and trained me as his apprentice. I love my work, Uncle Curtis. I practice medicine because it is my life, and because I can do some good for people."

"But, my dear child, the things you have seen and done! This is no life for a gently bred young lady! Medicine is a dirty business, and surgery in particular is a task fit only for craftsmen capable of removing bits and pieces. You might as well be an itinerant bonesetter as a surgeon."

"The surgeons I worked with were honorable and skilled, and my own father practiced surgery when it was necessary."

"Stuck out in the middle of nowhere, Horatio had no choice but to lower himself that way. No, that was not the life you were meant for, Charlotte Alcott!" He softened his voice. "I know you are used to keeping busy, and you wish to be helpful, and I understand that. But give me the opportunity to show you what you have been missing as a young lady. You may find you like it, and I expect once you meet an eligible young man or two these silly ideas about practicing medicine will no longer be an issue."

For that was what it was all really about. Dr. Wilson made it clear that his duty to her dead parents meant marrying her off to a suitable man, and a suitable man certainly did not want a woman used to treating the pox and administering clysters to strangers.

"But what if I do not find a suitable man to marry? My unconventional past could make this difficult. And I am honest enough to know that my looks will not drive men to compose odes to my features."

She didn't feel she needed to add that her status as a non-virgin wouldn't help in the marriage market.

He looked dismayed at her blunt self-assessment, but drummed his fingers on the table as he thought.

"Let us see what happens this year. Will you grant me that much? A year to see if we can find you a situation that suits you?" He reached across the table and patted her hand, wincing at the roughness of her skin. "I do not want you to be unhappy here, Charlotte, far from it. But you must give yourself a chance. And please, give me a chance as well. If you indulge me on this it would make me quite happy."

Charley lowered her eyes from his sincere gaze. She was ashamed at her temper, and chastised herself. Her godfather welcomed her and she threw his gifts back in his face.

"That does not seem at all unreasonable, when you put it that way, Uncle Curtis. I will do my best to fit in here, as you wish."

When Mrs. Norton arrived to make Charley's wardrobe, she didn't give the trousers a second glance. A slim, red-haired woman of indeterminate years, Mrs. Norton also did not affect a French accent, as so many dressmakers did. Most importantly, she listened to Charley's concerns.

"These styles constrict the movement of my arms. I cannot be comfortable in such a fashion."

"We can do with a different sleeve, Miss Alcott. Perhaps something in a bodice *a l'enfant*? It is fortunate that the fashion now is for fuller sleeves. But I must insist on the carnation pink. It is a color that suits you and will bring out the shine in your hair. In addition, it is a color quite in fashion!"

"Heaven forbid I should scare away a man by not being fashionable enough," Charley muttered, turning on the stool where she'd been ordered to stand. She shivered in the cool morning air, since she was wearing nothing but a hastily purchased chemise.

"Think of my reputation, if not your own, Miss Alcott."

She looked down at the kneeling seamstress to see if she was making a jest. She appeared in deadly earnest and Charley relented. She didn't want to make a fool of herself in public, and Mrs. Norton's reputation was formed by how people viewed her creations.

Besides, rather than be critical of her unconventional looks, as she'd always feared a dressmaker would be, Mrs. Norton was blunt in her assessment.

"You will do quite nicely in my gowns," the seamstress said as she rose to her feet and walked around the young woman. "You have a long and lean form, which is all the style right now. Also, your bosom is not overly large."

"That is a good thing?"

"It is when one wishes to be fashionable. I sell restricting corsets to women who long for a silhouette such as yours."

Charley shuddered at the thought of binding her breasts again. That was one thing she did not miss from her days masquerading as a man. Encouraged by the dressmaker's assessment of her form, she went further and insisted that some of her everyday dresses be cut to be worn without a corset. After years of being bound tighter than a sausage she was reveling in the freedom to go about unfettered. If one was "blessed" with a small bosom and slight hips, it made sense to take advantage of what nature bestowed.

When Mrs. Norton returned the next day with two finished dresses, Charley smiled to herself as the dressmaker turned her this way and that, taking in a stitch or pulling at a seam. She'd been afraid of wearing women's clothing, afraid of looking foolish. But once she realized how much more comfortable a lady's muslins and silks would be in this tropical climate than the heavy coats, waistcoats, cravats and boots worn by the gentlemen, she was quite pleased to play the part of a young lady of fashion.

If she had to be perfectly honest with herself, Charley would say that after all these years of masquerading as her father's son, and as Dr. Alcott, she was reveling in being a girl. She smoothed her hand over her arm, loving the feel of silky fabrics against her skin, light fabrics that moved with the breezes. Mrs. Norton explained how different colors added to her appearance, what colors to avoid, and how a strategically placed bow or ruffle could highlight one feature or disguise another. It was an art that was all new to her, but fortunately, she had good guides in Mrs. Norton and in Tilly, the maid engaged for her by Mrs. Mansfield.

In the privacy of her room Charley practiced sitting properly, like a lady, her legs no longer sprawled open like a man's. It was a harder task than she expected, remembering not to stride, but to stroll, not to sit any which way, but with ankles together and back not touching the chair.

There were moments she missed the freedom of her man's attire, and at other moments, too many of them, she wondered what David would have thought to see her dressed so.

But those thoughts brought tears, so she tried to lock them away.

At night there was no escaping her memories in her lonely bed. She had never known how much she missed the touch of another human being before she fell into Black Davy's arms. The pain rolled over her in waves in the dark and she clutched her pillow to her chest waiting for the heartache to ease, the tears to cease.

Physician, heal thyself. Easy to say, hard to do, but each morning when she awoke and saw the circles beneath her eyes, and Dr. Wilson's concerned face, she vowed to move forward with her life. Longing for David would not bring him back, so she could only go on, and she threw herself into the study of being a young woman, just as her godfather wished.

When she protested the amount Uncle Curtis was spending, he brushed aside her concerns.

"I should have made inquiries into your welfare long ago, Charlotte. You are my goddaughter and this is an opportunity for me to make up for not being there for you when Horatio passed on."

Charley conceded when she realized how much he wanted to do this for her, and she allowed herself to be swept away in a billowing cloud of sarcenet and silks as the clothing continued to arrive. After months of having two coats to choose from, and one pair of trousers for when the other was being washed, she was buried under slippers and fans, stockings and chemises, petticoats and shawls. There were hats for the day and for the night, and gloves for all occasions.

Tilly demonstrated in her gentle, unassuming fashion why a maid was vital to a young woman of fashion, to get her in and out of her complicated garments at least twice each day.

"It all seems like a great deal of bother," Charley groused following a tiring afternoon of fittings. "When I had only two coats and two pair of trousers I didn't have to think about an entire ensemble with the proper gloves, stockings, reticule—what a chore!"

"But you looked so elegant in your new riding habit, Miss Charlotte, the one with the gold braid and the military jacket" Tilly murmured. "Wouldn't you rather wear that for your outings than your old clothes? And what would that habit be without its own little hat? Not nearly as striking or fashionable."

"I bow to your superior judgment, Tilly," she conceded. She did love her new habit of bright green broadcloth, embroidered down the front and cuffs *à la militaire*. The riding hat was black beaver trimmed with gold cord and tassels, and she thought it made her look elegant indeed. It had been ages since she'd been riding and Dr. Wilson, himself an excellent horseman, was patient with her while she re-learned how to handle her spirited little mare. They would take morning rides around town, and he'd introduce her to matrons and their daughters, and on occasion to select young men.

"Some of these fellows are scoundrels of the worst stripe, Charlotte," he warned after one encounter. "They are sent to the islands because of their misdeeds in England, and you must be careful of them."

She looked at him sideways as the breeze ruffled the tassels on her hat, but her godfather appeared completely serious. Apparently he'd chosen to forget she'd spent months amongst American "scoundrels" who would make these English ne'er-do-wells look like choirboys.

"Yes, Uncle," she said demurely, hiding her own smile.

After a few weeks, the hairdresser Mrs. Norton recommended took Charley's short locks and brushed them forward from the crown, using his scissors judiciously. What had been a severely masculine style was transformed, with soft curls framing her face and fringing her cheekbones. She had to acknowledge the style was not only fully feminine and easy to care for, but it did interesting things to her eyes.

Finally, the dance master who'd been hastily found to teach her the dances she'd need to know pronounced her ready to be seen in public, and she was thrust into a whirl of social events.

Winter in Jamaica was an endless round of balls and picnics, teas and horseback rides up into the cool mountains. A new face was always welcome and she was introduced to the younger members of Jamaican society, the sons and daughters of the planters and merchants, and some children of the aristocracy.

Word also leaked out that Dr. Wilson was establishing a very nice dowry on his goddaughter. Charley found herself to be far more interesting than she otherwise would have been to the bachelors, many of whom had been sent to Jamaica to make their fortunes.

"I suppose marrying well is one way of making one's fortune," she said to her uncle as she sipped her morning coffee—then she paused. Wasn't that exactly what David Fletcher had felt compelled to do?

Despite her new wardrobe and her new skills, she felt adrift. She was trying, really, to fit in for the sake of her dear Uncle Curtis, but she simply could not work up any enthusiasm for conversations with other young ladies about ribbon trims and where the waistband on dresses would be this year. After one or two outings she also learned that what gentlemen wished to talk to young ladies about was themselves, or the weather, or other commonplaces.

Charley never expected she would miss conversations over who could piss the farthest after a night of drinking ale in a dockside tavern, but even that was better than talking about the weather! Uncle Curtis would not discuss his more interesting cases with her, insisting such conversations were inappropriate for a young lady. Her suggestion that she volunteer at the Naval Hospital in Port Royal was met with stunned silence. She did not make that offer again.

"I have high hopes for this evening, Charlotte," Dr. Wilson was saying to her now as they drove through the evening dusk. "The Erskines are famous for their hospitality and their home is one of the area's finest."

The Erskine home, or "great house" as these buildings were styled, was built in the combination of Caribbean and English fashion that was uniquely Jamaican. A broad stone staircase led up to the lower portion, while the upper story with its wraparound veranda, opened to the soft breezes, spilled light and music out into the evening.

The carriage rolled to a stop and Charley was assisted down the step by the footman, his shining black skin a sharp contrast to the white wig he wore for the occasion. Dr. Wilson took her arm and smiled.

"I am fortunate to be escorting the loveliest lady here. I will have to arm myself against the young men who will flock to you, Charlotte!"

Charley smiled, for she felt fine indeed. That morning Mrs. Norton had delivered her last creation, just in time for the ball. The evening dress was of blue crepe the color of a stormy sea, over a silver-gray satin slip. The combination made Charley's eyes glow and even her smallish bosom looked fuller with the double fall of silver lace framing the round neckline. No one would mistake her for a boy in this attire!

"That gown requires a certain sophistication to make it work," Mrs. Norton had said as she tweaked the hem. "On another those colors might look dull, and it's not for a young girl during her first season, but you are one of the rare women who can do a gown like this justice. And that means more accolades for me," she added with no bashfulness at all.

There were gray satin slippers with silver-gilt rosettes, a lace fan, and a shawl of deepest sapphire with silver thread that would provide all the protection needed from the tropical breezes.

Even Dr. Wilson had ordered new evening clothes for the occasion so he would complement his goddaughter, and Charley thought him dashing in his midnight-colored evening coat and sparkling white linen, and told him so.

He patted her hand where it rested on his arm.

"This evening is for you, my dear, and that is all that matters."

She tamped down her guilt, again. Uncle Curtis was trying so hard, and she should not be ungrateful.

"I vow, Uncle, the ladies of Jamaica must be sun-touched to have let such a handsome bachelor slip through their fingers all these years!"

Charley smiled at his fond chuckle. She would try tonight, truly she would. But she very much feared that if she had to endure one more conversation about whether or not it would be a nice day on the morrow, she couldn't be responsible for her actions.

She was introduced to her hosts, and received a pat on the arm from the rotund hostess, whose red face gleamed in the lamp light.

"Your godfather brought all of my babes into the world, Miss Alcott, and is practically one of the family."

"Not surprising considering how many hours I spent here setting bones, Mildred, after one boyish adventure or another," Wilson said.

"You know the lads thought being pirates and whacking each other with wooden swords was just part of what they owed their Jamaican forebears," Erskine added. He was as skinny as his wife was round, with a hectic flush to his cheeks that concerned Charley.

"Mr. Erskine has consumption, doesn't he?" she said in a low voice as they walked into the ballroom.

"Charlotte…"

"I know, I know, I'm not supposed to diagnose."

Wilson sighed. "You are correct, however. Jonathan Erskine does have consumption, and the fact that he's lived long enough to see his sons grown is a great blessing and a comfort to him."

"I wonder if the climate here in the tropics ameliorates the affects of consumption…"

"Enough, Charlotte."

"Yes, Uncle," she said, adding her own sigh.

Charley already knew some of the young people from previous social events, and other young men crowded around asking for introductions, so her fears that she would end the night as a wallflower weren't realized.

She danced, and if she wished each of her partners had been one particular man, at least she did her dancing master credit.

She listened to their banal remarks with a polite smile, and if she wished it were another speaking to her, one who would be sarcastic and funny and loving, she did a credible job of hiding it. Even from herself.

But as the evening went on Charley felt more and more like she was outside her body, observing a young lady who danced, and smiled, and made light conversation, but someone who bore little resemblance to the *Fancy's* Dr. Alcott. Bore almost no resemblance to the woman who had shared Black Davy Fletcher's bunk.

She had been invited to waltz, but had declined. The dance was too intimate, too enticing. There was only one man with whom she wished to waltz, and he was not here. Charley stood instead on the veranda, fanning herself while her last dance partner went to fetch her a lemonade. The air was full of the fragrance of flowering ginger and jasmine, and the scent of tobacco and the voices of young men also drifted up to her. No doubt they'd snuck out for a smoke before their mamas could drag them off for another round of dancing with eligible planters' daughters.

"…I think you exaggerated, William, she's not nearly the awkward long Meg you warned us about."

"'Lotta' Charlotte? That's what I call her because there's so much of her. At least a lot lengthwise. Not much up top for a man to hold onto."

Charley froze, her hand clutching her fan, and leaned closer to the veranda rail to hear. William Wilcox was one of the young men she'd danced with earlier. She remembered him more for his appearance than his dancing skills, but it was easy to pick out his voice as he discussed her.

The men laughed at his quip, and he took it as encouragement to continue.

"I would not complain, however. I understand Dr. Wilson is putting a very nice settlement out for whomever marries Miss Alcott. With his plantation shares and no heirs of his own, a man could do quite well by marrying his goddaughter, no matter what she looks like."

"Money's all well and good, William," an unknown voice chimed in, "but I heard from one of the officers off the *Caeneus* that Charlotte Alcott was living for months with Americans aboard one of their privateers. Doesn't that concern you?"

His reply was muffled, but Charley heard the lewd laughter of the men below. There was a sharp "crack" and she looked down to see the new fan she was using broken in half.

When her escort returned with her lemonade, he must

have seen something in her face. He stuttered about needing to find his mother, and he hastily beat a retreat after pushing the cup into her hands.

But Charley was not after his carcass. She had other prey in mind. She set her cup down on the ledge with a thunk, tossed her broken fan behind her and returned to the ballroom.

～

"...I do not know why everyone was so upset. I thought pointing out the sore next to Mr. Wilcox's mouth and suggesting appropriate treatment for his condition would be appreciated. Especially if he is considering marriage. But I assure you, after what I heard and saw tonight, the list of eligible women will not include me!" She strode back and forth in the library, her steps hampered by the cut of her skirts and she finally stopped and threw up her hands in frustration.

"You would think someone would want to know if he has the pox or not, so he can take steps to treat it! We both know that's not going to be the only sore on his person!"

She happened to glance over at her godfather, then rushed to his side and helped him to a chair.

"Uncle Curtis!" Charley pulled at his neckcloth, opening it to allow some color back into his face. "Do you have a weak heart?"

"I do not know," he said faintly. "I never suspected I might before this moment."

She hurried to get him a brandy. His color improved after he took a swallow.

"No, I do not think it is my heart. I think it was just the shock of envisioning you discussing syphilis with Mr. Wilcox. In front of everyone at the Erskines' ball."

299

He looked at her, really looked at her, much as she'd seen him look at his patients.

"Charlotte, are you happy here?"

Charley opened her mouth to tell him what he wanted to hear, but she couldn't do it.

"Uncle Curtis, do you know the story of Atalanta?"

"Atalanta? Something from the Greeks, correct?"

"Yes." She sat next to him, and smoothed out her skirts. A thin gold bangle set with pearls, one of the few pieces of jewelry she owned that belonged to her mother, winked at Charley's wrist.

"Atalanta," she began, "was a young woman who lived in ancient Greece. She was raised by bears, and thought herself a bear until one day she was captured by a bear hunter. He raised her as his daughter and told her she couldn't be a bear anymore, and had to be a human and marry a man."

"Charlotte, are you making this up?" he asked suspiciously, but there was a faint smile on his lips.

"No, Uncle, this is truly how the story goes. Atalanta knew she couldn't be happy as a human girl married to a human man. She was very fleet of foot from her years living as a bear, and proclaimed that she would only marry a man who could beat her in a foot-race. Many tried, none succeeded, but one, named Melanion, prayed to Aphrodite for help. Aphrodite heard his prayers. When Melanion raced against Atalanta, he had three golden apples. When Atalanta would pull away from him, for she was the faster runner, he would throw out a golden apple. Atalanta was distracted by the shiny object and stopped to pick it up. Melanion did this two more times, and deceitfully beat Atalanta and won her as his wife."

"I do not suppose the moral of this story is true love wins over all?"

Charley smiled sadly.

"No, Uncle, true love doesn't win in my version. However, I am like Atalanta in that I have been distracted from my goal by bright, shiny things." She stroked the rich satin of her silver gown, then raised her head and looked at him in the lamplight.

"I am sorry, Uncle Curtis. I have tried, really I have, but I feel like I am losing myself and losing my mind."

She knelt next to his chair, looking up into the lined face that was now so dear to her.

"I came to live with you, Uncle, because you are such a fine physician as well as a fine man. My father always said so and I know he was right. I thought if I was here, you would teach me as he taught me. But when you look at me, you don't see me, you see my mother," she said softly. "Who, I'm told, loved to go to dances and parties and wear pretty frocks."

"And you are your father's daughter, is that what you have been trying to tell me?"

"Yes, Uncle," she said with a sigh. "I have spent my youth being useful and practicing medicine with my father, and then again as a doctor at sea, not going to parties and picnics. There's nothing wrong with an occasional outing, and I adore my new clothes, but I miss helping people. I hate feeling useless when I could be useful."

She looked up at him earnestly.

"Try to imagine what it would be like for you if tomorrow you were told you could never do another examination, stitch another wound, heal another ill person."

"I cannot imagine that," he said. "But I cannot change what is, Charlotte. You are a woman, and I am not."

Charley's spirits fell as flat as her dancing slippers.

"However," he continue, "I do not want to see you unhappy."

She looked up.

"It goes against everything I believe is proper for a young lady, but I suppose you can help me in the delivery of babies, and treating women's diseases. And you can work in the still-room preparing medications, for that would be part of your education if you were my male apprentice."

He awkwardly patted the curls atop her head.

"Do not look so forlorn. I am no radical, and this is a huge step for me to take. Perhaps, with time, there will be more we can do…Charley."

She rose to her feet and went to refill their glasses.

"It will help. If I am busy, then I do not think so much about my time aboard the *Fancy*."

"Is this also about the man you met while you were at sea?"

She spun around on her heel.

"I am an excellent diagnostician, Charlotte, and I know the signs and symptoms of a broken heart. Too well."

Dr. Wilson was standing now. He walked over to his desk and opened it, pulling out a miniature, and motioned to her. She took it from his hands and angled it to see it in the lamplight. The girl in the picture was dressed in the fashions of twenty years earlier, and had a sweet smile and brown ringlets.

"Miss Johnson and I were to be married. I met her here in Jamaica when I came to establish myself. Her parents hoped she would marry someone of more status who would take her back to England, but they gave us their blessing." He gazed at the miniature Charley held. "Clara succumbed to yellow fever before we could be wed."

He took the picture from her hand, sighed, then put it away.

"I know the look of someone who has loved, and lost the one they loved."

Charley nodded. "I lost my heart to an American privateer, Uncle. He is gone now, but he took my heart with him when he died." She took a deep breath. "Working keeps my mind occupied so that I am not thinking about what happened. Or what might have been."

"A broken heart may ease over time, Charlotte."

She said nothing to this, so he patted her on the arm. "I am off to bed then. In the morning we will discuss your schedule. Goodnight, my dear."

The course of study Dr. Wilson set out for Charley on the healing plants of Jamaica kept her busy through the sunny days of winter, and into spring and summer, the change in seasons barely noticeable. She was assisted in her lessons by Mrs. Mansfield. The housekeeper came from a long line of healing women and was happy to share her knowledge, especially since she had no daughter of her own to pass the information on to.

"There's wisdom, and then there's women's wisdom, Miss Charlotte. Men don't concern themselves with women's health unless it affects them. They don't think about what a woman needs, or how her courses come in and out like the moon. They just think about her courses as something that inconveniences them, and how soon they can get back into bed with her after she births their sons. You will learn from me what women share.

"Some of this is information Dr. Wilson doesn't need to hear about," Mrs. Mansfield said with a steady look at Charley. "For example, how if a woman's courses are late, she can take calabash to get regular again."

"I understand," Charley said. "Women seem to be so woefully ignorant of how their bodies work."

"White women, maybe." Mrs. Mansfield sniffed. "Or rich women. Poor women learn, soon enough. They cannot afford not to know."

They had these discussions when Dr. Wilson was not around, lest they be subjected to his opinion on "native nonsense and superstitious trash," but Charley enjoyed chatting with the middle-aged housekeeper as they sat in her cozy parlor or worked in the stillroom. She learned Mrs. Mansfield had been with Dr. Wilson nearly since he arrived in Jamaica, and if she wondered if there was anything more between her godfather and the stoutly handsome widow, she also figured it was none of her affair. But the housekeeper's knowledge of the plants around them was invaluable, and Charley took copious notes and drawings.

Jamaica was a regular pharmacopeia surrounded by the ocean. The guaiac tree so common to the island yielded not just the valued lignum vitae wood, but also guaiacum for the treatment of syphilis. The "fresh cut" plant's bruised leaves were a plaster for lacerations, and red lily was good for skin sores. When called to the side of a birthing woman, Charley would fix "Juba's Bush" tea with a few drops of whisky to ease the labor.

Some of the women were uncomfortable at the idea of a young woman assisting Dr. Wilson, but most of them were easy enough to deal with, though they did not seem sure how to address her. Was she a servant like a midwife? Dr. Wilson's niece, and therefore a young lady?

One or two ladies made it clear that they did not want anyone but their trusted physician to assist them during their lying-in, and Charley tried to take it with good grace.

But it was hard. It was especially hard after months of being "Dr. Alcott," the final word in the health and welfare of a hardened crew of privateers. Did these pampered women with their homes full of slaves and servants to wait on them hand and foot think they were better than the men of the *Fancy?*

She had to bite her tongue more than once, but it paid off in those cases where she could establish a good relationship, and the reward was helping someone deliver a healthy boy or girl.

Somewhat to her surprise after the Erskine ball, Charley still was active in society, and was approached by men at dances and suppers to partner them. They were all quite pleasant, some of them were quite handsome.

None of them, however, were Black Davy Fletcher.

Her months at sea seemed now almost a dream, a time where she had been transformed into something different from what she had been, but also a time that transformed her into the person she was now. More confident about herself and her abilities, more comfortable as a woman.

And she was a woman who having had the heights of rapture was not willing to settle for less.

While her days were full now, taken up with her work with Dr. Wilson, she was still unsatisfied with her life. She had never wanted to be a midwife or an apothecary, but that seemed to be her fate in Jamaica.

That was why she was thrilled one July morning when James, the younger houseboy, tracked her down to the patio garden where she sat in the shade writing notes on native plants. Pirate kept her company, sunning himself on the flag-stones, lazily blinking at a doctor bird hovering over a hibiscus.

"Miss? There's a gentleman here, says he needs to see the doctor."

"You told him Dr. Wilson isn't in?"

"Yes'm, but he says it won't wait."

"Take him to Dr. Wilson's examining room, James."

Charley's heart beat just a little faster as she smoothed down the lavender-striped muslin of her skirt. Maybe he needed to be sewn, or have a bone set, or would present an interesting disease! She could dazzle her mentor at dinner with tales of how she'd dealt with the emergency, efficiently and competently, and Dr. Wilson would give her more responsibility.

She hurried into the examining room where a man stood with most of his face turned toward the window. But she knew in an instant who it was. She must have made some noise, for he turned his head. The sunlight coming into the room seemed too bright, and Charley heard a buzzing in her head that wasn't from the insects in the garden. She put her hand on the wall to steady herself and wondered with detachment if fainting was the normal response to seeing a dead man standing before you.

"Charley? Is that you?"

David Fletcher looked as startled by her as she was by him, for different reasons. He stared at her, and she stood there, rooted to the floor.

"But...you are dead! I saw the explosion!"

"It was a near thing, Charley," David Fletcher said, turning fully toward her. For all of her experience Charley couldn't stop the gasp as her hand rose up to cover her mouth.

She slowly walked over to him, and said, "Step into the light."

He did, and the bright tropical sunlight pitilessly revealed the extent of the damage. His left eye was covered by a black patch, and a deep scar twisted along his cheek up past his forehead into his hairline, where a swath of white stood out in the black hair around it.

"Take off the patch."

He slowly reached up, watching her with his good eye, and undid the patch. The socket was empty, the burned flesh around it pitted and scarred.

"After I was blown off the *Fancy* I managed to cling to a hatch. A full day I drifted, but then I had the good fortune to be picked up by a whaler returning to Nantucket. I made it home to Baltimore. The doctor there did what he could for me, but it was too late." He looked down at the ground, then back at her, and took a deep breath. "I suppose I should have written to you, especially with the war over. But I was not sure you would want me, Charley, since I no longer had a ship."

He swallowed, his brown throat moving, and she pressed her fingers harder against her mouth to keep from touching him.

"I was not sure you would want me, now that I can no longer be called 'Handsome Davy.' Look at you, Charley Alcott! You are so beautiful and I am—" He didn't finish, his voice trailing off.

Charley stepped closer to him and he seemed about to take a step back, then stopped, his hands loose at his sides.

"Mmmm," she said, putting her hand on his chin and turning his face so that she saw the undamaged right side, the clean lines a parody of what had been before. The skin she remembered so well was warm beneath her fingers, pulsing with life and vitality.

"Is there any residual pain, Captain?"

"Not to complain of," he said. "I sometimes get headaches."

"Are you having one now?"

"No."

"And what about here, on the undamaged side. Any pain at all?"

"No."

"You are certain?"

"There is no pain in my head."

"Good," she said, and hauling back her arm, slapped him for all she was worth—on his undamaged side.

"Ow! What the hell was that for?"

She was pleased to note that while she may hit like a girl, she'd hit him hard enough to rock him back on his feet.

"You think all I care about is your *face*?" she hissed at him. She shook her hand to make sure she hadn't broken it. "Honestly, I have never been so angry in my entire life! You show up after all this time worried about how you *look*? You know very well that eye patch only makes you look more dashing, you pirate! And who cares about your ship? It is you I wanted! Oh, go away! You are a prize idiot and I am an even bigger idiot for falling in love with you!"

She turned to stomp back into the house but he stopped rubbing his reddening face and grabbed her arm, ruining her dignified exit. He compounded the transgression by swinging her about, and kissing her within an inch of her life.

While one part of her was pleased to note that he hadn't lost an iota of function or skill with his mouth due to his injury, another part of her was encouraging her to forget everything else and leap into his arms.

But she was made of stronger stuff than that, and eventually broke away from him with a sigh.

"Oh, Charley my darling, I have missed you so much! And I am very glad I never taught you to box! Damn, now I really do need a doctor." He moved his jaw, somewhat tentatively, then he smiled, that beautiful dimpled smile that led her to many evenings in his bunk. "I'm glad I am more to you than a pretty face. I truly was worried that my ugly phiz would scare you away."

Charley reached up and put her hand on his face, on the

injured side, and gently pulled him down to her level. She put her lips over his battered and empty socket, then rested her hand on the injury, her long fingers brushing back the hair that was still silken, even if it was now streaked with silver.

"You are more to me than your bits and pieces, David Fletcher. You are the beautiful pirate who snatched me off the *Lady Jane*, and you will always be my Handsome Davy, no matter what happens.

"Besides," she said, her lips curling up, "you thought that I'd find *you* ugly, after we both gazed upon *Señor* Martinez's arse?"

"That is a good point." He retied his eyepatch on, then pulled her closer to him and she felt her skin come alive for the first time in months, all her senses sharpened. "I also waited to come to you until I had another ship. Come sail away with me, Charley, for I am headed to China!"

This was too much information for her to process all at once, but one thing stood out. David Fletcher needed to marry to get the funds for his ships. If he had another vessel then...

"What about Miss Dixon?"

"You mean Mrs. Fletcher? She is back in Baltimore."

All the blood rushed from Charley's head, and then rushed back in, a red hot flame through her veins. The same clinical corner of her brain that wondered at her syncopic reaction to seeing him alive now wondered if one's head could explode from anger. She shoved herself away from him, her hands fisted in front of her.

"Captain Pirate indeed! You would leave Mrs. Fletcher in Baltimore and take your fancy piece with you sailing to China! I might have known! You haven't changed one bit, Black Davy Fletcher!"

"Don't scream at me, it makes my head hurt. More." He looked at her and had the gall to smile, the reprobate!

"Charley Alcott, there are many ways I would describe you, but 'fancy piece' isn't one of them. Although that is a very becoming frock." He grabbed her hands. "Oh no you don't! You don't want to bruise these hands that save lives, Doctor!"

He put a kiss on the knuckles of the fist he held tight.

"My fancy piece? I never think of you that way. I think of you as my annoying medico," he said, punctuating this with a kiss on her other hand. "My all too vocal conscience," ending this statement with a kiss on her forehead as he pulled her closer. "My very succulent bed partner…"

This kiss, on her lips, and his arms banding tighter around her nearly brought her to swooning, again, but that was probably his plan all along, especially when he broke away to whisper in her ear, "…and my dearest heart."

He put his lips on hers again, and she was sure her brains were leaking out because she was listening to this litany of lover's talk without punching him for his arrogance.

"Stop kissing me. I cannot think when you do that!"

"Good. Say yes, Charley, and sail with me to the ends of the earth."

She marshaled her defenses for one last try.

"Scoundrel!"

Which would have sounded better if her voice hadn't come out as a squeak. She tried again. "What will Mrs. Fletcher say about this when she hears of it? And don't think she won't!"

"Would you sail away with me if you thought she'd never find out?"

To her shame, Charley hesitated, but fortunately, David was still talking and didn't notice.

"You mean you would consider coming with me anyway,

a scoundrel and a pirate? And why should my sister-in-law care about who I take with me to China?"

"Your sister-in— Miss Dixon married Henry?"

"He snuck behind me, the rascal, and married Miss Dixon after he took the *Trinidad* up to New York. Turns out he's loved her all along, and it seems she feels the same way about him."

Charley blinked at this new development. "But what about your family's finances?"

"Between the sale of that cargo and Henry's marriage, all is—wait a minute, that's not what I want to talk about. Were you really willing to sail away with me in sin? A morally upright person like yourself? I'm shocked, Dr. Alcott! Shocked! But very happy at this evidence of your dissolution. You will fit right in with my salty crew! Ouch—don't kick a wounded man!"

"You let me think you were married! I am going to administer to you a black draught that will have you locked in the privy for a month!" she hissed through her teeth.

"That would certainly put a damper on our wedding trip!"

Could one's heart explode in joy? The clinical part of her brain still functioning was exploring this newest possibility.

"Wedding? You want to marry me?"

"Yes, my good doctor, I want to marry you just as quickly as I can secure a license and set out to sea. So, do you want to sail to China? As the other Mrs. Fletcher? And let me just add that the new ship is a hermaphrodite, making this an especially appropriate choice for us."

"A hermaphrodite?"

"Combining two types of rigging. Come with me and I will teach you all about it."

"I thought you said you didn't want women aboard ship?"

"I have come to think about many things in a new way. I suppose I, too, underwent 'a sea change'. And besides, it's only good common sense to take a surgeon with you on a long voyage. Remember? 'I sail, you doctor'? It was a good arrangement, wasn't it, Charley?"

He said this with hesitation in his voice. She stopped fussing and looked at him. Really looked at him. She had never seen Black Davy Fletcher like this, unsure of himself, waiting for an answer from her—her, Charley Alcott—as if she were the prize diamond of the season.

"You need a wife who will complement you, Captain Fletcher. An ornament to you."

"Do not tell me what I need. I know what I need!" He was angry now, and pushed her at arm's length, holding her by the arms so she could not escape him and so he could look into her eyes. "I do not want an ornament, Charley Alcott! I want someone who will snap at me and be sarcastic, even though sarcasm is the captain's prerogative, and tell me when I'm wrong and sew me up when I bleed. I want someone who will make me laugh, and smile, and feel like there's no place I'd rather be, because you're by my side."

"But what about your crew. Will they be prepared to let me physic them?"

"I am confident that I can find a crew so desperate for a qualified doctor that they would even take a woman's assistance."

"Oh, thank you, that makes me feel much more wanted!"

"I will make you an offer, sweetheart. If anyone complains, I will run him through."

"That only creates more work for me," she grumbled, but she was thinking furiously. "I give you fair warning, I will wear trousers aboard ship."

"You can be stark naked for all I care. As a matter of fact, I wish you would be stark naked, at least when the crew isn't about. But say yes, Charley. Please say yes." He gripped her hands and looked down at them, rubbing his thumb over her knuckles. "Every day I was gone from you, I felt like my heart was at the bottom of the ocean with my ship. If you tell me you do not want to go to sea, then…I will find something else to do. But whatever I make of my life, I cannot do it without you, my dearest heart. I love you so much. You are the greatest treasure I ever stole."

Charley wondered if one's heart melting from love as hers was now would be a chronic condition. There was only one way to find out, and that was to do a study of it for the rest of her life. At the side of Black Davy Fletcher. She put her hand up to his damaged face, still more handsome to her than any man she had ever known.

"A ship needs a good doctor, David, and a great captain. And I have always wanted to see China."

He pulled her back into his arms and the light in the room that smelled of medicine and spices seemed to grow even brighter as she lost herself in his kiss.

"Miss Alcott!"

Charley turned to the doorway, where Mrs. Mansfield stood watching them a look of startled delight on her freckled face.

"What do I tell Dr. Wilson?"

"Tell him she was carried off by an American pirate!" David said cheerfully, lifting Charley into his arms and starting to stride to the door.

He didn't get very far.

Charley sternly told him to unhand her, and see to arranging their marriage.

"If I am going to be the doctor aboard the—what is the name of your ship?"

"The *Harpy*."

She looked at him sharply but his face was bland as sick bay gruel.

"If I am going to be the doctor aboard the *Harpy*, then I

will need time to organize my supplies and check out the ship's stores. And my godfather is entitled to see me properly wed, even if it's to a pirate such as yourself!"

And so it happened.

Dr. Alcott (as the Harps were already calling her, many of them being former hands on the *Fancy*) and Captain Fletcher were wed in a flower-laden church with the bride given away by her beaming godfather.

Charley wore a gown of carnation silk with a ruff framing her graceful neck, and stars shining in her eyes. Her groom was in midnight blue broadcloth and fawn trousers, and the smile on his face was for her alone. There were those in the church who wondered how such a strikingly handsome girl could marry such a scarred and damaged man, but they kept their opinions to themselves.

If you asked the blissful couple, they would say they were not ducks nor were they swans. They would compare themselves rather to the paired dolphins who frolicked joyfully in front of the *Harpy* as she sailed out to sea, bringing good luck and blessings to the happy voyagers on their journey to China.

ABOUT THE AUTHOR

Darlene Marshall is an award-winning author of historical romance featuring pirates, privateers, smugglers and the occasional possum. She loves working at a job where business attire is shorts and a shirt festooned with pink flamingos and palm trees. Marshall lives in North Central Florida, a convenient location for researching sites of great historical significance, which also happen to also be at the beach and serve *mojitos*. Her books have been published in English, German and Estonian.

You can learn more about Darlene by visiting her website:

https://darlenemarshall.com

Want more of Doctor Murray? Read **Castaway Dreams** **(High Seas #2)**--Aspen Gold Reader's Choice Award—On sale now in ebook and print:

After a lifetime in the Royal Navy, surgeon Alexander Murray knows one cannot exist without a brain, yet Daphne Farnham may be the exception. Her head contains nothing but rainbows, shoes, bonnets, pink frills and butterflies. Even her fluffy dog is useless. But the war with Napoleon is finally over and Alexander is sure he can put up with the cloth-headed Miss Farnham only for a couple of months until they reach England.

Did that naval officer have his sense of humor surgically removed? It is bad enough Alexander has no fashion sensibilities, never smiles at Daphne like other men do and doesn't adore her darling pup Pompom. He had the gall to proclaim her "useless" when everyone knows it's Daphne who's the best at picking out just the right ensemble for any social occasion. Fortunately, she has to put up with the sour Scotsman only for a couple of months until they reach England.

But when their ship goes down, the dour doctor (after a fashion), the dizzy damsel (more or less) and the darling (and potentially delicious) doggy are about to embark on the adventure of a lifetime as unlikely companions, castaway on a desert island. One of them may have fleas, but it's the two humans who will find themselves wanting to scratch a certain itch.